To Love a King

Shona Husk

sourcebooks
casablanca

Published by Sourcebooks Casablanca, an imprint of Sourcebooks, Inc.
P.O. Box 4410, Naperville, Illinois 60567-4410
(630) 961-3900
Fax: (630) 961-2168
www.sourcebooks.com

Printed and bound in Canada
WC 10 9 8 7 6 5 4 3 2 1

Chapter 1

THE SILVERY TRIANGLE OF MIRROR SPUN IN THE BREEZE. That was the one Felan wanted to gaze into, but he waited. Instead, first he examined a few others that gave him general glimpses across the veil, into the mortal world. He could pretend he was studying the damage the breaches in the veil were having. While people were watching him, he was always careful about what he did.

The Court was waiting for him to do something.

In two mortal weeks, his mother would be executed for treason. Which meant he only had two mortal weeks to get a Queen, and get her pregnant, and take over, thus restoring the magic of Annwyn and saving both worlds from unnecessary hardship. More hardship. Annwyn was sliding into winter as his father weakened. Felan closed his eyes for a moment before pushing aside the thought. Everywhere he looked there was a reminder that his father was dying.

The trees that formed castle Annwyn had once been lush and green, but now they were bare skeletons as the magic failed. The veil between Annwyn and the mortal world was tearing, and death was bleeding through. There were plagues in the mortal world. Death tolls were rising and governments were getting twitchy. They were looking for the cause in all the wrong places. No one believed in fairies anymore.

Jacqui doesn't believe in me.

The memories of that day still had the power to draw fresh blood from the wound. He'd lost the one person he'd ever loved in a few short moments. However, he'd only realized it was love when it was too late.

While he'd been recalled to Annwyn—a move orchestrated by his enemies, he was sure—something had happened to her. When he'd returned to her, Jacqui was no longer pregnant and she no longer wanted to see him. There'd been something in her eyes that day and an ice in her voice that he hadn't recognized when she'd asked him to leave. He'd left because he didn't know what else to do at the time.

He touched the mirror that was charmed to view Jacqueline Ara across the veil. What felt like months to him had been seven mortal years since he'd last seen her—in person. It had taken a long time before he could even bring himself to check on her in the mirror, and yet, eventually, he'd been unable to resist.

She'd been the one he'd wanted by his side to rule Annwyn. He'd been ready to claim the throne—almost. But all his plans for their future together had unraveled faster than he'd ever thought possible.

No Queen, no heir, no claiming the throne of Annwyn. He was partially responsible for the winter.

The mirror flickered with color and life. He held his breath as Jacqui appeared. She put on a dab of lipstick, pulled her dark hair back, and with a final glance, walked away, unaware that he was checking up on her. How could he not when she was still lodged in his heart? A faint smile formed on his lips. She looked happy. Happier than he'd seen her in a while.

She'd moved on.

He wished he could say the same.

At first, he'd let time slide past unnoticed as he'd struggled to keep his grief hidden from the Court. He'd been determined to show no weakness and give his enemies no crack to slide a blade into. Back then he hadn't known who was trying to trip him. Now he did, and Sulia was watching him as closely as he was watching her. Who would make the first move and bring their human consort to Annwyn?

Probably Sulia, since he'd let the Court assume he had one. Not a lie, but not the truth either. He was dancing on a very fine line, being caught out would not help his cause.

He needed to find a way to take over Annwyn without repeating his father's mistakes. He wanted more than the cold, hate-filled relationship his parents had. Two weeks wasn't long enough, and yet it was too long. The longer he stalled, the more time Sulia would have, and the worse it would be for mortal and fairy alike. If possible he wanted to avoid a civil war like the one his father had been forced to fight.

Sulia had already bested him once. If she won this time…at least he wouldn't be alive to see the result. He was sure she'd continue with his mother's cruel games. He should've known that someone would challenge him for the throne. Fairies loved power too much to not attempt a coup.

With Jacqui he'd never had to play games. Even now he longed to go back to the way it had been with her. But not even fairies had that power. He'd screwed up everything.

Felan watched Jacqui for another heartbeat before

letting the mirror go. The surface returned to silver, so no one else would be able to watch Jacqui through it. Only him—unless someone was peering over his shoulder. He checked just to be sure that no one was close, but the other fairies were staying well away from him, as if sensing the turn in his mood.

He missed her. He almost let himself be dragged back into the darkness of those first few days after their breakup. The evil thoughts of what he could've done differently, the unanswered questions he had about what had happened. Back then, he hadn't known how to voice them. Maybe if he had, he would've been able to let her go instead of watching her through the mirrors and wondering if she still thought of him.

He drew in a breath and released it slowly. He needed to know. With measured paces, he strode through the hall, looking as though he had somewhere to be. He always had somewhere to be, something to do. Even as he slept, his enemies worked.

If he was going to beat Sulia to the throne, he needed to move forward, and to do that, he had to face his past, even if he wasn't sure he was ready to see Jacqui again. Maybe he would never be ready to hear what had happened to their baby and the love they'd had.

It's gone. He still heard the echo of those words when he slept.

Dead, before a soul had even had a chance to take hold. He'd never even had a moment with his child's soul. His throat closed.

Maybe facing Jacqui again wasn't a great idea, but at the moment, it was all he had. He needed to know what had gone wrong so that he wouldn't repeat it. Most of all, he needed to know that their love was dead even though he still longed for her. She'd carved out his heart and kept it, and he'd never asked for it back.

He left the castle, the branches of the overhead canopy that served as a roof now bare of leaves. Ice crunched under his boots where the dew had frozen. Annwyn, and the mortal world may not even have two weeks. As winter settled in Annwyn, so the plagues would worsen in the mortal world. He didn't want to drag either world through a fairy civil war. Sulia would though, and she'd laugh while she did it. A shiver traced down his back. She was so much like his mother.

Felan walked across the field toward the main doorway in and out of Annwyn. Two large trees formed the entrance that faced the castle. From here, he could go anywhere he wanted. It was the doorway he chose to use, rather than a back way, as it was harder to track his movements. And anything that masked where he was going and who he as seeing was a good thing right now.

And if he couldn't find love and the right woman in two weeks?

That was something he didn't want to consider.

The thought of ending up like his parents wasn't unbearable. Stepping aside and letting Sulia rule was just as bad. Her heart was as black as his mother's.

Felan stepped through the doorway and into Californian sunshine. Salt air touched his tongue as he walked from the cemetery toward the beach. The idea of living this close to such a large body of water was enough to make the hair on the back of his neck draw tight. But the sun and warmth was a welcome change to the cold of Annwyn that lingered in his blood.

He'd spent more time in the mortal world in the last few months than he had in seven years. He'd forgotten how much he liked it. He expended a little magic, casting a glamour so people could see him dressed like any other human, in jeans and a white shirt. Classic and simple. His elaborately embroidered knee-length waistcoat would look out of place here. He pulled a pair of sunglass out of his pocket and slipped them on. As he walked, his heart sped up, as though he'd been drinking too much coffee. The idea of seeing Jacqui in person again was making him nervous.

He stopped a passerby to ask the time and set his watch. It had been a gift from Jacqui to help him keep track of time, but it had never worked in Annwyn. There it had simply been a pretty piece of metal with a ceramic bezel and strap that had refused to even tick. But he'd kept it, unable to let go of the gift that she'd put so much thought into, knowing he wouldn't want to wear iron-based metal against his skin. The white ceramic was cool around his wrist as he put it on. One second in the mortal world, and it had sprung to life as if it had never stopped. If only it were that easy to pick up the life he wanted.

Despite not having seen her for years, he knew where she was in the mortal world. He could sense her. He could feel her in his heart as if no time had passed. It was only the twinging of his scarred heart that reminded him to be careful. Things had changed. She was no longer the nineteen-year-old woman he'd once known.

While he'd recognize her face anywhere, he did not have as much confidence when it came to knowing the woman she'd become.

The coffee shop where she worked came into view. He paused for a moment and tried to gather his thoughts. There were seven billion people in the world. Half of them female, a good portion of them young, pretty, and smart. Even if only one percent of them were willing to leave everything they knew and come to Annwyn, that was still a lot of potential women he could make Queen. But he didn't love them and they didn't love him—neither had Jacqui the last time he'd seen her. Yet he was here.

He was an idiot.

He was desperate.

He wanted to undo the last seven years and put everything back the way it had been.

But he'd settle for knowing the truth. This time, he was ready to listen, and he hoped she'd be ready to tell him.

—∾∾—

Something fluttered in the corner of her vision. Jacqui was used to ignoring the things that no one else could see. It had taken a while, and had become easier after she had stopped taking the meds the psychiatrist had given her. She'd had lots of labels—delusional, paranoid—and had even been on suicide watch for a little while.

But she knew the truth.

There were monsters, and if they thought you could see them, they followed and tried to draw attention to themselves. They'd make trouble. Mentioning the monsters had convinced her parents that the loss of her baby had pushed her over some edge. They'd tried to use their money and connections to fix her.

She'd had to fix herself.

The little blue wren bumped against the coffee shop window again as if trying to get in. For a moment, her heart fluttered like the bird's wings. She couldn't help it. If she saw a fairy wren, she thought of him.

If a wren was around, it meant the monsters weren't. It did mean that a fairy was, though, and they were far more dangerous and far more powerful. She'd learned that the hard way when she'd given her heart to one. Her fingers strayed to the crescent-shaped iron pendant that she never took off. Fairies didn't like iron or water.

She'd done everything she could to protect herself from fairies. All those years of lying and saying they weren't real hadn't changed what she saw. These days, she didn't talk about them or even look at them. It was safer that way.

"That bird is going to hurt itself." Ashleigh put the cake back into the display.

"I can't go and shoo it away." There were a half dozen coffees waiting to be made. "It's only a bird; it's probably checking out its own reflection and thinking it's found a mate."

Ashleigh shook her head as she rang up the order and handed the customer her change. "Get an order ready and I'll take it and shoo the bird away."

Jacqui almost said no but then shrugged. How could she explain to Ash what the bird meant? "Whatever."

Why should she even care if a fairy was nearby?

Ever since Felan had burned her life to the ground, she'd sworn to ignore all things fairy. She'd had to spend years rebuilding, but her life was back on track. She was studying part-time, working part-time, and was living on the other side of the country from her parents. Truthfully, that was what had really turned her life around and made it hers again.

They never let her forget how she'd screwed up and how they'd helped her. Help. It was their help that had made her believe she was crazy.

A man walked into the coffee shop. For a moment the sun cast him in shadow and he seemed to flicker, as if she couldn't be sure what she was seeing. He took a few more steps, and she saw him for what he was. His purple, knee-length waistcoat swirled around his legs. Her gaze lifted slowly, taking in the rest of his odd clothing, the black pants and dark shirt. But it wasn't just his clothing—he was too pretty to be human. Fear balled in her stomach and punched up into her chest. He was the fairy the wren had been heralding.

She looked at him for a moment too long. Something about him held her gaze. The curl of his dark brown hair against the collar of his shirt, the way he moved as if he owned the place. She glanced away sharply. Had he realized that she could see him? Was it already too late?

No one else was staring at the strangely dressed man. She held her breath as he walked closer. Then Ash walked back into the shop. Her gaze was firmly on his butt. She winked at Jacqui, and Jacqui forced a smile. At least Ash could see him, so Jacqui didn't have to pretend she couldn't. Sometimes it was hard to tell, but when in doubt, she ignored them, no matter how pretty they looked. She'd seen fewer of them since moving to the seaside.

The fairy man took off his sunglasses, revealing pale green eyes like the edge of a glacier.

Her heart stopped. Or time stopped. That split second hung incomplete as her brain tried to rationalize what she was seeing. It couldn't be him. Not here. Not now. Her heart gave a beat and noise rushed back in to fill the silence she hadn't noticed. Felan, the fairy Prince who'd ridden away with her heart and never thought to return it, was in the coffee shop. She blinked and glanced away, pretending she didn't recognize him.

The doctors who'd told her fairies weren't real had never been confronted with the truth—the truth that was walking steadily closer to the counter as if it wanted to order a cup of coffee.

Last time, it had been hard to say anything with her mother standing there. He'd never come back and given her the chance to speak or explain what had happened. And she'd never had the chance to ask him to send the monsters away. Everyone had just thought she was crazy. Then, as the years had passed in drug-induced grayness, she'd begun to hope that she would never see him or any fairy again. It hurt too much.

As he strolled toward her, the old doubts began to rise. Why was he here now? Had he come back, thinking it wasn't too late, that maybe only days had passed when it had been years? Or had he come to take her to Annwyn? Why would he bother chasing her? He could have any woman he wanted. She was just the girl who he believed killed his baby.

If he wanted revenge, he was a little late. She'd been to hell and back, and she had nothing to say to him.

He glanced at her and looked away as if he didn't recognize her.

Maybe he didn't. She'd grown up and changed. She'd had to.

He hadn't changed a bit. His cheekbones could still weaken women's knees, and the curve of his lips could melt hearts. But it was the way he acted, as if he didn't know women were watching him over their coffee cups. The trouble was she knew it wasn't an act. When he'd been with her, his attention had always been on her. He'd made her feel like the most beautiful woman in the room even if she wasn't. He'd had a confidence she'd always lacked.

He'd seemed stable, calm, and wise, while at the same time he'd craved freedom from Annwyn. That her parents had hated him had been the cherry on top. He'd been her rebellion. Even though he knew that her parents didn't like him, he'd always insisted on being polite and behaved himself around them, as if he thought he could eventually win them over. He believed family was important. And she'd lost his baby. She'd never forget the look on his face when her mother had said it was gone. Felan calling her name even as the door shut. She'd cried until her mother had forced her to take a sleeping pill. She'd slept so many hours away, hiding from reality.

He really had no right to be here, messing up her new life with his charm and looks.

Ash almost raced around the counter to take his order. Her eyes were bright and unable to look away from the fairy. That had been her once, stumbling into his arms, head over heels in love. Crawling out had been much harder than getting in. It was kind of like those coils of barbed wire and the mud pits army recruits have to slog through and over, only it had lasted for years.

She busied herself wiping the coffee machine and filling the next order on her list. It was better this way, that he didn't recognize her. Easier if she never had to explain herself or listen to his reasons for abandoning her. Love. Fairies didn't know the meaning of the word.

"Latte, please." His voice was soft and smooth, just the way she liked to remember, not the tortured cry she'd heard last from his lips.

Jacqui had to close her eyes to hold back the memories. She opened her eyes, expecting him to be looking, but he'd taken his table number and found a seat by the window. Then he busied himself reading the newspaper. He had always liked to follow news from around the globe.

She frowned. How long had it been since he'd been in the mortal world?

Ash slapped the order in front of her. "How gorgeous is he? I bet he's an actor or something."

Or something was closer to the truth. "Trouble I bet." Jacqui glanced at the till, wondering how he'd paid. When they'd been together, she'd helped him set up a bank account. Did he still use it, or had he simply tricked Ash into thinking he'd paid?

"I wouldn't mind that kind of trouble." Ash sighed.

Jacqui looked at Ash. She wasn't even twenty, but she was pretty—she'd be prettier if she didn't bleach her hair to within an inch of its life and she quit the fake tan. She looked like every other girl here. Didn't everyone go through that phase of trying to fit in? Jacqui had dyed her brown hair black and straightened it every day through high school, partly to fit in, but mostly because her parents had hated it.

"You would when he left you heartbroken." The words came with more bitterness than she'd planned.

Ash raised her eyebrows. "You have to kiss toads to find a prince."

"I don't want a prince." She'd had that once, and she wouldn't make the same mistake again.

Chapter 2

FELAN TRIED TO CONCENTRATE ON THE DAY'S HEAD-
lines. The death toll in Africa from a new strain of Ebola.
The overcrowded hospitals in China from a SARS vari-
ant. Russia was controlling the smallpox outbreak by
shutting borders. The humans were trying to stop the
spread of the plagues, but how could they fight what
they only half understood? He felt the weight of every
death. He could've prevented it all if he'd taken bigger
risks and played a better game.

That Sulia had been one step ahead of him rankled.
His mother's protégé was still one step ahead of him.
Perhaps he didn't deserve the throne if he couldn't win
it. But it didn't feel like a game anymore when so many
lives were at stake—his included.

From the corner of his eye, he watched Jacqui and
her friend. The blond was cute, but could never hold
his attention the way Jacqui did just by being in the
room. Her curly brown hair was pulled back, but a
ringlet kept falling out and brushing her cheek as she
made the hot drinks.

She'd been studying business management. They'd
been in the same ethics class—all fairies could do with
lessons in ethics. He'd gone to college to learn more
about the mortal world and start looking for a Queen,
and had found more than he'd ever expected. So what
was she doing making coffee?

His leg began to bounce with nerves, but he shut it down. He was the Crown Prince of Annwyn, yet around her he was nothing except Felan. This time, that wouldn't be good enough. He forced out a breath. He was here for answers only. Nothing more. Although, given the way she was carefully not looking at him, he was willing to bet that even getting answers would be difficult.

Did the past matter so much that he couldn't get beyond it?

He glanced at her again, and the scar that she'd left on his heart tore a little. He wasn't over her. How could he move on and find a Queen when he was still thinking of her? It wouldn't be fair to anyone. Was she over him?

It was hard to tell.

And if she wasn't, was there anything worth saving?

He turned the pages of the newspaper and hoped to find some celebrity gossip, anything to distract him for just a few moments from the wreckage of the world and his relationship.

He lifted his gaze as footsteps approached. He'd expected it to be the blond girl, but it was Jacqui. He let himself be caught in her blue eyes, deep as the ocean. He'd once believed he could happily drown in them. Seeing her in the flesh was different from watching through the mirror. Here, he could see that she'd lost the wild edge; she was more careful, more restrained, and getting closer by the heartbeat. But her eyes didn't look dull, the way they had the last time he'd seen her, and that gave him hope. There was a flicker of recognition and a shimmer of fear she was trying to hide.

He drew in a breath and hoped she wouldn't toss his coffee in his lap.

—⁓—

Jacqui placed the coffee down without meeting his gaze. Her hand betrayed her by shaking just a little and the cup clinked against the saucer. He'd watched her walk over, but his face had revealed nothing. Once, she'd been able to read his mind just by looking at his lips.

She wasn't angry anymore, or hurt. When it came to Felan, all she had left were the hollow ache and the knowledge of the damage he'd caused. Did he realize or care? Or was this a game to him and she was just the gullible human who'd fallen for his act? She wasn't that girl anymore and it would take much more than a pretty face and a killer smile to get her to fall into any man's bed.

Carefully, she lifted her gaze and met his stare. He didn't look older, but he had changed. There was something in his eyes, a razor-edge she hadn't seen before—or perhaps she hadn't cared to notice. He didn't blink or flinch away, and for a second, she thought she saw something more familiar before it was smothered. If he wasn't here to torment her, why was he having coffee by the sea? She knew fairies didn't like water; it was one of the many reasons she'd moved to California. That it was miles away from her parents and had great weather were all excellent features in her book. California had been her fresh start. Somewhere Felan shouldn't have been able to find her.

"Why are you here?" She kept her voice calm and low. No one needed to realize that she knew this overly good-looking man. No one, especially him, needed to know that her heart had beat a little harder at the sight of

him. She blamed her fear of fairies, but she might have
been lying to herself.

Everyone can see him. I am not crazy. But she was
still talking to a fairy, something she'd vowed never to
do again. Fairies were bad news. Especially fairy princes.

He looked at his coffee, and she knew he had no good
reason to be in this shop.

Felan glanced up. "I needed to see you."

"Well, here I am. Have you seen enough?" She tilted
her chin and tried to sound much braver than she felt.
He could grab her and take her to Annwyn in a heartbeat
and there wasn't a damn thing anyone could do about it.
Her necklace felt heavy against her skin, and while the
iron gave her comfort, it wasn't enough to stop him, just
enough to give him a nasty burn.

He attempted a smile, but it had lost the luminescence it once had. What had happened to him since their
breakup? "We need to talk."

Jacqui shook her head. She'd wanted to talk to him
every hour when he'd first left, prayed he'd return soon,
and then…then she'd come to fear his return and what
she'd say to him. Now she tried to tell herself she didn't
care even though she wanted to run and hide.

It was a shock to realize that he could still have an
effect on her. Although it wasn't desire anymore; it was
fear. She didn't want anything to do with him or any
fairy. She swallowed and tried to appear cool and calm.

"You're seven years too late." Then she turned on her
heel and walked away.

"Give me a chance to explain," he said, loud enough
that people lifted their heads and looked.

Jacqui stopped and cringed. She hated being watched.

What if he used his glamour to make himself invisible, so it looked as though she was arguing with air?

He's here and he's visible. She'd much rather he be somewhere else. She'd moved on; she had a new life that didn't involve fairies, shrinks, meds, or anything out of the ordinary. She was normal. Normal women didn't know fairies existed, much less date them.

Pretend he's a human ex. No one else knew the details of what happened.

She glanced over her shoulder, not trusting him enough to get close. "Why should I?"

"You weren't innocent."

The hell she wasn't!

How dare he insinuate… She spun and stalked back over to his table and placed her hands flat on the wood. She leaned close and looked him square in the eye. "It was an ectopic pregnancy. I almost died." Her words were clipped as she whispered the things she'd wanted to tell him so long ago, in what seemed like another life, when she was someone else. "You strolled back into my life two months later and looked at me like I had killed our baby." She swallowed the lump in her throat, but there were no tears left. They'd dried up long ago. "You never gave me the chance to tell you the truth, so no, you don't get a chance now. You don't have the right to come here and ask to talk to me."

She straightened up. That had felt rather good. She'd waited seven years to tell him what had happened, and while she would never forget the look on his face when he'd realized she was no longer pregnant, at least she got to see the look on his face as he realized how wrong he'd been.

A frown formed, as if he was struggling to understand.

He'd never get close to the confusion and agony she'd gone through, followed by the realization that it was over. He could have fought his way into the house; he could've rescued her from her parents' control. Instead, he'd left her there to drown in a medicated haze. She wanted to hate him for that. That would be so much easier than actually wanting to ask why. Why hadn't he tried harder? She'd needed him and he hadn't been there.

Had he cared more about the baby than her? It was an insidious thought that she'd had many times before. Maybe if she hadn't already been on meds when he'd shown up she would have fought harder. She might have pushed past her mother and flung herself into his arms, but she'd been tired and listless, and it had been easier to obey. Maybe, maybe, maybe. Too many maybes and no answers.

She wanted to know why he hadn't been there for her. Why had he stayed away for so long? Why didn't he give her a chance? Would the answers change anything?

No, so she didn't bother asking him. It was done and in the past, and she had moved on.

"It's too late, Felan." She left him sitting there with his cooling coffee.

<center>~~~</center>

Jacqui's words echoed around Felan. He knew other patrons were looking and whispering, but he didn't care what they said or assumed. This wasn't Court, where he had to hide everything he thought and watch every step he took.

It was an ectopic pregnancy. I almost died.

He didn't know what ectopic was, but obviously it had almost killed her and it was something to do with the baby. His knowledge of the mortal world, while better than most fairies, was inadequate.

He needed to know what she meant. In his shock, had he made a grave error of judgment? Had her mother deliberately led him astray? He closed his eyes for a moment and tried to examine those few fateful moments again. The dead look in her eyes, her smiling mother. His own grief that he'd allowed to blind him.

She was right; he'd never given her the chance to tell him more. He'd left before she could see him fall apart, believing that she had betrayed him unforgivably. Felan opened his eyes and glanced at her. She was cleaning the counter hard enough to wear a hole in the wood, determined not to look at him. If he was kinder, he might walk away and let her be. But he was fairy and on a very strict time frame. He didn't have the luxury of nice.

His chair scraped over the floor as he stood; then he walked over to her. "Jacqui."

She flinched and turned away from him.

He deserved that. He hated that his life in Annwyn had stolen the time he should've been here. Always the worst of both worlds. "Please."

"I'm working. I have nothing to say to you."

"I know you hate me, but I need to understand, and I don't." Admitting that wasn't as hard as it should have been. Those words would've been dangerous at Court, but around Jacqui, he'd never had to pretend or plot or scheme. He'd never needed a poker face and a secret plan. Around her, he was able to relax. Her head lowered and she sighed. "I don't hate you, not anymore.

You can't help what you are." She turned and looked at him. "Do you really want to know, or is this a...trick?"

She'd almost said *fairy* trick—he could hear the unspoken word ringing in his ears. But there were too many people around for them to be totally honest—too many people pretending not to listen to their little drama. Their little drama was wrecking two worlds.

"I never played games with you." Not once.

"Fine. I finish at five. If you aren't here, you've blown your one and only chance to talk to me." She pulled a pendant free of her clothes.

Iron. He almost laughed. A human drawing iron on a fairy lord was an act of war. At one time, it would have started battles that raged over Ireland until firstborn children were promised and human consorts were taken to sooth the bruised pride of the fairy Court. But back then, the Court had spent more time in the mortal world and humans knew who they were. These days, most lords and ladies never left Annwyn except to create a child. They had become pale, greedy shadows of what they once were. However, Jacqui was wearing iron because of him. Because she'd hoped it would keep him and other fairies away. That stung him to his core.

"I won't harm you. My word." A fairy's word was their bond.

She snorted and shook her head. "I trusted your word once before. Not again." Then she went back to work, dismissing him as if he were a servant of no consequence.

He'd never broken his word to Jacqui; he'd come back just as he'd promised...though he admitted to himself it had been too late and he hadn't returned to her side and helped her. He'd fled. While he hadn't technically broken his word, he hadn't truly kept it either. In her eyes, he'd failed. Damn the Court dramas and plots to the river and the troublemakers with them.

He looked at the other girl, then at the people watching. He gave them a slow, steady glance that made them look away and mind their own business. He would not be gossiped about here. He got enough of that at home—and most of it wasn't good. Too many thought he would fail to take the throne in time and too many backed Sulia. He should've realized she'd been acting against him sooner, but her tracks were well covered by his mother and her schemes. Not that his mother would be doing much now from her cell. Her games had turned and bitten her hard.

With measured paces, he went back to his table by the window. He pretended to watch the waves roll against the shore, as he drank his cool coffee. He could feign indifference; he'd rather do that than storm out of here. Yet he couldn't sit here all day and wait for her to finish, nor could he go back to Annwyn, in case he missed five o'clock.

While his body was still, his mind was tumbling. His fingertips whitened against the cup. He didn't know what to say to her at five. He glanced at the newspaper and the death tolls. It wasn't about him anymore or what he wanted and needed. He'd thought Jacqui would make a good Queen once before, and even if there was no love, maybe it was a case of better the devil he knew beside him on the throne.

Chapter 3

IT WAS ONLY WHEN FELAN LEFT THE COFFEE SHOP that Jacqui let herself breathe fully, instead of the tight, half-panicked breaths she had been taking. Just because he wasn't watching her didn't mean he wasn't aware of her and that he wasn't listening to everything that was going on. She knew him too well. *Had* known him too well.

And she wanted nothing to do with him, so why had she told him to come back at five? The words had fallen out of her mouth before she could think them through.

She shook her head and squirted whipped cream on the coffee she was making. The whole time they'd been together, he'd flitted in and out of her life. A year of never knowing when he was going to be around and when he was leaving. At eighteen, it had been exciting.

At nineteen, she'd tried to pretend he could be normal and they could be a family.

Now she looked back and wondered how she could have ever been so gullible.

Ash nudged her. "You know him?"

Jacqui just nodded. She didn't want to talk about it anymore. She just wanted him to go away so she could get on with her life.

"Why didn't you say something?"

"I did. He's trouble."

"But you're thinking about him."

Jacqui looked up. "I'm reminding myself why it was a good thing we went our separate ways."

Ash raised one eyebrow and didn't look convinced.

And while Jacqui knew their breakup, which hurt at the time, was probably a good thing, it didn't stop her from wondering why he'd come back now and why he was suddenly so interested in finding out the truth. From what she knew of fairies, they thought themselves always right. Was it possible he'd changed?

"Getting back with the ex never ends well…how about I take him off your hands?" Ash grinned.

The idea of Felan with someone else pressed on the jealousy she thought she'd left far behind. The old fear that she wasn't enough to hold his attention, that when he wasn't with her, he was with someone else, bubbled back up. He'd been away seven years—what did she think he had been doing? He had probably been off cavorting in Annwyn with lots of beautiful fairies. He hadn't come back here to hook back up with her. No, all he wanted were some answers. That, she could give him.

"You don't want to get mixed up with his kind."

"Crime?" Ash lowered her voice as if Felan had possibly planted a bug and was now listening to every word.

She realized she was dangerously close to revealing how delicate her hold on what people perceived as reality was. *No, he's not a crime boss; he's the Prince of Annwyn, you know, the Underworld. Heaven, Hell, and all of that.*

She wished he'd never told her the truth, that he'd let her drift along in ignorance. At least then her recovery would have been simple, not complicated by things that shouldn't exist.

Jacqui glanced at Ash. It was just simpler to agree. "All kinds."

"So you agreed to see him after work because…?"

"Because he owes me." And she owed him. This was the conversation they should have had years ago. He should have been with her in the hospital, instead of being given the brush-off by her mother.

"Should I call the cops if you don't come home?"

Jacqui smiled. If she didn't come home, there was nothing anyone could do for her. Still, it was nice that someone cared if she vanished. "Give me a few hours with him."

"Is he why you moved from Chicago?"

She bit the inside of her lip and didn't answer.

Ash put her hand on her arm. "Are you sure this is a good idea? He's tracked you down. He must want something from you."

"He won't hurt me." She wouldn't let him hurt her again. There was nothing she could give him that he hadn't already had and thrown away. But Ash had reinforced the nagging question of what he wanted. There was more to it than finding out what had happened to their baby. She hadn't spoken about it to anyone in so long, but he had the right to know. Maybe that was all he wanted, peace of mind that he couldn't have done anything different. She knew now that it wasn't her fault either. It was just one of those unfortunate things.

While it wasn't his fault, what had happened, it was his fault that he wasn't there to grieve with her and stop her from falling apart. It was his fault she saw things she shouldn't. When she saw him after work, she'd make him explain what he'd done to her and take it back.

Then, she could go back to being normal instead of pretending to be normal.

---*m*---

The street was busy with people enjoying the warm weather. It was nice to feel the sun on his skin instead of the chill of Annwyn, but even here he could feel the cold as if it were part of him. No one was paying any attention to him as he walked by. It had been a long time since he'd felt his heart thump with excitement instead of warning.

He was used to living dangerously, but he'd forgotten what it was like to be in the mortal world, doing simple things, not worrying about Annwyn falling down around him. He knew he couldn't ignore it forever, or even for very long. But for the next few hours, he would. Felan pushed up his shirtsleeve and checked his watch. He had a couple of hours to kill.

He hadn't let himself plan beyond seeing her and getting her to acknowledge he existed. That part had been surprisingly easy—although not entirely painless. Now he needed to work out what his next step was. Which meant he had to decide if this was just a chance to clean wounds and let the past heal in peace, or a chance to resurrect and resuscitate what had once been between them. And the whole time, he had to consider Annwyn and the mortal world.

Sometimes what was best for the two worlds wasn't what was best for him. He understood that now. Before, he'd thought he could have it all, which had resulted in him losing everything. He walked around shops, aimlessly looking at things he didn't need while at the same time assessing every woman he passed. None of them made his pulse quicken. He didn't want anyone else. He wasn't ready to move on.

Yet he knew if Jacqui really didn't want him, he couldn't drag her to Annwyn. He'd have to find someone else. Within two weeks. Plenty of people had married for business and eventually found happiness.

Happiness wasn't love. Nothing could substitute love, and while his father believed he didn't have the luxury of love as King, Felan believed differently. Love wasn't a luxury; it was an essential. He stopped at a flower shop. She'd given him a chance, and he wasn't going to let it go to waste. The fate of two worlds hung on what happened next.

It was times like these he envied his changeling son. Caspian only had to worry about his life, not the lives of billions.

—⁓—

At a quarter to five, Felan waited outside the coffee shop. He took a table on the sidewalk and placed the flowers down. They were probably not the right gesture, but he appreciated that she was seeing him. He was also watching everyone around him very closely. He'd spent the afternoon making sure he wasn't being followed by any fairies—including those who had been banished or exiled from Court. Just because he knew Sulia was moving against him didn't mean he knew everyone who was on her side, or those who pretended to be on her side. Being seen with Jacqui would only draw unwanted and dangerous attention to her—the same as it had always been.

He raked his fingers through his hair. Everything he did was a risk to someone or something. It would be nice to make a simple decision once in a while. He'd spent longer than necessary picking the damn flowers because he was worried about the message they'd give her. He couldn't even work out what to say to her. What had been very little time for him had been years for her. And yet, the flicker in her eyes when she'd seen him was enough for him to know that there was something there—something other than fear and hate, but they had been there too. He didn't like that he'd been the cause.

She came out of the shop, a bright turquoise handbag slung over her shoulder. "Not here," Jacqui said with barely a glance at him. Then, she walked past him without pausing.

Felan grabbed the flowers and followed, not wanting to give her any opportunity to walk away—not yet, anyway. But he'd already reconciled that he might have to let her go. She might have changed too much; he might have changed. The ashes might be too cold.

She stopped at a bench facing the ocean and sat down. The noise of the waves rolling against the sand curdled his blood. No doubt she'd picked this place deliberately, instead of walking inland. Reluctantly, he sat too. He'd have preferred to keep walking.

"These are for you. To thank you for seeing me." *Tread carefully*. The ice he was on was as delicate as the ice forming at the edge of the river of damned souls. If he fell in, it would be no less dangerous.

People walked by, paying them little regard. Here, they were just another couple. It was reassuring that he wasn't the only man to ever have to try and win his lover's heart back. As soon as he thought this, he knew that was what he wanted to do. Since meeting Jacqui, he'd never wanted anyone but her. But unlike his plots and games at Court, he really had no idea where to start or even how to play. He was going to have to throw everything he had at getting her to at least smile at him and agree to see him again. The alternative was really unattractive.

Jacqui looked at the flowers, then him. Her gaze was wary, as if she expected a trick of some kind.

He tried not to fidget under her scrutiny. He didn't feel like a Prince when she looked at him. He felt like he should be on his knees, apologizing for not being there when she'd obviously needed him. Apologizing didn't happen in Annwyn, as that would mean admitting to being wrong in the first place. "They are still your favorite?"

"Yes." She smiled, the tiniest curve of the corner of her lips. She took them from him and placed the bouquet between them on the bench. Then she watched him carefully, clearly expecting him to go first.

At least she hadn't thrown the flowers at him. He took that as a good sign. He leaned forward, resting his forearms on his thighs. He'd had plenty of time to think about what to say, the things he should've said that day, things he should've done differently. He decided to go with the simple truth. "I got called away. I lost track of time in this world."

From the corner of his eye he saw her nod. He'd used the same lines so many times before. She knew what was a few hours there could be days here, weeks at worst.

"That's not an apology."

Maybe not but it was the truth, and he wasn't sure

how to apologize for something he couldn't have avoided. What he should've done was take her with him, but she probably didn't want to hear that. "I'm not sure I'm ready to give one. I was doing my job."

Jacqui turned, one leg resting on the bench, her knee jutting toward him. "You were gone eight weeks, Felan. In those eight weeks, my life as I'd known it ended."

He got that, he really did, because the life he'd hoped to have with her had been destroyed, but telling her that now wasn't the right move either. Not when he still didn't understand the reason why. "What is ectopic?"

She pressed her lips together and stared at him before answering. "How can you know so much about some things and yet be so oblivious about others?"

"It's not a word I've come across in my interaction with the mortal world." There were plenty of things he didn't understand, but he tried to keep a grasp on the basics. How could he judge souls when he became the King of Annwyn if he didn't understand the life they'd led?

"The baby was growing in my fallopian tube—you know what they are?"

He closed his eyes. He knew, and he could also figure out the rest. If he'd known back then... Instead, he'd thought the worst of Jacqui's mother—and Jacqui. Mrs. Ara had let that happen. She'd have done anything to get him away from Jacqui. No doubt his mother would've approved of that power play—he should've seen it coming, instead of believing that mortals weren't as conniving as fairies.

"I was hoping you'd come back soon, so we could tell my parents together. I waited and waited. They worked it out when I passed out and started hemorrhaging. They were less than thrilled."

"I can imagine." Mrs. Ara would've hated Jacqui being pregnant by him.

"Maybe I should have listened to them."

He flinched at the sharp tone of her voice. "I thought your mother…" He couldn't even say it.

Jacqui drew in a sharp breath. "Had forced me to terminate?"

Felan nodded.

She shook her head, her disbelief etched on her face. "No. I would never have done that. Did you really think I had?"

"I didn't know what to think. I didn't know what was wrong with you, but I knew something wasn't right. Why didn't you say something?"

"Why didn't you stay?"

He closed his eyes. He'd barely been able to hold himself together. Jacqui had needed him to stay, and he'd let himself be swallowed up by his own concerns. He knew then what he should be apologizing for and what she needed to hear. However, it still took a few moments for the words to form, as they were so foreign on his tongue. "I'm sorry I wasn't there for you." He opened his eyes and looked at her. "You know I wanted to be there to tell them."

Jacqui shrugged and shook her head. "Really? You were always taking off with no notice for unspecified amounts of time, to God knows where."

"I was in Annwyn." It sounded like a lame excuse even as he said it.

She went on as if he hadn't spoken. "Then you'd

come back and expect to pick up where we'd left off. You should have seen the look on your face when you realized I wasn't pregnant. I'll never forget it."

"Babies are precious. It is so difficult for a fairy to have a child, even with a human." He'd been shocked, gutted. That had been the lowest point of his long life. He'd barely walked away before crumbling. It had taken hours to pull himself together enough to go back to Annwyn. He hadn't been able to let anyone see how shattered he was, so he'd kept it to himself all the pain and disappointment, the broken trust and lost love. He'd been tempted to go back to her, but the situation in Annwyn had worsened—looking back, he knew it had been deliberate—and then it had become too hard to even look at her in the mirror. Those memories were still sharp.

"So you assumed the worst?"

He had, and he should've known that she would never do that. When he didn't answer straight away, she stood up.

He stood too. If he was to have any hope, he had to be honest with her. "You're right. I thought your parents had found out and had talked you around. I thought you'd gotten scared. Hell, that you'd changed your mind about everything I'd said. You told me fairies weren't real, as if you were denying my existence, our child's existence. What was I supposed to think?"

"You could've come back and asked me. You could've done something instead of run."

"I didn't know how to deal with it any better than you."

"You should've been there for me." She was almost snarling, as if all the old hurt was rising back up.

He took a breath and refused to drown in those emotions again. "Yes, I should have been. But I can't change that. It's been seven years for you; for me it feels much more recent.

She crossed her arms and tilted her head slightly. He'd seen that look before, when he'd told her he was fairy. "You've been in Annwyn this whole time?"

Except for a few mortal hours here and there. "Politics are bad, factions are working against me. I was trying to numb the pain and pretend it never happened." He shook his head. He didn't know what else he could say. Nothing he did or said could change what had happened, as much as he wished otherwise. All that wasted time. If he'd been with her, they could've gotten through it together. Sulia and her schemes had taken the one thing he valued more than the throne of Annwyn.

———

Jacqui looked at him again, and this time he didn't bother to hide the hurt in his eyes. It would be so easy to believe him. And if he'd been there when she'd needed him, she would've believed him without a doubt. The bright yellow flowers lay on the bench, and he was apologizing for something that had happened years ago as if it were recent news. While it was nice to hear, she didn't need it. She didn't need him.

"It happened; you ran." She looked away and stared at the waves, the happy couples and families on the beach, all without a care. Maybe on the inside there was turmoil, but to the casual observer, they seemed to be enjoying life. That could've been them. It could still be them. He was here...seven years too late, but he was here. She pushed the thought aside. "I fell once and I got hurt. I can't do it again."

"I never meant to hurt you. Things were dangerous."

She spun back to face him, the breeze tugging at her curls and pulling them free. "You always said that. Has nothing changed for you?"

He paused, and she could see him thinking, trying to work out how to answer her. He wouldn't lie, but it wouldn't be the whole truth either. *Secret fairy business.* God, she didn't miss that. The never knowing when to expect him or for how long he'd stay. Could they have even lasted as a couple?

"Things have changed. None for the better." He smiled, but it was forced. "Tell me about those missing eight weeks. You always used to fill me in on what had happened while I was gone."

"That's because we were together. We aren't anymore."

"I didn't stop caring, even when I was convinced you'd cut out my heart and dropped it on the floor."

The retort she'd been about to make died on her tongue. She realized that from his position on her parents' doorstep, that day looked very different. By the time he'd returned and knocked on the door, she'd listened to too many people bad-mouth him and popped too many pills to think clearly. She'd been numb, and seeing him had only brought back the pain and the feelings of abandonment. She couldn't do that again, and yet talking to him now felt natural—as though they were just catching up.

"When my parents wouldn't let up about where you were, I told them you were a fairy." That had been her first mistake. It had been rapidly downhill from there.

Felan winced. He knew them well enough to know what that meant; he'd had dinner at their house a number of times. They still hadn't trusted him. He was too smooth, too rich, too something. But the more her mother had interfered and tried to discourage the relationship, the more Jacqui had enjoyed it, reveling in the rebellion and him. Around him, she'd always felt special.

"I'd also started seeing things, flickers at first. Then, after I'd been in hospital, they became solid." She knew what went bump in the night and it wasn't pretty. "Anyway, I wasn't coping with the loss, and then I was talking about seeing monsters and fairies, so they took me to a shrink who put me on meds. When you finally showed up, I didn't want to see you. You had wrecked my life without a backward glance." She picked up her handbag and the flowers, hoping he'd be happy with the answer and that he'd gotten what he needed to leave her alone.

"I'm sorry." He touched her hand for a moment and her skin warmed.

"It's too late for sorry." She gave an awkward shrug. Was there anything she wanted from him anymore? She looked at him without getting caught in his cool, green gaze. He still had the power to make her heart flutter like a butterfly in the breeze. There was one question she had left unanswered. "What are the monsters I see?"

He looked at her for a moment, shock on his face for a second before he masked it. He'd always been able to set his expression to unreadable very quickly. It wasn't natural, but then again, he wasn't human.

Felan took a few paces and turned to look at her, as if expecting her to fall into step like she once had. He'd always liked to be moving when having difficult conversations. Maybe that was a habit that came from being at Court—if he stopped too long, someone would overhear. She'd always suspected his life in Annwyn wasn't easy, but he'd never shared the bad bits. If he wanted to be moving for this, it wasn't going to be a nice, simple answer. Her heart sank a little. She'd wanted simple with a simple solution. She caught up with him and they started following the path that ran alongside the beach.

"They aren't monsters. They are banished fairies."

"Banished fairies? They don't look like you." Did all fairies look like him? Pretty, sharp, and sensual all in the same heartbeat.

He raised one dark eyebrow. "Greys are cut off from the Court, so they lose their looks as they slowly fade away to ugly nothing. It's a slow death and our harshest punishment."

Right, that explained why some were big and some were small, but all were ugly. "I thought it was being pregnant with a fairy child that made me see them, but it didn't stop afterward." She'd thought it would, had hoped it would, but instead it had become worse. "You didn't send them as punishment for losing the baby?"

"No!" He looked aghast. "I never wished you ill. Mostly I just wished I'd been with you instead of in Annwyn." He sounded so wretched about it that she began to realize that he was still coming to grips with the loss. How deep did his feelings for her run? It didn't matter. She just wanted to be rid of the monsters.

"How can I stop seeing them?"

"You will always see Greys."

She stopped walking. "What do you mean? I'm stuck

seeing *Greys* for the rest of my life?" He'd never told her that would be a side effect of being pregnant. She didn't want to always be watching where she looked in case she gave herself away.

Felan turned and looked at her. "When a human eats or drinks food from Annwyn, it binds them to the Court as well as giving them the ability to see fairies."

"I've always been able to see you." When had he fed her food from Annwyn?

"Because I use magic to be seen while I am here."

"Like now?"

He nodded and started walking again, and she followed. "The wine we celebrated with was from Annwyn. I was so sure we'd be together I didn't think anything of it. I didn't realize seeing the Greys would scare you."

It took a couple of steps for her to realize what he'd said. "You gave me wine from Annwyn, deliberately?"

"I thought we were going to be together. I wanted you to be able to see any threats, instead of letting them sneak around you."

"You never told me that." What a fool she'd been to ever trust him. She took a step away from him, certain he wasn't back in her life just to catch up. Her grip on the flowers tightened. Should she have accepted them?

"I didn't get around to it." He smiled and his face softened for a moment. "We were too busy celebrating."

And then he'd left and hadn't come back until it was too late.

Felan stopped. "What fairies have you seen?"

"None recently. I stopped taking meds and learned to ignore them. When the monst…Greys believed I couldn't see them, they stopped bugging me."

"That's good. Ignoring them is the best way to stay safe. Have you seen any Court fairies, pretty fairies?" His gaze slid across the people around them, never stopping, yet she knew he was taking in everything.

"Only a couple, mostly in a crowd—none since I moved to California. Why?" She shifted, suddenly concerned. The old fear of fairies and being viewed as delusional returned and gave her heart a squeeze. This wasn't a normal conversation, and she'd spent years trying to be normal again. A few minutes with Felan and it all came undone.

"You knew every time I saw you it was a risk. That someone might follow me and try to use you against me. That hasn't changed. If anything, things are more precarious."

"And you decided now was a good time to drag your baggage to my door?"

"I wasn't ready to come back sooner. This is all fresh for me. It hasn't been years in Annwyn."

She sighed and tried to remember how she'd felt only a year or so after their breakup, but it was a drug-induced haze. Part of her life had been absorbed into a place where time seemed to stand still and days bled into each other. While he might still be dealing with the fallout, she wasn't. "I've moved on, Felan."

"You're with someone?" He stepped back as if surprised.

She was so tempted to lie and say yes so he would leave. But she couldn't say it. She couldn't lie to him. There'd been too many half-truths and misunderstandings. He'd been honest with her, and she had to be honest with him. The way they had been once…maybe.

He'd lied, or at least left out the truth about the wine. What else had he misled her on?

"No, but I know you. I know that you come and go as you please, and I need more. I *deserve* more." If he could promise to never leave, that he'd be there when she needed him, she'd be tempted to play with fire again—it was hard to let go of something that had felt so good when it was going well. Of course, when it all went wrong, it hurt far worse than anything she'd ever known.

"I have responsibilities—"

"Exactly." Somewhere in her teenage heart, she'd once hoped that he'd give them all up for her. She knew now that was never going to happen.

"Annwyn comes first. It has to." His voice was soft and sharp. She glimpsed the Prince and the man he was in Annwyn. There was no joy, only work. She had been his fun times, R and R in the mortal world.

"And that's never going to change." She turned around and walked away, half expecting him to follow and put up an argument, half hoping that he would. He was a mistake she'd happily make again.

Don't look back. Just keep going.

Chapter 4

FELAN WATCHED HER WALK AWAY. HE TOOK A STEP after her, then changed his mind and started back toward the cemetery where he'd crossed the veil. She was right. Annwyn was always going to come first; he didn't have a choice about that. He blinked slowly and let the glamour go, invisible now to everyone except those who could see fairies, like changelings and people who'd tasted fairy food or wine.

Even though most people could not see him, they still avoided where he was, as if unconsciously sensing he was there.

Hearing the truth from Jacqui's lips had only made him realize what he'd lost. No, not lost—thrown away because he'd been unable to see past his own pain. Talking to Jacqui had only reopened the wound. He wanted her the same way he always had. Time away hadn't diminished that, but it had changed the way she felt about him.

He was no longer enough.

He was a virtually immortal fairy Prince, and she wanted more. He shook his head and tried not to let the bitter laugh escape. He could give her a life beyond the mortal world, one that would last for centuries, and it wasn't enough. It wasn't enough because he'd never directly explained what he could offer her. She could have a life few even dreamed of, and she'd live for centuries with him as they ruled Annwyn. He'd just assumed, once she knew he was fairy—and the Prince—that she also knew they would live in Annwyn.

But he'd never actually asked her to be his Queen. Perhaps he'd been a little afraid she'd say no—he *still* wasn't ready to hear that response—nor had he ever stated exactly what would be required of her to save the mortal world. He'd just expected that because they were in love it would all fall in place.

Apparently not. He kicked a soft drink can and watched as it scuttled down the sidewalk. And they weren't in love anymore. They were someplace where love cast a long shadow but it hurt to step into the sun.

Any other woman would've jumped at the chance to take what he had, but not Jacqui. It was her refusal to grab the power being offered that kept drawing him back to her. Even if he didn't still love her, that quality still made her an ideal candidate for Queen. She wouldn't be corrupted by Court. That she still looked at him with more heat than she should if she were truly over him—and he was damn sure he hadn't hidden his feelings very well—gave him hope that perhaps there was still some love.

He still didn't know the answer to his problem. He could pursue her and hope their love grew back, risking making her unhappy for millennia, or find someone else and risk a cold, power-hungry bitch like his mother who would sacrifice her grandson in a heartbeat if she thought it would bring her more glory. After his mother had involved Caspian in her plot with her lover, and a subsequent attack on the woman who was now Hunter of Annwyn, he wasn't bothering to try and defend her. Annwyn was safer with his mother locked up.

He really didn't want to end up married to someone like her because he was in a rush—just like his
father had been. Damn his father and his deadline. In
the same breath, he knew his father didn't have the
strength to give him any more time. He wasn't ready
to lose his father.

A few blocks away from the shore, he reached the
church and the cemetery. It was quieter here—the tour-
ists and shoppers stayed close to the beach—and he was
glad to put some distance between him and the ocean.

He buttoned up his knee-length waistcoat and made
sure his clothing was neat. Then he ran his fingers
through his hair and hoped he looked calm, as if he
hadn't been anywhere interesting. At least he could use
monitoring the tearing veil as an excuse to spend more
time away from Annwyn.

Just before the threshold, he hesitated. His skin was
still warm from the California sunshine, but he could
feel the chill of Annwyn in his blood. Even before he
was fully across, the cold was crawling over his skin and
sucking away the heat.

This was why Annwyn had to come first.

Through the doorway, the ground was crisp with
frost. The grass was virtually dead; the field where
people had once played boule and watched the doorway
was now more like a muddy paddock with frost rimming
the edges of the puddles. The trees were bare, all but
the last few leaves had fallen, and there were no new
buds. His breath clouded in front of him as he walked.
It wouldn't be long until snow not only fell but settled.

The castle was grim, a skeletal reminder of the summer days now past. The Court had just celebrated the

midsummer festival. They'd danced and ignored the falling leaves. The festivals were tied to the mortal world, while the seasons of Annwyn were tied to the King and Queen. With the Queen imprisoned, things were getting cold fast. Felan was almost missing California, ocean and all.

He walked into the castle. Where once the ground had been a lush carpet of grass that always sprung back, it was now mud churned up from being walked on. In the main hall, people were dining and dancing as if nothing was wrong, but the hems of their dresses and cloaks were now edged with dirt, not gold or silver.

They chose to ignore the failing magic and carry on playing, hoping the problem would get solved. Some were on his side; others were on Sulia's. Some were hedging their bets and watching both sides while committing to none. Those were the ones he really needed to watch.

"So glad you could join us." Sulia stood, a glass goblet in her hand. The cut of her dress emphasized the gentle rounding of her stomach, revealing how she threatened the throne. She was not far along but enough that she looked like a sure thing to claim the throne; plus, she now had her human consort here. She'd snuck him across the veil while Felan had been away. He gritted his teeth but refused to let the tension show.

The man next to her stood and gave Felan a look mortals usually reserved for gum stuck to a shoe. Others at Sulia's table turned to look at him, none of them with the slightest bit of respect. It was as if he were interloping on a private dinner.

Nice. Felan didn't acknowledge the mortal.

The chill in the air thickened and settled around him like a wet, heavy wool blanket. Sulia was holding court—or at least pretending to. She had the man she wanted on the throne with her, a mortal willing to give up his soul to save Annwyn, and a child growing in her belly that would secure succession. It was no wonder that she was gaining supporters.

She was looking brave and strong while he was looking weak and afraid, as if he couldn't protect his future Queen if he brought her here. To many that would be a sign that he wasn't fit to rule. Yet Sulia had made no public declaration of her claim.

Felan carefully noted each fairy that was in the chamber and was relieved to find that the ones he considered loyal to him weren't there. But that could've been because they were being careful. He didn't know whom he could trust these days.

"Someone has to stop the veil from totally disintegrating."

Sulia shrugged, her white-blond hair trailing over her shoulder in a long braid elaborately threaded with silver and gems. "What are a few less humans? There are billions of them. They won't miss a few."

Her Court laughed as if she was making a joke.

"I'm sure all mothers miss their children, and children miss their mothers." He crossed his arms and leaned against the wall made of a tree, trying to look as relaxed as ever.

Her hand brushed her stomach and she smiled, as if she didn't care what he thought. He knew her goal, just not how she planned to achieve it or when. He really needed to act first and cut her off before she could finish what she'd started. That meant he had less than two weeks.

When the fairies looked at her, did they see the Queen they wanted to rule them? Or simply a return to spring and summer? Probably both. They knew Sulia would continue with the parties and gambling and deal making that his mother had encouraged. It was familiar, and Felan wanted change—not that he'd said it in as many words. After all, to most, he was nothing but the wastrel Prince. A part he had played too well.

Sulia walked toward him, her red dress trailing in the mud and a cruel smile pasted on her lips. "You haven't brought your beloved to Court?" She trailed her fingers over his chest, but he kept his face a perfect mask. He was used to hiding everything at Court.

"Why would I bring her so soon?" He caught her hand and kissed her fingers.

"So we can judge her worth."

"My choice of consort is of no one's concern but mine."

"Or maybe you don't have one." She plucked her fingers free and grinned at him.

That was what everyone thought. And they'd be right. But he didn't need to let anyone know that. He would have someone before the two weeks were up. Sulia would be taking the throne only after she'd drowned him in the river of damned souls.

"I value her safety. I know our history, Sulia, even if you don't. Human consorts have been murdered before by rival factions." His father and uncle had fought viciously for several years, killing many lovers in an effort to secure the throne. It was how his father had ended up with Eyra. She hadn't been his first choice, or even his second, but she had been there and she knew how to rule, and at the time, that had been important.

Sulia's back stiffed and she half turned. "Do you not trust me?"

"I'm the Crown Prince of Annwyn." He paused and let the words sink in. Let her supporters think again about who they were backing. But perhaps they didn't have a choice. Many of them would've made deals and promises, and wound up trapped and on the wrong side. "I don't trust anyone."

Sulia tossed her head. "You are too much like your father." It was aimed as an insult, and to many it would be. They saw Gwyn as a King who'd let his wife control everything, when, in fact, he'd been mitigating any damage Eyra would do for well over a human millennia. Now Gwyn was old and tired.

"And you are too much like my mother." Now that was an insult.

"I know how to run the Court. I have broken no rules."

Yet.

"Let's keep it that way. I'd hate to send the Hunter after you."

She laughed, and it echoed in the cold hall. "That little chit barely knows which end of the sword to hold."

That may have been true at the start, but Taryn merch Arlea was doing everything a good Hunter should, including supporting King and Prince. She'd quite happily stick the blunt end of the sword through Sulia too if she thought it would get her back to the mortal world faster. The love that Taryn and Verden had was what he wanted. Not even Verden's banishment had touched it. It was possible for a fairy to love and be loved so deeply they forgot about status and deals and the things that most Court fairies considered important.

If Sulia ever caught on to the half-truths Felan was telling, there would be trouble. He couldn't appear to be lying or no one would trust him. He trusted Taryn, Verden, Dylis, and Bramwel, and also Caspian. That was five people, not enough to win the throne if it came to war. But it might be enough to steal it before Sulia sat on it and proclaimed herself Queen.

He'd still back himself in the battle for the throne—but not for much longer if he didn't do something soon.

"You mock the Hunter?" Aside from the King, the Hunter held the most power and sway. Taryn, who was only doing the job until a new King, or Queen, sat on the throne, could arrest fairies if she thought they were committing treason. She was also spending a lot of time training with Verden and was far more dangerous with a sword than Sulia gave her credit for. Not that Sulia needed to know that.

Sulia rested her hand on the human's shoulder. "No, just stating a fact."

"I'd hate to think you were questioning my father's choices—he is King after all." Felan walked out of the hall before Sulia could think of a retort. He wanted her followers to question what they were doing and why. While he couldn't free them from the deals they'd made, he could at least make them think about where they were placing their loyalty.

Felan walked down the corridor, shadow servants hovering at the edges, waiting to be commanded. There were more of them than there had ever been. What was his father doing?

What was he going to do?

Since his father wasn't in the main hall, he would be in the Hall of Judgment.

The doors opened as he approached. The last time he'd been in here, his mother had been sentenced and Taryn had been made temporary Hunter after Verden had been banished. While Taryn wouldn't have been his first choice, she was the best choice, given that it was only for two weeks, especially as she was going to leave Court at the end. Usually the Lord of the Hunt was a coveted role, but this close to the end of a King's rule, no one wanted to be on his Council, as all knew the new King, or Queen should Sulia win, would pick a fresh Council.

Gwyn sat on his throne as a procession of almost-transparent souls filed past. When the King was judging souls, doors on the sides of the room opened to allow the souls passage. From one side they came in; then they paused by the throne, only to be sent to one of the two doorways on the other side. One was a doorway that led over the river, in much the same way the veil divided the mortal world from Annwyn, and the other went down to the river. Felan had been shown both but passed through neither—doing that would result in his death.

The door the souls entered the Hall through was the center of Annwyn. Once, long before fairies took over Annwyn, souls would have arrived here and had to figure out their own afterlife. Some would have found it easy to cross the river while others would have naturally drowned, and others would've been trapped and unable to move on until they finally worked it out. Back then the river had been more like a choppy ocean, or so the singing stones said. When he was younger, he'd made a point of learning everything he could about the past, including the way the fairies had taken over the sorting of souls and the creation of the Hall of Judgment.

With the King now judging and the souls passing through quickly instead of lingering, the battle between life and death in the mortal world had turned. Fairies had allowed humans to multiply and spread, and in exchange, they had forgotten about the old ones who held the mortal afterlife in their hands.

Jacqui would lose her soul, and her afterlife, to save two worlds, but in return, she'd live for centuries and have a life she could only imagine. To him, losing a soul didn't seem like an issue—fairies had no souls and therefore no afterlife. There was no gambling that it would be better once they died, as all they had was now. Jacqui, or any human Queen, might feel differently. He needed to tell her what was required. No, he needed to ask her to be his Queen first. After all, if she said no there was no point in continuing with the details.

His father carefully looked at each soul, then sent them off with a flick of his hand. There were only three choices—across the river to the Elysian fields, into the river, or becoming a shadow servant. Granting shadow status meant the souls had a chance to redeem themselves, to eventually cross the river instead of drowning forever. That was why there were more shadow servants—his father didn't want to condemn everyone who was dying of plagues, yet not all were ready to cross. A sudden and unexpected death left souls unprepared for the afterlife. Those that were ready to become shadows approached the throne instead of a doorway and took on the solid gray of the shadow servant. No voice, no face. Felan would have to decide when they'd served their penance…or not.

Too soon, this would be his responsibility. Some days it was enough to make him want to run across the veil to the mortal world and never look back. He drew in a breath. Today was one of those days. Even if he won the throne, there was still a lot of work to do to put things right. Jacqui didn't see that. That Annwyn came first didn't mean he loved her less. However, he didn't even know how to begin that conversation, or even if he had the time to have it. If she couldn't understand the importance of what he did, it would always come between them.

He looked at his father. At a casual glance, he didn't look a day over twenty-five, but Felan saw his true age in his eyes. Ancient and dull, he'd lost…not weight, but there seemed to be less of him. It wasn't just Annwyn failing. His father was dying, wasting away while the Court partied.

The anger that he'd felt at the two-week deadline faded. His father deserved more than spending his last few days judging souls and waiting for death.

Felan stepped into the room and shut the door. "Do you want some help?"

―――

Gwyn looked up and focused on his son. "Don't you have more pressing things to do? This will be yours soon enough."

The souls that had been filing past in a flicker of light and color stopped. They would wait until he was ready to begin again. So many were muddied and confused, angry and uncertain. Many longed to go back across the veil to the living, but they couldn't. The sheer number of souls now waiting was enough for him to know how bad it was on the other side of the veil, and if Felan didn't do something fast, it would only get worse—for everyone.

"Not if Sulia has her way."

Gwyn grunted and let a few more souls pass. "She thinks she is popular, and people are thinking she might succeed because of the child she carries. You need to quash that and prove you have someone." He glanced at his son. "You do have someone selected?"

Felan walked over and took the throne next to him, the one meant for the Queen—not that Eyra had ever helped judge. She was more interested in parties and power plays, and would have sent them all to the river just to get it over with. However, there was still time for Gwyn to hunt and feast and gamble. His work didn't consume all his time, even now. Felan slouched in the throne, his legs out straight and his eyes on the bare branches that formed the roof.

Gwyn had tried to save his son from the bitter fight he'd had to win the throne by having only one child. Unfortunately, his brother, Edern, had made many children, most of which Gwyn had ensured were born in the mortal world and were no threat. Someone, however, had protected Sulia's human mother and made sure the child was born in Annwyn, thus making Sulia a fairy. He'd failed to protect Felan from threat. Although, the fewer who knew of Sulia's direct claim to the throne, the better. It was a secret Gwyn was happy to die with—he certainly didn't want to legitimatize her claim by admitting her lineage.

"Yes—maybe. I don't know." Felan scrubbed his hand over his face. "I don't know what I'm doing."

"No one does until after it's done." He paused to look at the soul in front of him and didn't like what he saw. Some still had the power to make Gwyn stop and wonder what they had done to be so damaged. This one wasn't truly evil, but it had caused enough damage to others that it wore the marks in slashes of black and red. Could this soul be redeemed and sent over the river, or was it too far gone? In his heart, he already knew the answer. *River*. This soul would drown forever. Once assigned, the soul had no choice but to go. They never knew where they were going until they got there. He'd stopped feeling guilty about sending souls to the river a long time ago. "If you don't do something soon, you will lose by default."

"I know that." Felan's hand slapped the arm of the throne. "But I want a proper marriage. I want more than…" He grimaced, as if realizing he'd gone too far.

"More than what I have?"

"I'm sorry." Felan bowed his head.

A century ago, he would've taken Felan to task for speaking so boldly. "I think the time for delicate manners is behind us. You see the end result. You don't remember the start. We were happy." Gwyn smiled and let the early decades of summer and joy fill him for a moment—back when Eyra had acted loving even if it wasn't in her heart, before she learned that she could control others through trickery and games. "It took a while, centuries maybe, for her to be corrupted."

"And your mother?"

Gwyn frowned and tried to pull up memories that

were millennia old. "She wanted everyone to be happy. She brought music and dances from the mortal world. There were grand processions…back then more mortals came to Court. Perhaps that was good for us and I shouldn't have stopped the practice." But he had because Eyra had used them cruelly.

"So it is possible for humans to keep their humanity here?"

"Many do when they are brought here." Though it had been a while since anyone, before Sulia, had dared bring their mortal lover to Annwyn. Eyra didn't tolerate it. If she couldn't take a human lover, then no one could.

"They don't have to give up their souls," Felan muttered. His face was set somewhere between a frown and deep thought.

While it pained him to see his son struggling, there was nothing he could do. "Sulia will not let you live if you walk away." The same way Edern had promised Gwyn's death. If Edern had let him walk away, then the war between them would never have happened, but his brother's insecurity and paranoia had gotten him killed.

Felan nodded. "I know, but the woman I want…it's complicated. And now…I don't know if I should continue or start afresh."

"You are talking about love, not a Queen."

"In my mind they are the same."

"No, in your heart they are the same." Gwyn stood. He'd had enough of silent souls for the moment. "I want you to be happy. I know you've made mistakes in the past—like with Caspian's mother—and maybe that is my fault for not being clear. I would never have fought you if you wanted to step up sooner. I would have thanked you for it. We don't get the luxury of love. Maybe it can grow, maybe you find it with a mistress, but Annwyn needs the soul of the human consort. Nothing more; nothing less."

Felan lifted his gaze. "What would you have me do? Grab the first woman who walks past? Does she not deserve more?"

Gwyn shrugged. "Most humans come to love Annwyn once they get over the shock." He crossed his arms and looked at his son. Felan looked so young, and yet he was already far older than many. The overlap between King and the heir assuming power was long so that the heir had the chance to learn. Half his life had been spent preparing; the other half would be spent ruling. Fairies lived much longer in the heart of Annwyn than those on the fringes or those in the mortal world. Millennia instead of centuries. In truth, Felan had been ready to rule years ago, but taking over was never easy. Gwyn knew that from bitter experience. Sometimes it was easier to leave things as they were until change had to happen. "Tell me, if Annwyn wasn't your concern, what would you be doing? Would you be trying to win back this woman?"

"Yes," he said without hesitating.

"Then you have your answer."

"It will take longer than two mortal weeks."

Gwyn smiled. He could've given Felan two Annwyn weeks, which would've been far longer in the mortal world, but his son had had plenty of time and had squandered it, and Gwyn no longer had the time to be generous. He was dying and Annwyn was killing him faster. "Then try harder. If you think she's worth fighting for, then fight."

Felan looked at him. "How can I convince a woman that giving up her soul and living in Annwyn is a good thing?"

"Maybe you don't. You just bring her here and let her grow to love it."

"Or maybe she just grows to hate me instead." Felan pushed himself out of the throne.

"Maybe. But you won't find out by lingering around here like a lost shadow." Gwyn took a few paces, then turned to face his son. "I have a favor to ask."

"I may not have time to grant it."

Gwyn gave a low laugh. He deserved that. "I want you to go to your mother's grove and free her statues."

Felan's head snapped up. "Why me?"

"Because I know that you know where it is. I do not."

Felan raised his eyebrows. "How long have you known?"

"The time doesn't matter. I want them freed before she is executed." The word didn't stick in his throat the way it had when he'd first given the order for her arrest. He'd had to choose between the Queen who hated him and his son. To give his son the best chance of succeeding, he'd had to bring the full force of the law against his wife. If he'd let her go with a warning, it would have strengthened Sulia's campaign. Even still, it hadn't been an easy decision, and he knew he wouldn't be able watch as the Hunter carried out the sentence. Poor Taryn—she hadn't volunteered for any of this, and yet she had risen when required, just like her mother. He had no doubt Felan would do the same. When the time came, his son would make sure Annwyn remained free of Sulia's grasp.

"Very well."

"Sooner rather than later...I have heard whispers that Sulia is planning to cut down the trees." The statues were actually trees that had once been fairies who had somehow crossed Eyra. While trees, they lived; if they were cut down, they would die. Before his rule ended, he would try to unravel the edges of Eyra's work to give his son a head start.

Felan drew in a sharp breath. "She wouldn't."

"Sulia wouldn't even blink. Those fairies are a threat to her simply because they hate Eyra." He didn't need to say that if they were bad for Sulia, they could be good for Felan's cause. Gwyn unhooked a plain drinking horn from his belt and handed it to his son.

"She doesn't waste time either." Felan fingered the cup of life, then tucked it beneath his waistcoat. "I will be across the veil."

"Saving trees and winning hearts." Gwyn smiled, but it was forced.

Felan didn't return the smile. He bowed and left the chamber.

For a moment, Gwyn didn't move. He closed his eyes and let the silence wash over him. He'd hoped to avoid handing Annwyn in winter to his son. He'd wanted to avoid the horror of what he'd gone through—his father pitting his sons against each other to see who was worthy to rule. Knee-deep snow stained brilliant blue with blood and trees frozen solid with ice. It had taken a long time for the snows to melt and the river to settle—longer for the bitterness to go. And here he was again, but on the other side.

It wasn't any easier.

Chapter 5

By the time she'd gotten back to the share house she called home, Jacqui had her emotions locked down. It wasn't right that Felan could waltz back into her life, spin her around, and then wander off again. She had to stop letting herself be swept into his arms. She had to say no and let him find another dance partner.

She knew what happened to humans who danced with fairies—they became trapped in the dance. Was she trapped, unable to let him go because of fairy magic? Or did she still care?

Unfortunately, she cared. It had been nice to talk to him, and she'd been able to do so without breaking down. Three years ago, even one year ago, she wouldn't have been able to do that. Her lips turned up into a smile as she realized how far she'd come from being the scared, medicated nineteen-year-old she had been when he disappeared. There was nothing wrong with caring about an ex. She was kind of sad for him that his life hadn't gotten any better the way hers had. But she had to admit that he still scared her—not because she thought he'd hurt her, but because he still had the power to turn her life upside down. She didn't want fairies in her life.

She opened the front door, dropped her handbag and the flowers in her room, then went looking for Ash. She was watching TV in the living room. Their other roommate worked in a bar and must have left for work already.

"You're back way before I thought you would be." Ash turned down the volume, while the news reporter kept talking about a disaster in Africa.

Jacqui plonked onto the sofa, her legs suddenly tired. "We didn't have much to talk about." Or rather, there wasn't much to say. What had happened was in the past. He wasn't the jerk she wanted him to be—that would be so much easier—he was just torn between two worlds. The same as always.

Ash leaned forward as if expecting more details. While Jacqui had kept her relationship with Felan a secret for years because she was afraid people would think she was crazy, she wanted to talk about him now. He had been an exciting part of her life...a part she'd thought she'd always have at the time.

"We dated for over a year, but we broke up..." She didn't want to tell Ash the full story, about the baby or about where Felan came from—some things were best kept secret, even from her friends. Like the three awful years that had followed the breakup. "It was part misunderstanding, part wounded pride." Part parental meddling.

"Ah, ended badly and neither of you ever got over it."

"Not really. We got over it—it was years ago—but I guess we both needed the chance to air the wound and let it heal." She leaned back against the sofa and closed her eyes. In her mind, she saw Felan the way he had been when they'd first met, smiling and laughing as if he didn't have a care in either world. He'd changed. He was more serious, more cautious this time. She wanted to see him grin without the edge. She wanted him to be happy.

"So that's it? He didn't beg for another chance?"

Jacqui opened her eyes. He hadn't. In fact, all he'd

done was ask about what had happened. She had been the one to jump to the conclusion that he was looking to rekindle what they had. "No, he didn't."

He hadn't behaved the way she'd expected at all. She'd seen the look in his eyes, the heat half-hidden behind his cool green gaze. But he hadn't acted on it the way he once would've. He'd kept the distance between them, even though she was sure he wanted more than the truth. So why hadn't he done anything? What game was he playing with her?

"You know he's going to be back." Ash flicked her hair over her shoulder, her gaze somewhere else. Jacqui was sure she was picturing Felan and imagining what it would be like to be with him. He had that effect on women.

"I hope not." But her words didn't ring true. Even now there was a place in her heart that belonged to him, though she'd gotten used to living with it being empty and unfulfilled. Today had reminded her of what was missing, but also of the danger of being with Felan. He was too seductive, like a drug that she knew was bad for her but she couldn't resist. She couldn't go back. She didn't know if she'd have the strength to rebuild her life when he left her again. Which he would. He'd even admitted that Annwyn was still the first thing in his mind.

"You wouldn't give him a second chance? Man, half the women in California wouldn't kick him out of bed in the first place."

Oh yes, they would, and if they knew what he was, they wouldn't even get into his bed. But that was how he worked: he'd let her think he was human for six months before revealing he was the Prince of Death. He'd proven he was fairy by holding an iron nail on his palm while she'd watched his skin burn. Then he'd vanished for two weeks and left her to dwell on what he'd said.

"His job is more important than me. It always was. Besides, he didn't ask for a second chance." And he probably wouldn't. She hoped he wouldn't. Would she be able to say no? "He doesn't think of me that way now." The words tasted wrong as she spoke them. He hadn't sought her out just to learn the truth. Ash was right. He would be back. What did he really want from her? That she didn't know scared her more than a little. She knew fairies always had an endgame in sight. What was Felan's?

"Well, if you're not interested, you won't mind if I take a shot at Mr. Tall-Hot-and-Trouble." There was a glint in Ash's dark eyes that Jacqui didn't like.

Her heart gave a nasty clench, and she had to bite her tongue and take a moment to make sure she didn't turn an unflattering shade of green. Felan would've had lovers since her; she'd had lovers since him. But none had stolen her heart the way he had—none had ever destroyed it like he had either. And even though she'd thought he no longer had a claim on her heart, she had been wrong. She still wanted him—maybe even loved him. However, that didn't mean they were ever going to work. Sometimes love wasn't enough when there was a whole other world standing in the way.

Jacqui looked at Ash, trying to make her voice light. "How would you feel if I dated one of your exes?"

Ash shrugged. "If I was over him, what does it matter?"

She couldn't argue with that. She couldn't say no,

unless she admitted she wasn't over him, and she wasn't ready to do that, not even to herself. "True. If he comes back, you can serve his coffee and see if he bites."

And if he bit, she was sure that would end her attraction to the overly handsome Prince.

———

It was night when Felan stepped back into the mortal world. The air smelled different here—drier and ancient.

"Where are we?" Taryn, Lady of the Hunt, glanced around. She had her sword drawn, ready to fight as if she'd been wielding a blade for years.

Felan hadn't been sure what they'd find when they stepped through the doorway closest to his mother's grove. His sword was a comforting weight in his hand. He paused and listened before answering, but he heard nothing but the soft rustling of holly trees.

"Middle East."

"Are you trying to get us killed?"

He'd been concerned that the trees would be damaged by a stray bomb, but they were far enough away from civilization and the fighting that the grove remained untouched. "Be more worried about my mother's spies than human weapons." He'd been here only twice before—once when he'd followed out of curiosity, and once when he'd filled a promise and freed Bramwel, who'd been trapped here as a tree. There was a very good possibility that his mother had upped the security since. "Guard the doorway."

If that were destroyed, they would have a long walk to the next one—which would no doubt suit Sulia perfectly, as he'd lose precious days.

"Don't take too long," Taryn whispered.

"I don't intend to." He gave her a nod and moved away from the doorway. His soft-soled boots were quiet over the rocky terrain.

As before, the skin on the back of his neck prickled from both the magic in the air and the tension. They weren't alone. Flitting along, almost hidden by the trees and darkness, were wild fae. The wild fae were what all fairies had once been—bound to nature and existing only in the mortal world—until millennia ago, when some had discovered Annwyn and claimed it as theirs. Now the wild fae and fairies were two different creatures, but they weren't at odds. On this old hill, the wild fae were drawn to the magic of the grove and the trapped fairies. They'd watched him last time, their skin rough and dark like bark, silently waiting to see what he'd do.

Freeing Bramwel seemed to have made them happy. And if he'd cut down the tree instead and killed Bramwel? He doubted they would have interfered. Wild fae rarely interacted with anyone; they merely watched.

If there were wild fae here, what else was here? Did his mother or Sulia now have the area guarded? He hoped he wouldn't need to use his sword tonight. He didn't like killing.

Maybe he was too soft to be King.

He pushed the thought away. He didn't have to kill to be a good King. His father hadn't killed to rule the Court—but then, his mother had done enough for the both of them. The trees grew closer together, and he could feel the resonance of the grove now. The wild fae fell back, unwilling to enter the place that had been desecrated, used to bind and torture.

His mother had gone to great lengths to hide it, away from a natural doorway yet close enough that the distance could be covered with a captive, and in a place of reverence for the wild fae. What she'd done had driven them out of the grove. He paused before entering. There were seventeen trees. Well, they looked like trees to the casual eye, but when he looked closely, he could see the fairies reaching for the sky and silently crying out. Their feet were embedded in the earth. They were alive and yet not.

Bramwel had refused to discuss what the experience had been like after Felan had freed him—except to say that it was nice to have a stretch and a scratch. After the successful recovery of one fairy, he knew all could be saved. The trouble was, he didn't know what they'd done to be put here. With his mother, it could be anything from daring to be the King's mistress to beating her at cards.

He drew in a breath and tried to center himself. A little wine from the cup of life around the roots of each tree, and the spell would break. For a moment, he considered each tree. Did he make his case now, while they could listen? Or wait? Or just let his actions say everything that needed to be said?

He sighed. This was bad business. But it would have been worse if he'd arrived and found them all cut down. He sheathed his sword and pulled the cup of life from his belt. He knew he wouldn't be handing it back to his father this time. His father had been surprised when he handed it back after the last time he'd used it. Felan had been shocked his father would hand it over to him so readily. Only the King should use the cup of life. He looked at the relic from another time and saw it as more than a magical object, more than an ancient animal horn. His father trusted him to do the right thing and become the next King of Annwyn. His father would do anything to ensure that happened.

That was why Felan was here and not his father. It was important that he was seen to be these fairies' savior. He pulled the cork from the small bottle of fairy wine he'd tucked into his waistcoat pocket and filled the drinking horn. Then he walked widdershins around the grove and spilled a little at the base of each tree. The ground immediately sucked up the offering and the branches began to quiver and then lower. He took a step back and watched. A slow smile formed as the bark fell away and the fairies began lifting their feet out of the dirt where they had been rooted for too long.

A few stumbled, their legs unused to movement. Felan helped them up. He poured more wine, and let them drink and heal. They thanked him, not caring who he was, just that they were free. Their clothes were fashions he'd forgotten—the flowing white dress on a pregnant lady; gold-embroidered robe on a man; tight, multicolored hose on another. Some had been here for a very long time. It was a cruel punishment that should never have been allowed to happen.

How had Eyra even learned this magic? And who else knew how to trap a fairy forever? That was something he'd yet to find out. He made a mental note that he needed to see his mother—and possibly Sulia—for a private meeting. His to-do list was getting longer and yet his time was getting shorter.

He checked his watch, well aware Taryn was by the

doorway alone, then looked at the gathered fairies—one was little more than a child. Felan pressed his teeth together and wished he had better news for them.

"I'm here to take you back to Annwyn."

"No, I can't. The Queen." The woman in white placed her hand over her stomach and Felan knew immediately what her perceived crime was. His mother had refused to allow her ladies to take lovers or get pregnant after she had been denied the chance to have a second child. As a result, the numbers at Court had been slowly dwindling. The Court of Annwyn had been in decline for longer than he'd realized—or maybe he just hadn't wanted to see it because he wasn't ready to take over. He still didn't feel ready.

"Annwyn is in winter." He let his word settle like icy flakes of snow.

A few blinked, as if not understanding; others shuddered, as if feeling the chill in their blood. He could feel it in his, an ever-present chill that couldn't be warmed away.

"The Queen is imprisoned for treason, and while there is the possibility of war, if you remain here, you will face certain death when the power shifts."

The man in the purple-and-gold robe with sleeves that dragged on the ground folded his arms. "And who are you? Which side are you on?"

"Side?" Felan didn't want to be standing here discussing a war he wanted to avoid.

"For war there has to be two," the man insisted. A whisper rustled through the grove as the fairies started talking for the first time in many years. The man caught the edge of the conversation and stiffened as he realized his mistake. "Prince Felan?"

Felan inclined his head.

The man bowed. "I'm sorry, my Prince, I didn't recognize you. You were knee-high last I saw you."

That was longer than Felan had expected. Had there been others trapped over the years? If so, what had happened to them?

"Come on. There is a fair walk back to the doorway." He started moving, then stopped. "I would recommend that you go to a village or the outskirts of Annwyn if you wish to avoid the Queen and her supporters."

"You don't want us at Court?" one of the freed fairies asked.

"I don't want retaliation. I have freed you, but if it were known, I suspect there would be trouble, and not just for me."

A few fairies exchanged nervous glances, and that was the first time Felan considered that he might have also freed a spy, someone who would report back to his mother. But who? They'd all met his gaze and smiled gratefully. Was he overreacting and being overly suspicious? He'd like to think he was, but given his mother's record and Sulia's conniving, he suspected his concern was justified.

After noting each of their faces, he led them back to the doorway. When they arrived, Taryn was wiping her sword clean on the clothes of a Grey. The Grey looked like a cloth-wrapped bundle of sticks, his limbs gnarled and twisted, his face caught in a wizened grimace.

Felan reached for his sword and the freed fairies stepped back. "Just the one?"

"Yes." She sheathed her sword and looked at the fairies who had followed him to the doorway. Was she also noting who they were in case of later trouble? "Let's not wait around to see if more follow."

He nodded and led them back through the doorway to Annwyn while Taryn followed behind. Seeing Annwyn after so long would be a shock, even though he'd told them it was winter. They stumbled through the doorway, and some gasped in horror at the ice and bare trees. He was used to it, but it still cut to see Annwyn in such a condition. He was sure it got worse every time he came back.

A few glanced at him with blame in their pale eyes.

It was his fault. He should have acted years ago. He should be doing something now. The time for stalling and delicate games was over. He needed to go back to Jacqui and ask outright if she would be his Queen.

Chapter 6

A FAIRY WREN FLUTTERED ONTO THE FOOTPATH IN front of him and hopped around as if looking for crumbs. As Felan walked into the coffee shop, it followed, landing on the windowsill and watching. As before, Jacqui and the other girl were behind the counter taking orders, making coffee and serving cake, and then carrying the offerings to their respective tables.

It took a moment for Jacqui to notice him. When she did, her body stiffened and she glanced at the blond girl. Was she worried he would look at her coworker the way he had once looked at Jacqui? Or had they been discussing him?

He walked over and placed his order. The girl handed him a table number, her fingers deliberately contacting his, her smile a little too wide. The whole time Jacqui watched, and he had the distinct impression he was being set up. At Court, he might've had some fun and returned the blond's smile, maybe even flirted a little to see where the game was leading and if he could turn it to his advantage. But not here and not in front of Jacqui. He didn't want her viewing him with suspicion. In truth, he didn't feel like flirting or laughing. He had nothing to laugh about.

The table he'd used last time was empty, so he sat there and watched the waves. So far it was only the rivers affected by the tearing veil. He was sure the oceans hadn't been affected when his father had taken over. His stomach rolled like the waves on the shore, and he looked away. Even looking at that much water was uncomfortable.

"Latte?" The blond tilted her head and smiled. He was sure it would have worked on a human male, but he'd seen it all before and on a hundred different faces.

"Thank you." He purposefully added sugar to his drink and stirred, aware she was still standing there. Waiting for him to acknowledge her. "Can I help you?"

"I just wanted to make sure everything was okay?"

"It is." He held her gaze until she looked away. "Maybe you could get Jacqui to send over a piece of cake. Her pick."

That wiped the smile of the blond's face. "You know she's not interested."

"I never said I was. We have a past. I still consider her a friend. And friends don't date another friend's ex. It gets messy. I don't like messy." He had enough of that at Court. Here was supposed to be simple. It had always been simple with Jacqui. He wished he could take the watch off and start rewinding time. He'd do things so differently. "Actually, tell her to wait five minutes until she finishes, then she can join me. My treat."

She took a moment to process what he'd said, and when she'd worked it out, all sweetness left her face. "Fine."

He looked at Jacqui as the blond relayed the message. It was clear the blond was unimpressed—she hadn't expected to be brushed aside so quickly. When Jacqui lifted her gaze and looked at him, it was as though she was steeling herself for battle; that was much better than running.

Five minutes later, Jacqui came over with one piece of cake. "Carrot cake okay?"

"Perfect. Thank you." He smiled.

She didn't return his smile, but she sat opposite him. "Why are you doing this?"

"Having cake?"

"Don't be like that. Why are you here?" Her fingers flexed against the table but that was the only sign she was nervous. She didn't trust him.

That was nothing new. Even his son hadn't trusted him completely because he was fairy. But Jacqui knew him better than that. She knew who he was. Maybe the easiness they'd once shared was gone, but that didn't mean they couldn't build something new. The old attraction was there; it was just buried under layers of old hurt. He had to start peeling back the bad stuff. And that started with admitting he'd screwed up and apologizing properly.

He would never admit anything close to that at Court, even if he was at fault. He took a breath and held her gaze. "I wanted to apologize for leaving you. For not finding out the truth, and for blaming you. For letting my own fears get in the way."

She tilted her head slightly, as if trying to gauge if he was telling the truth or if it was a clever lie. "You have fears? You are the Prince of Death." Her voice was little more than a whisper.

He had a list of fears a mile long. However, they weren't the sort that humans had. He didn't fear death or spiders or heights. He feared for Annwyn, for the mortal world. He feared that he wasn't good enough to be King, but then he feared that Sulia would make a worse Queen. He feared he'd end up like his father and that he'd lose Jacqui forever.

She watched him as if waiting for him to reveal some of those fears. He didn't want to give them voice. The silence stretched a little longer. He was going to have to say something, so he took a sip of coffee and formulated his words. "I don't want to be trapped in a loveless marriage, like my father, for the sake of Annwyn. I worry that I will end up marrying a woman who only wants power, not me. You have always hated what I do, what I will become. But never me…" He needed to believe that she didn't hate him. That what he wanted was possible.

"I can't imagine living without love forever." She picked up the fork and helped herself to his cake. "I never thought I'd lose you, but you hurt me so bad I lost myself."

He nodded, knowing exactly what she meant. He'd thrown himself into Court politics instead of facing up to yet another failed relationship. He sucked at these things far more than the average fairy. But then, his relationships had far more pressure than the average fairy. Yet he also knew he wouldn't stop trying to find love right up until the last second of his deadline.

—∞—

Jacqui chewed and thought. She was quite happy that he hadn't shown the slightest bit of interest in Ash, but then she hadn't expected him to. It had also gotten Ash off her back. Jacqui had learned something of fairy games from Felan when they'd been together. "I'm glad you know the truth. I wanted you to know for so long, if only so you wouldn't blame me." She'd also hoped he'd be able to get rid of the monsters she now knew were

Greys, but that wasn't to be. "And while it's nice to see you again, why are you here?"

He hesitated, looking at his coffee before looking up at her. "It was always you I wanted on the throne next to me."

She blinked, sure she'd misheard. "You wanted me to be Queen? Of Annwyn?" His plan had been for them to live there? "I thought you wanted to live here."

Felan frowned. "I can't do that. I thought you understood I would be King."

"I did, but I thought you didn't want that."

"Some days I don't, but that doesn't mean I'm going to walk away."

She leaned back in the wooden chair and stared at him. He hadn't come back to find out the truth…or maybe he had, but it was only part of the reason. He'd come back because of Annwyn. Because he wanted her to be Queen of the fairies. "You only came back to me because of Annwyn."

"It's in trouble."

She shook her head. "It's always Annwyn. It always was and always will be. Can you hear yourself?"

"You never used to care when I talked about it."

"That's because I was young and gullible. You're a workaholic and you don't even realize it. You call it duty, loyalty, saving the frigging world. What do you want? Why did *you*, not the Prince, come back?"

She needed to know that he'd come back because he loved her, that he'd missed her, something other than the expectation that she'd help him with Annwyn. She could fill in the gaps now, and she knew what he wasn't saying—which was good, because she didn't actually want him to ask in case she accidentally agreed. There was no way she was ever leaving the mortal world to live in Annwyn.

"I thought I'd been in love before you, but it was only after we were over that I realized what we'd had and what I wanted."

Jacqui raised one eyebrow. "But it took you years to realize it."

Felan leaned forward, his coffee forgotten. "Time moves differently."

"So you say." He had the same excuses even after all this time. It was infuriating yet strangely reassuring. He hadn't lied to her all those times. It had always been the truth.

"You want to go and find out for yourself?"

"No. Because I might never return. I don't want to live in Annwyn. I had always hoped we'd have a normal life here." She really had been young and dumb. And desperately in love. Even now, just sitting with him made her heart flutter. When he smiled, it was just for her. It was easy to remember why she'd fallen for him.

"If I wasn't Prince, I would."

"You have always got a reason."

"Jacqui, how long do you think we would have lasted if I lived here? I wouldn't age and die, yet I would be forced to watch you age and die. I don't want that—you wouldn't want that. You would come to hate me."

She glanced away and busied herself with another bite of cake. How could she have overlooked his immortality? It had been one of the things they'd never really discussed, along with where they would actually live. "You can't become human?"

He shook his head. "If I walk away from Annwyn

now, I will be banished or exiled. Probably banished, which means I will become a Grey."

A Grey—like the monsters she'd seen. Withered and ugly. She didn't want to see him like that. She was used to his beauty, his light, and Greys had none of that. "I didn't realize. And if you're exiled?"

"That is a social death. I would be unable to return to Annwyn, but I wouldn't be cut off from its power. The woman who wants to steal my throne won't let me walk away easily. She would probably prefer my death." He picked up his coffee and finished it.

He didn't seem bothered that it would be lukewarm at best, more likely cold. She tried not to think about him being cold and dead. She'd never wished him dead, even when at her lowest. "Can she really steal the throne?"

"If she wins enough support. You had planned on asking me to give up the throne." There was a glimmer in his eye, as if he'd just caught her out.

She glanced away. "I'd hoped that you would without me asking, that you'd love living here and love me so much that you'd do whatever it took to make me happy."

"I always wanted to make you happy." He took a breath and then placed his hand over hers. "Would you be my Queen if I asked?"

His fingers were cool against her skin, but a shiver of heat traced through her body at his familiar touch. She'd never be able to forget him, but she didn't think she could ever be with him again. Maybe once, she would have agreed to be Queen, if things had gone well and she'd realized that he was never going to be able to live here. "No. I have spent the last seven years rebuilding my life. Not even you can undo the damage or time that has passed."

"We could start over." There was that smile, the one that could derail all of her good intentions, the one that warmed her blood like she was standing in the sun and basking in its heat.

She knew if she lingered too long she'd get burned. "To what end? We both know it will end badly again."

"It doesn't have to."

She pulled her hand back and crossed her arms. "If I do what you want. If I go to Annwyn and give up everything I want. Is that about right?"

He clenched his jaw and looked away. She doubted he was watching the sunlight on the waves.

"You would be asking me to give up my whole life." The very thing she'd once thought he'd do for her. It seemed neither of them was able to make a compromise. "You could have any woman you wanted. I'm sure many would like to be Queen of Annwyn."

He looked back at her. "But I don't love them."

Her heart did an erratic dance, and spun. Her lips curved and the words to reply automatically formed on her tongue. When she met his gaze, the words froze. In his pale green eyes, she saw so many shadows. Love shouldn't be followed by so much darkness. It should make you happy, not afraid. When she'd been around him, she'd always felt safe and loved and happy. Even now, she was tempted to give him another chance—right up until she remembered he was fairy and wanted her to go to Annwyn. Even now, he wasn't telling her everything.

"I can't trust you."

"I won't take you back to Annwyn without your permission. No tricks or glamours. Can you at least think about giving us another try?"

"It's not us that concerns me. It's everything else." She couldn't imagine being surrounded by fairies all the time. If being in Annwyn didn't make Felan happy, how was she supposed to like it? She was human, not fairy. And compared to them she would be dull and boring. A waitress couldn't be Queen.

"I have twelve days, Jacqui. I'm running out of time." For a moment, he looked tired and worn out, as if his long life was catching up with him.

"Why twelve days?"

"The magic is failing and damaging both worlds."

"Right." So he'd come to her to save the world—*worlds*. She could barely keep her life together. How did he expect her save the world and rule Annwyn?

"Read the paper, watch the news. Tell me what you think." He stood. "I'll come back tomorrow."

"I'm not working tomorrow." She glanced up at him. Should she have told him that?

"Then I'll come to your house. Seven okay? Maybe we could go out somewhere."

"Like a date?" He was asking her out on a date? When had they agreed to that? She hadn't even agreed to see him tomorrow, and yet she didn't want to say no. She wanted to see what he'd do, and she wanted to know more about Annwyn and what was happening. Would he tell her about his life in Annwyn, the parts he'd never shared?

"Only if you want it to be." He walked around the table and placed a kiss on her cheek.

She turned and her lips brushed his. He smelled the way he always had, like summer and fresh grass, as if she could close her eyes and all her troubles would vanish on a sultry breeze. His lips were warm and tasted like coffee.

Half a second later, she realized what she'd done and pulled back. He gazed down at her, and for a moment she thought he was going to lean in and kiss her properly. She wanted him to. The old lust reawakened, filling her belly with heat, and she was so tempted to fall back into his arms and pretend everything would work out fine.

He brushed a stray curl from her face, his fingers lingering for a moment. "Enjoy the cake."

Chapter 7

ASH SLID INTO THE SEAT OPPOSITE HER. "WELL?"

Jacqui snapped her gaze from Felan's back and the way his red waistcoat swung about his knees as he walked away. He always looked good no matter what he wore. However he'd never worn fairy clothing around her before; yet today and yesterday, he had. He wasn't bothering to change into human clothing the way he once had—although she was sure that he was using a glamour, so that everyone else saw what they expected. For the first time she was seeing him as the Prince.

Her fairy Prince had kissed her. She pressed her lips together, still feeling the heat of his mouth and the taste of his lips. Damn him. He'd done that deliberately. But as much as she'd like to blame him, she'd been the one who'd turned her head and met his lips, revealing how much she still felt for him.

She shrugged, not sure what to say or even how to describe it to Ash. She wanted him, the same way she always had, but she didn't want the baggage that he came with. She didn't want to live in Annwyn, and she didn't want to be Queen. She just wanted a nice, normal life, without fairies or Greys or anything.

"Are you getting back with him? You know getting back with the ex is never good. There was a reason you broke up." Ash rested her elbows on the table. There was more than a touch of attitude in her tone.

Jacqui sighed. "Our breakup wasn't simple—it was almost accidental." If she hadn't had the ectopic pregnancy and it had all gone well, would they still be together? She'd have a six-year-old child…and be living in Annwyn, according to Felan. Would she be Queen? Or just his wife, waiting for the old King to die? Was that even what happened?

"An accidental breakup?"

She nodded. "We were both young and made mistakes."

"Someone cheated?" Ash leaned forward as if expecting juicy gossip.

"No. Never that." She'd had a boyfriend or three since, but nothing that had lasted, and she'd been almost paranoid about getting pregnant again. The idea still terrified her. However, there had always been something missing with the other guy—a snap or sparkle, a longing that pulled when they were apart. With other boyfriends, she wasn't upset when they went away and had hardly noticed their return. Was that what Felan had meant, that he hadn't realized how big their love was until it was gone? She drew in a breath. That was what had been missing from her other relationships—love. He still had her heart, and he was keeping it in Annwyn. "I think I still like him."

She wasn't going to admit to loving him—she wasn't sure she still did, but she knew she had, and she thought if she gave him half a chance she would love him again. And if she loved him, she might agree to go to Annwyn. The idea of giving up everything and going to live in a place most people didn't even know existed made her blood run cold. It was one thing to move across the country, but another to leave the only world she knew behind.

Ash leaned back and pulled her hair out of the bun. Long blond hair fell over her shoulders and she looked even younger. "He still likes you."

"I know. He said as much." That made it even harder. The attraction hadn't died; it had laid dormant, waiting for a chance for the warm coals to catch again and relight the fire. If she kissed him again, it would be like adding tinder. Every touch was like a light breeze, fanning the sparks. And then what?

How were they ever going to make it work when he couldn't live here and she refused to live there? Maybe they could live between both worlds. He could commute—weekends with her, weekdays in Annwyn. She bit back a smile at the idea and knew it would never work. They were never going to work. No matter how much she liked the idea of being with Felan again, he wanted more than she was prepared to give.

—⁓—

He tried not to think of the kiss as he walked to the cemetery to cross back to Annwyn, but his body wouldn't let it go. No one since Jacqui had heated his blood and made him hungry like she did. It had taken all of his strength not to cup her face and kiss her again, deeper. He wanted to taste her lips, feel her embrace, and revel in desire. Instead, he'd walked away, half hoping she'd call him back. She hadn't.

However, she hadn't told him not to come back tomorrow.

At this rate, it would be time for the Yule festival before they got back together. Not fast enough. He had twelve days until his mother was executed. If the veil was in trouble now, that would tear it to shreds. Without a King and Queen, Annwyn would fall, and death would race unchecked across the mortal world. Perhaps it would stabilize after a time and the humans and fairies would take a new direction with their respective civilizations, but he didn't want it to get that far.

As soon as he stepped through the doorway into Annwyn, he turned around, thought of a different location, and went back to the mortal world to check the rips. The desert sky was hot, and the air sucked the moisture from his skin even though it was early morning. Here he didn't bother using magic to allow himself to be seen. He just wanted to do his job and leave.

While he couldn't fix the veil any more without new tears opening up, he was monitoring and contemplating a temporary fix—if it could be called that. The only problem was that the fix meant sacrificing one area to save the rest of the world. How could he choose which country to let die of disease? Which continent should face such devastation? Maybe it was better all countries suffered a little.

Felan walked from the tombs cut into the hill and down to the river Nile. There was no one about, but it was still early. However, in the few days since he'd last checked it, the rip had worsened. The smell made him gag before he even got close. In front of him was dead vegetation clotted with rotting fish. His stomach heaved and he almost threw up. It took several slow breaths to get his stomach to obey. The rip was obviously bad for there to be this much death.

He closed his eyes and reached out, feeling the magic and the death pouring out of the river in Annwyn and into the Nile—all the poison bleeding out and spreading. It was like a festering wound. Even if he bandaged it, without treatment, the patient would die. Both worlds would die. The reeds whispered in the warm breeze that spread the sickly scent of death. He opened his eyes. He needed to check other rivers, determine which ones were worst hit, and maybe see if he could redirect damage there to save somewhere else. That would at least keep him occupied until he saw Jacqui again.

He didn't know if he was gaining ground with her or wasting time he didn't have…and yet he wasn't prepared to walk away. He should have come back sooner. He hoped the mistake wouldn't cost him the throne—or her heart.

The sun beat down on him. He shrugged out of his waistcoat and slung it over his arm. He stopped and turned his head. The wind caught in the reeds and made them rattle like dry bones. They had never been that loud before. Then he realized that was the only sound he could hear. He turned around and looked at the river again. There were no boats on it. It wasn't just the dead fish or the birds lying on the ground. There was no sound of life at all. There should be bustling around the river, boats, and people yelling and singing.

Nothing.

The silence of death echoed around him. The music of the reeds was hollow and mocking.

If this was happening in Egypt, what were the other countries like?

———

Usually Jacqui didn't watch the news, as it was too depressing. There was never any good news—summer wildfires, war, violence. But tonight she sat and watched, simply to see if what Felan was saying was true. Was the magic failing, and if so, why?

Not that the news would tell her that. She was pretty sure they wouldn't mention magic or Annwyn. Yet he'd asked that she watch and see what was happening. She could do that; she wanted to do that to understand his world better.

Ash had decided to go out; she'd wanted Jacqui to go, and usually Jacqui would've but not tonight. The news started and death tallies ran across the bottom of the screen. The reporter talked about outbreaks of disease, not just in one country but all over the world—smallpox in Eastern Europe, bubonic plague in India, Ebola in Africa, SARS in China, and measles in America.

Jacqui blinked, hoping she was dreaming.

She'd known there was something happening, but she hadn't paid much attention—there were always disease scares. Some scientist thought something was going to mutate and cause grief, but it had never happened. Until now.

And it was everywhere. It was like the world was suddenly breaking free and all the diseases humans had thought safely contained or eradicated with medicine were back. How was that possible? Panic danced along her nerves, and she wiped her palms on her pants. This couldn't all be caused by Annwyn, could it? Why now? Why not ten years ago or a hundred years ago?

She watched on even though she'd rather have turned it off. Some countries in Europe had closed their borders because they didn't want to be infected. Some speculated it was too late and that, with air travel, the viruses were already worldwide. Already there were cases of smallpox in the United States—but the reporter assured the viewers that quarantine rules in the U.S. were strict and that it had all been contained.

The words *so far* were unspoken.

But Jacqui heard them. This is what Felan had been talking about. *The magic is failing and damaging both worlds*.

If disease was creating havoc in the mortal world, what was happening in Annwyn? Were fairies dying? The reporter kept talking as if this were the only story. Maybe it was. She picked up the remote and turned off the TV, completely numb.

Her world was falling apart and there was nothing anyone could do. Quarantine and modern medicine couldn't combat fairy magic—not totally. She'd have to find out what was happing and why.

And how she fit into Felan's plans.

She couldn't do anything to stop this. She wasn't a doctor; she wasn't anything at the moment except a café worker. She couldn't be Queen. She didn't know the first thing about being a Queen. And aside from what Felan had told her and what she'd researched in New Age shops, which hadn't been very useful, she knew next to nothing about fairies.

No, he needed a woman who knew what it was like to rule and to lead. Someone who wasn't afraid and who was willing to take on the responsibility. Someone who would relish the chance to leave this world and go on the adventure of a lifetime.

That wasn't her. She liked her life the way it was. Normal. Without fairies.

Without Felan.

She wished he'd never walked back into her life. Now she was involved in his problem, and she knew he was expecting her to be the solution.

Chapter 8

THIS TIME FELAN MADE AN EFFORT TO LOOK HUMAN. He had put on mortal clothes, jeans, and a white shirt that he left untucked and casual—a look that was always in fashion—instead of using a glamour that wouldn't work on Jacqui anyway. He wanted Jacqui to see him the way he had been, and maybe she'd remember why they were good together. He'd also brought her a gift—one he'd prepared for her and had planned to give her the day they had, instead, broken up.

He knocked on her front door and waited. The sunlight was sliding away and staining the sky pink. The mortal world could be beautiful, but lately all he saw was death. Everywhere. Death had its place—even fairies eventually wasted away to nothing—but at the moment it was out of control. It was one thing to see the towns where bodies had been left to rot, rivers clogged with the bodies of animals and people, but another to pick up a newspaper and see the cold numbers.

The blue front door swung open to reveal Ash. She stepped back, startled, while he smiled and wondered why she was here.

"Jacqui in?"

"Yeah." She stepped aside to let him in, her gaze raking over him as if she didn't think he was worthy of entering.

"You're early," Jacqui called down the corridor.

"Only by five minutes." He walked down the corridor toward her. It was better to be early than late. He'd been late too many times.

She came out of a bedroom and closed the door before he could peek inside. Dressed in a knee-length denim skirt, a red top, and sandals, she looked relaxed, almost happy to be going out with him.

"You look great," he said. Which was true except for the iron crescent hanging against her collarbone. It was a reminder that even though he was dressed as a human, he wasn't one.

Jacqui smiled. There was glimmer in her blue eyes that gave him a flicker of concern. He pushed it aside. What could go wrong on a simple date that wasn't a date?

"Where are we going?" He hadn't made plans. With Jacqui he was happy to go along with what she wanted.

"Dinner, but the location is a surprise."

Okay, he generally didn't like surprises, but he smiled anyway. He'd do anything to win back her heart.

"I brought you something." He didn't mention how long he'd had the gift. Instead, he just held out the wooden box. Carved in a floral design, it was very beautiful itself, but the true gift was inside.

"You didn't have to."

"I wanted to. I thought you might appreciate it."

She raised one eyebrow, then opened the box. On a bed of green velvet was a small round mirror on a length of silver chain. She lifted it up and watched it spin for a moment.

"A mirror?"

He nodded. "It's trained on me, so when I'm away, you will be able to see what I'm doing. You'll be able to glimpse Annwyn, the people I talk to…anything really." He was trusting her with a very important fairy-made object. If it were to fall into the wrong hands, Sulia or any other enemy would be able to follow his every move.

She looked at it. "I think it's broken. I only see me."

"That's because I'm standing right here. I have to be away from you. Would you like me to put it on for you?"

She glanced at him and then the mirror. For a heart-beat he thought she was going to say no and hand the gift back. "You told me once not to accept gifts from fairies."

"I didn't mean from me. This will do you no harm, and if you want to negate all implications or assumption of a debt owed, simply give me something in return."

"Like what? I have nothing to give you." She frowned as if thinking.

"It is the act of giving, not the value of the gift." Humans had created the legal profession because they had kept getting bound in deals with fairies, though those origins had long been lost.

"Right. Um. Just a moment." She turned and went back into her bedroom, leaving the door open so he could see in. Her bed was made, and there was nothing on the floor. She'd never been neat when he'd known her. Back then, her clothes were often on the floor and her bed had never been made. When she came back, she was holding something in her hand. "This is for you."

She placed a silver earring in his palm. It was a small fleur-de-lis that glittered with tiny diamond chips. "It was my favorite set, but I lost one and couldn't bear to throw the other one out."

"It's very pretty, thank you." He took the back off

and pinned the earring to the pocket flap on his shirt. "We are square."

Jacqui handed him the mirror and turned around. He put it around her neck and did up the clasp. When she turned around, the iron crescent was above the silver mirror he'd given her. The mortal and fairy worlds were meeting. He much preferred her in fairy silver to mortal iron, but he wouldn't ask her to take it off. Not yet.

Her fingers brushed the surface of the mirror as she glanced down to look at it. "Thank you." She looked up. "You aren't worried I'll catch you in the nude?"

Felan laughed. "No. You've seen it all before." And he wouldn't be doing anything he would be ashamed of her seeing anyway.

"True." She grinned as if remembering. A car honked out the front. "That'll be the cab. Shall we go?"

He agreed and they left—no doubt Ash was scowling somewhere in the house. "So you and Ash live together?"

"Plus another girl. It makes the rent affordable."

They got into the cab and Jacqui gave directions. Neither of them spoke for the ride, but his gaze would drift to her, and a few times he caught her looking. When the cab stopped, they were at the waterfront. A cold worry grew in his gut as he paid the driver.

Once the cab had pulled away, Jacqui spoke. "You used real money."

There had been times when he'd taken her out and he'd tricked the human with leaves instead of notes. He'd shown her the trick after telling her he was fairy, and she had taken him to the bank. "I still have the account I set up when I was dating you. It's actually quite useful."

"I thought you'd have just paid with leaves."

"Sometimes. It depends on what I'm doing and where I am. When I'm with you, I want to fit in." He knew she didn't like him ripping people off by using glamours on them. Most people fell for it—except in Ireland. They had kept fairy law alive. It was hard to get away with anything there.

They walked down the road toward the pier and the unease in his gut swelled. On the pier was a sign advertising a boat cruise. A dinner boat cruise. On the water. He stopped before his feet hit the pier. "We aren't eating dinner on the boat."

"Yes we are. I thought it would be nice." That glint was back in her eye. She was enjoying this.

"There's water." He really didn't want to sit in a boat on the ocean. He could think of many things he'd rather do.

She took his hand. "There usually is with boats."

Her palm was warm against his skin, and when she gave it a gentle tug, he followed. If he wanted to see her, it was going to be on her terms. She'd grown up and gotten tougher. He kind of liked this sharper Jacqui, even if he didn't like where she was leading him.

Beneath the wooden pier, water sloshed and slapped against the supports, and the cold swelled and flooded his blood. He had to concentrate to take each step and not turn and run to get off the pier. He could do this. He was the Crown of Prince of Death, Guardian of the Veil, and soon-to-be King of Annwyn. He wouldn't let a little water freak him out. It wasn't like it was touching him. He'd be floating in a boat. It would be fine.

"The boat won't sink?"

"No." She stopped and faced him. "Do you not want to have dinner with me?"

She was expecting him to change his mind and walk away. He met her gaze and held it. "I would have dinner with you on the shores of the river of the damned if that's what you wished."

Other couples passed them, making their way to the boat at the end of the pier. The boat where Jacqui was expecting him to go.

Jacqui stared at him, her lips slightly parted. "You are trying to get back together with me."

"Is that a bad thing?" She was still holding his hand. He stepped closer so their bodies almost touched. "Tell me that you haven't dreamed of me, that the love is dead and buried, and I'll walk away." More like crawl away and spend the next millennia slowly dying because he'd lost the one woman he truly loved.

For several heartbeats she was silent. "Let's just have dinner, okay?"

While she'd seen the boat in the evenings, and always thought it would be romantic, being here with Felan, it was almost like no time had passed. But she couldn't forget about the past seven years or that Annwyn always came first for Felan—not that he'd ever made her feel like she was second best when she was with him; it was only when he left.

They boarded the boat, walking past other diners already perusing their menus, and went to their table. As the boat rocked on a gentle swell, Felan looked as comfortable as a cat about to be given a bath. She almost felt sorry for him. Almost. Except that he hadn't told her the whole truth about what was going on. She'd wait until they'd cast off before she started asking the hard questions.

"It'll be fine." She touched his hand, not sure if she was reassuring him or just fulfilling her need to touch him. She'd forgotten how magnetic he was, and now he was in her blood again. "Just read your menu."

A few minutes later, the boat was under way. Felan gripped the table and drew in a sharp breath as if he were about to be thrown into the ocean. "I can't swim."

"Now you know how I feel when you talk about me being Queen of Annwyn." Then she lifted her menu and purposefully ignored him while she tried to pick what to eat. It was an act; her heart was pounding and her palms were getting sweaty. She was as nervous as if it was their first date.

The boat motored out into deeper water. Other patrons were taking photos of the lit-up shore and talking animatedly while she and Felan were sitting in silence. Had she pushed him too far? She peeked over the top of her menu. He was reading, his fingers pressed too hard against the cover of the menu. But he wasn't complaining; he was going through with her dinner date on a boat. What else would he do to get her back?

The waiter made his way around. Felan ordered mushroom risotto—he always ordered risotto; it was as if he'd found a human food he enjoyed and was sticking with it—and she had prawn curry. She also ordered a bottle of white wine. Neither of them were driving, and she knew Felan would pay. He always did. In those small things, he was predictable. She was actually surprised he'd gotten on the boat. She'd expected more of a fight.

She leaned forward and placed her elbows on the table. "I watched the news."

That got his attention. "Then you know how bad things are."

She nodded. "But how does it relate to you and…" She glanced around then lowered her voice. "Annwyn."

He joined her in leaning on the table. To anyone else, it looked they were having an intimate conversation—not a semi-argument. "You want to have this conversation here? Now?"

"I wanted to make sure you were going to answer my questions and not take off when it got hard." They were trapped on the boat for the duration of the cruise. It had seemed like a really good idea at the time. Now she wasn't so sure. If he couldn't escape, neither could she.

Felan looked offended. "Have I ever done that?"

"Not technically, but you have a knack for half-truths."

He grimaced but nodded. "That is more habit than deliberate. What do you want to know?"

"How do the plagues relate? Why do you only have twelve…eleven days?"

"I told you, the magic is failing."

She looked at him blankly. This was going to be like pulling teeth, her own teeth. "You're going to have to give me a bit more detail. I need to understand."

He glanced at his hands and didn't look up. "It's not simple to explain. The King and Queen keep the magic alive, but my parents have been fighting for centuries. All those little outbreaks that happen here are the result of them bickering. In eleven days, my mother is going to be executed for treason."

She gasped, and her hand covered her heart. "I'm sorry. That's awful." While she hadn't spoken to either of her parents in over a year because they hadn't wanted her to move away, she wouldn't wish them ill.

Felan gave a one-shouldered shrug that was supposed to mean he didn't care, but she saw through the act. "If you knew my mother, you'd be surprised it had taken this long for her to be caught."

The waiter brought the bottle of wine over and poured two glasses. Felan immediately took a drink, then turned the stem of the glass in his fingers, as if dwelling on a giant problem.

"She's still your mother."

"I know, but there is nothing I can do for her, and she would do nothing for me if the situation were reversed. She lost her humanity a long time ago." She saw a flicker of sadness before it was carefully masked. He was trying to be unaffected, but whatever was going on ran deep.

"Why, what happened to her?" And if she'd lost her humanity, had she once been human?

"My parents married because of necessity, not love. She was a human princess and she loved the power of being Queen. The more she got, the more she wanted. That is why I have to be so careful about whom I choose." He lifted his gaze and he looked tired—not his face so much, but it was something in his eyes. Almost as if he just wanted all this business over so he could get on with his life again.

"I still don't get why you need a wife so fast. Can't your father rule?"

The corner of his lips curved in the slightest smile. "There has to be a King and Queen, and it is my turn to step up. Besides, my father is old. He has the wasting but is hiding it well."

"Wasting?"

"Come on, Jacqui, think about it. You know I don't age and yet fairies have to die somehow."

There was the reminder he was a Prince and not a servant to answer her every question. If fairies didn't age, then maybe it was as simple as they wasted away and died. She took a sip of wine before she spoke again, gathering her thoughts and rephrasing so it wouldn't be a question he needed to answer.

"No King and Queen, and all hell breaks loose here." That was why he wanted her to be Queen. He needed someone beside him, and she was safe and familiar.

"Pretty much."

The waiter placed their meals on the table. Both of them took the opportunity to eat and let the truth settle. Around them there was the murmur of other voices and the gentle slap of waves against the hull. It would have been very relaxing if her mind wasn't full of disease and death. Is that what was on his mind all the time? No wonder he looked tired.

She looked out across the water. From here everything seemed fine with the world. If not for the news reports, she'd be oblivious to what was happening elsewhere.

—⁓—

Felan tensed every time the boat gave the tiniest rock. It wasn't a small boat, but he figured it would sink just as fast as a little boat. Yet Jacqui seemed perfectly relaxed. She sipped her wine, ate her dinner, and gazed out at the ocean as if she couldn't bear to look at him.

He forced a breath out through gritted teeth. As much as he wanted her answer now, if he pushed too hard, she'd run. He should be happy she was here with him.

"So, how far does this boat go?"

She turned and faced him, her blue eyes catching the light and glittering like gems. "Not far. We'll be turning around soon and making our way back. Not too traumatic for you?"

"I'll let you know once I'm back on land." He smiled and tried to make light of the fact she'd made him do something most fairies—no, *all* fairies—would run from. "I'm glad we could have dinner."

"So am I." She looked at him for a moment, and he saw the old heat in her gaze. She wanted him, even if she was trying to pretend that they were nothing more than old friends.

He wanted her to fall in love with him again, to believe that they could save the world together. He needed to believe that was possible and that with Jacqui everything would be perfect. Because if he let himself think of the alternative—that he'd end up like his father—he'd abdicate in a heartbeat, condemning two worlds to Sulia's rule. Yet when he looked at Jacqui and saw the life in her eyes and the smile on her lips, he didn't want to change that. He didn't want to take her to Annwyn and expose her to all the corruption while hoping she'd be all right. He didn't want her to lose her soul to save both worlds.

Yet he couldn't see another option except choosing someone else, and his heart wouldn't let him choose anyone else. He wanted it to beat for a reason, not just because it had to. Jacqui had broken it and yet it still beat for her.

He closed his eyes for a moment and wished he wasn't the Prince. Maybe he was overthinking things and worrying too much. He opened his eyes and smiled at her. He had to believe that she loved him. Even if she had insisted they have dinner on a boat knowing he didn't like water. Her lips curved in a small smile that had once meant only one thing. If she asked him to come home with her, would he?

He wanted to. His blood burned. The raw lust hardened his flesh, and for a few moments, he forgot about the boat and the water and Annwyn. It was just them. He covered her hand with his and then brought it to his lips; he needed to taste her, to feel her skin against his. He wanted to be alone with her, and yet at the edges of his mind, he knew he was rushing. The salt air was on her skin, but he didn't care. She was watching him, and she hadn't pulled back.

The boat touched the pier, and he resisted the urge to jump straight up. He'd kept it together this long, and he could last a few more minutes. It really wasn't that bad, except for the rocking motion—and the knowledge that if he fell in, he'd sink to the bottom and drown. He didn't release her hand as they stood, and they walked hand in hand off the boat, caught in the tide of other passengers.

Stepping on the pier was sweet relief.

Halfway along, he stopped and drew her closer, so the heat of her body invaded his. He needed her. His body ached, and his skin craved her touch. He brushed a strand of hair off her face, his fingers caressing her skin. His thumb touched her lip, then he leaned in and kissed her—properly this time, so there could no doubt about how he felt about her. Her tongue flicked against his lip as her arms went around his neck. It was all the invitation he needed to wrap his arms around her and pull her closer, so their bodies connected. He didn't care if anyone else saw.

Her breasts pressed against his chest. As she sank into the kiss, she moved her hips against his in a tease that sent shivers down his spine. He'd dreamed so many times of being in her arms again that he didn't want to let go, not even when the kiss ended and they were nose to nose, their breath mingling.

"That wasn't supposed to happen," she said, but she was breathless and smiling, her fingers brushing the back of his neck.

"I know. But I'm glad it did. I missed you."

"I missed you too...do you have to rush off?" Her fingers paused for just a fraction and there was a catch in her voice.

He swallowed and knew if she asked, he would follow. "No." His voice was husky, as if he could no longer fight the desire.

"Did you want to come back to my place for a drink?"

No was the smart answer; he had things he needed to do in Annwyn, plus the longer he spent with her, the greater the chance they could be seen together. But he couldn't say it. His heart was beating hard and his body was screaming yes; his shaft was pressed against her in a way she had to have noticed. And then what? What happened tomorrow? Were they good or was this just for old time's sake? *Think about it in the morning.* "I'd like that."

He eased his hands off her hips so they could separate and find a cab.

While again the cab ride was silent, he could almost taste the tension and anticipation. Her hand rested on his leg, her fingers always moving, inching higher. He wished she'd just touch him and run her hand over his shaft instead of hinting.

They stumbled out of the cab and up the front stairs. Before she could get the key in the door, he pressed her against the door and kissed her hard, his body against hers. It had been too long since he'd been with her—years felt like centuries. He wanted to rediscover everything.

She moaned against his lips. Her hands slid around him and gripped his hips, her fingers kneading into the muscle of his butt. He wanted to ask if she was sure— but she was meeting him every step of the way. He took the key out of her hand and got it in the lock. They managed to get through door and close it again before stumbling down the hallway. She kicked off her shoes as she went. His shirt was half-unbuttoned by the time they reached her bedroom and closed that door behind them. That was when they paused. In the pale light that filtered in from outside, they looked at each other, both breathing hard.

Her lips were parted and her eyes dark with lust. He undid the rest of his buttons while she watched, her gaze flicking from his face to his body. Her tongue darted over her lip as he let the shirt fall to the floor. Then he toed off his shoes, undid the top button on his jeans, and took a step closer. She stepped back and her legs hit the edge of the bed, so she sat and beckoned him forward.

Who was he to refuse?

A couple paces and he was able to kiss her again, drawing off her top then easing her back onto the bed. She wriggled back to give him room, and as she did, he took off her skirt. She'd put on matching bra and panties for their dinner. Red and lacy. She'd have never worn something like that when he'd first known her. He traced up her leg, letting his fingers relearn the texture of her skin.

Instead of continuing to undress her, he knelt on the bed and moved over her. Taking another kiss, he let his hips sink against hers. He really wished he didn't still have his jeans on. He was harder than he'd been since… well, since he'd last been with her. Her hands slid down his back. He kissed down her neck and lower, to the exposed curve of her breast. She arched her back, pressing her peaked nipple toward his mouth, so he obliged.

His tongue caressed the lace, then he drew the peak into his mouth. Her fingers scraped up his back and dug into his scalp as if to keep him there. He moved his hips against hers, enjoying the little movements of her body and the sounds of lust locked in her throat. He had never forgotten them, and hearing them again was better than any music on either side of the veil.

Her hands glided over his skin and her hips lifted to meet his, tempting him to do more, faster. But he didn't want to rush the first time. He wanted to be able to remember it as the moment they got back together, when everything had started going right.

Slowly he kissed down her body, enjoying the taste of her skin. His finger brushed over her mons and between her thighs. The lace of her panties was already damp. He slid his fingers beneath the lace to feel the slickness of her skin. Her hips jerked at the touch, but she didn't pull away as his fingers glided over her delicate folds and pressed into her.

He lowered his head for a taste. She was sweeter than fairy wine and definitely headier than the nonalcoholic drink. He wanted to be burying himself in her and rejoice in being back in her bed. Back with her.

"I want you," he murmured as he worked his way up her body, kissing, tasting, teasing. Tonight was going far better than he'd let himself dream.

"I know." Her voice was soft and her breath danced over his skin. Her fingers traced over his skin to his jeans, then she hesitated. She blinked, and he could see a shadow cross her eyes. "Do you have condoms?"

"No." He drew back, a sinking feeling dragging desire further away. Fairies never worried about contraception. He should have remembered, but he hadn't expected it to get this far. "The odds of you getting pregnant are so small."

"Yeah…that didn't work out so well last time."

Last time they used condoms, until he'd told her what he was. He'd also stopped pretending to be human around her. Yet that was exactly what he was doing tonight—trying to be human. It wasn't going to work. Not when she could see through any glamour he tried to cast. She had to accept him as he was, not for how well he could fit into her world. That didn't mean he was ready to give up tonight. "It took more than once." She gave him a look, and he immediately regretted saying that. The distance was growing and he could feel her mood cooling. "You don't have any?"

"No. Usually, I don't invite anyone home. You can't magic some up?"

Felan raised one eyebrow. "No." But he wished he could. He needed her. With Jacqui he could lose himself for a few precious moments. He wished he'd never opened his mouth. If he'd said nothing, then maybe she wouldn't have called a halt.

She closed her eyes. "I can't do this. It's too much too soon." She opened her eyes, the lust gone and replaced with something colder. The shadow of fear was back. She pushed at his chest and he rolled off her, not resisting even though he didn't want to put any distance between them.

He took a breath, tried to find calm, and failed. "You invited *me* home." What did she think would happen? Felan stared at the ceiling instead of looking at her. He couldn't look at her without wanting to kiss her and more. There were other things they could do, and he was half tempted to suggest something, but he didn't want to push. He shouldn't have accepted her invitation. He should've walked away after the kiss and left her wanting more. Now she was turning him away. He rearranged himself and tried to think of something other than sex and how much he wanted her.

"I know...I didn't think. You make me stop thinking." She leaned over him and placed a kiss on his cheek. "But I can't risk getting pregnant again after last time."

How could he tell her that to become Queen of Annwyn she'd need to be pregnant when that was the one thing she wanted to avoid?

His fingers threaded into her hair, not wanting to lose contact. "I get it." He did, but it didn't make it easier. This is what drowning felt like. The air he needed was so close, and his lungs were burning—yet he drew a breath anyway. He turned his head and looked at her. "Will it happen again?" Would they lose another baby because it was growing in the wrong place? Would he lose Jacqui? He wouldn't survive that.

"Probably not. But I don't want to risk a baby right now. You can't come back and expect to pick up as if no time has passed and nothing happened."

"You don't want to pretend we can." He smiled and let the back of his knuckles graze the side of her breast. He wished he could erase those years and make everything the way it should have been, but no one had that power. Not even the King of Annwyn.

She swallowed and blinked slowly as if she were fighting to resist. "I do. But I can't. I'm sorry."

"Perhaps I should go." He didn't want to, not now when they were actually talking and kissing and…and she didn't want a baby. There was so much more he needed to tell her about Annwyn. He should have said more on the boat while she couldn't run from what he needed to say, but what they had was still too fragile.

"You don't have to." Her touch lingered on his skin. She'd just pushed him away and now she was inviting him to stay. The ground beneath his feet kept shifting and he couldn't work out what she really wanted.

True, but he couldn't stay either; otherwise, his erection would never go down. "Yeah, because we've always managed to sleep in the same bed and do nothing. We could do something?" He smiled and let his fingers trailed up her thigh.

Jacqui's cheeks turned pink and she drew away. "It's not that I don't want you…"

Felan sat up. He kissed her shoulder blade and then her neck, torturing himself but enjoying it at the same time. But the heat of the moment had died several minutes ago.

It was best to let it go. Sometimes it was better to lose the battle so you could win the war. "Maybe it's better this way. You're right; it's too fast." He had to force those words out and make it sound as though he meant them while hoping she'd change her mind.

He needed fast. He could almost hear the clock ticking on his time left as Prince. And yet he couldn't sleep in Jacqui's bed while still keeping things from her. The truth was on the tip of his tongue. They could talk tonight and solve it all…except the only thing he saw happening was him getting tossed out the door and being told never to come back. He couldn't risk that. He closed his eyes and breathed in the scent of her skin. He didn't want to destroy the magic of tonight with the truth. He wanted to give their love time to strengthen before he tested it. Tonight had proved that it still existed, and that had to be enough for the moment.

She tipped her head back. "You always knew what to say." Her cheek curved. She was smiling.

No, he just knew what not to say. "Not always."

Sooner rather than later, he was going to have to tell her everything and hope she was willing. But the uncertainty was there. She might want him, but she still didn't want Annwyn, no matter how much Annwyn needed her. He couldn't bring himself to use trickery to get Jacqui on his side. And when he only had two days to go, what would he do then? He didn't like the answer that echoed his father's words—she'd grow to love Annwyn.

He moved away and buttoned his fly. His heart was still fluttering and his blood was still hot. He wanted her—he had never stopped wanting her. All he'd done was fool himself that he'd stopped loving her. He ran his hands through his hair and then glanced across at her. Where did they go from here?

Nowhere tonight.

"I'll see you tomorrow." He stood and grabbed his shirt off the floor.

Jacqui stayed on the bed and watched, the hunger still in her eyes. That just made it harder to leave. Perhaps he should stay. It was tempting, better than going back to Annwyn, but even if he did stay, they weren't back to where they had been. She'd said that. At the moment, all they had was lust—while that was plenty in Annwyn, it wasn't what he wanted with Jacqui. Slow was better.

"What are we doing, Felan?" She crossed her legs, giving him a glimpse of her lace knickers.

He hoped he'd get a chance to take them off her another night. "Reconnecting? Seeing if the attraction is still there?" Seeing if she was still the one who could save Annwyn with him?

"I think that's obvious. I meant—"

"I know what you meant, but I don't know. I don't know what I'm doing. Here or there." It was funny how clear everything was and how he had planned how it would all go down, and yet, when it came to the pointy end of the sword, all of his deals and plans meant nothing if he couldn't get a Queen. And the Queen he wanted had just kicked him out of bed. He drew in a breath and looked at her. "Tell me what I need to do to make it right."

She just looked at him. "I don't know." Then she slid off the bed and pulled on her skirt. "I'll show you out."

He bit back the sharp retort that it wasn't necessary as he shoved on his shoes. "Thank you."

The walk back to the front door was much more subdued. For a moment they stood on the front step. He shoved his hands into his pockets to keep from reaching out and touching her.

"Thank you for dinner. I hope you enjoyed it."

"Only for you would I get onto a boat." He placed a soft kiss on her lips and drew back before it became something more. He still hadn't told her that the Queen needed to give her soul and be pregnant with an heir, as children couldn't be conceived in Annwyn. And once she had no soul, she wouldn't be able to conceive his child anymore. One parent needed a soul. That was the reason fairies needed humans. But that was a conversation for another day. He could imagine her horror at hearing that now.

He turned and walked down the steps without looking back. He didn't want to know if she was watching because if she was he might be tempted to turn around and stay. He could go without; this wouldn't be the first time he'd walked away. However, he'd have much rather stayed and sealed their reunion, even though he wasn't keen on the condoms. It went against everything he'd always believed. If a child happened, it was a blessing. The odds were already against her conceiving in such a short amount of time. He knew why his father hadn't asked for the return of the cup of life. His father saw through Felan's careful sidesteps and half-truths and knew how unready he was to be King.

He walked back to the cemetery to return to Annwyn. He knew the rules there. And while he'd like Jacqui to be with him, he couldn't do that to her. They had time to get it together. He'd give her as long as he could. It was all he could do. He let go of the magic that let him be seen.

He'd barely crossed the threshold into Annwyn when the Hunter approached. Taryn looked grim as she handed him a note.

Mortal paper and mortal handwriting. No fairy would write with such a crass hand—if they could write at all.

Meet me in the grove. I will be waiting.

"Sulia? How long ago?"

Taryn raised her eyebrows. "Do you know how hard it is to judge time here?"

He did, but Taryn had been raised in the mortal world and had only recently come to Court and more recently been made Hunter. She was used to the mortal obsession with keeping an eye on the time. "Yes, but I've been in the mortal world checking on the damage."

"Everyone knows that's not all you're doing." Taryn looked at him closely. He was still in jeans and a shirt. As long as they didn't know with whom, that was fine.

"I was handed the note today. And because I hadn't seen you for a while, I thought I'd wait here, as I knew you'd need to cross here at some point."

So not that long really. "Are you coming with me?"

"You can't smell trap all over that?"

"I can, but that won't stop me from going." He could imagine how angry Sulia would be because he'd already freed the trapped fairies. It almost made him smile.

Taryn shuffled and glanced at the ground. "Why not ignore her?"

"I can't afford to ignore her. Fetch my sword." The

idea of a fight was beginning to sound appealing, a way to burn through some of the tension that wouldn't leave him and maybe clear his thoughts of what had happened and what Jacqui had said.

Taryn walked over to a tree and picked the sword up. She'd had it ready for him, knowing that he'd read the note and go. "Did you want more weapons or people?"

"No. Sometimes less is more." Except when it came to Jacqui, he just wanted more and more and more. But he still didn't have her heart—or even her trust. "I also want you to hang back so it looks like I came alone."

"Are you sure?"

"Yes." It was definitely going to be a trap, but walking out of it would prove more than avoiding it. If he avoided it, Sulia would make sure people found out he was a coward. He had to prove he had nothing to prove and nothing to worry about.

Chapter 9

JACQUI LAY DOWN ON HER BED. EVEN THOUGH FELAN had only touched the sheets for moments, she could smell him like a hint of summer. Heat and flowers. It would've been so easy to stop thinking and worrying, and just fall into his arms. Some things didn't change. She closed her eyes. The memory of his hands on her skin was fresh now. It had been hard to let him go, but she knew it was the right thing to do. She wasn't ready to let him back into her heart—or rather let him know he'd never left. Being with him was dangerous, and yet she couldn't help herself when it came to Felan. If he hadn't been fairy, would their relationship have been half as much fun, or did she love the danger and secrecy that came with knowing him?

He was truly like no other man she'd ever known. For a moment, she wished he was still here. Her hand slid over her stomach and under the waistband of her skirt to finish what they'd started. Her fingers brushed the scar on her abdomen and the lace of her panties, then slipped underneath them. In her mind it was his touch, his fingers. The heat in his eyes. He'd looked at her the same way he always had—as if the world spun around her. Then she stopped.

She couldn't do this thinking of him. He should have stayed…she'd wanted him to stay, but he was right. Something would have ended up happening. And no doubt she would've ended up regretting it. There was always a price with him, and she was always the one paying.

If she hadn't have said anything, she'd be in his arms and calling out his name…and waking up alone. He wouldn't have stayed the whole night. She knew that—she'd seen the dilemma in his eyes when she'd asked him to come over and had known he was tossing up between her and Annwyn. She'd won, temporarily. However, it didn't feel like a victory.

It felt like he'd breached her defenses and walked straight in. All the time she'd spent moving on had been erased, and once again she felt like the teen waiting for him to come back. That he could still do that to her…and that she enjoyed it scared her. And yet part of her liked that he'd come back to her and that he'd got on the boat for her.

He'd changed. Some part of him was now willing to go further than he ever had before. He didn't just want her. He needed her. He needed a Queen.

That really freaked her out. That he'd left without the evening going further was a good thing. She needed to reclaim the distance. She wasn't going to fall into his bed. She wasn't what he needed. He wasn't what she needed…only what she craved.

A tiny seed of doubt raised its head. If she resisted, she was going to lose him again. This time it wasn't so easy to believe that was a good thing. And she wasn't sure she believed that she didn't want him in her life. Felan wasn't any fairy; he was the one she'd once loved more than anyone. He was the one who'd broken her heart. Perhaps he was the only person who could put it back together.

She closed her eyes and took a breath, determined to push all thoughts of fairies out of her mind. He'd gone back to Annwyn, where he belonged, and she was here, where she belonged. However, the expectation that had built in her body didn't evaporate. She'd never get to sleep if she didn't take the edge off.

Her fingers moved slowly. Next time, she'd have condoms ready—because that would fix everything—because the lack of birth control was what was broken with their relationship.

Don't think of Felan…think of that hot actor…

She pressed a little harder, and her breath hitched. Then Felan was back in her mind, doing what she'd wanted—drawing off her panties and running his tongue over her clit.

No, anyone but him.

But it was his lips she wanted to be kissing as he eased himself into her. What was it about him that made her body crazy, that made her want to take chances a sane person wouldn't, that made her want to throw logic out the window?

Her fingers circled her clit, then she gave in and let thoughts of Felan fill her mind. It was too easy. She groaned as she came, wishing he'd actually been there—then wishing she'd never invited him in and left her in this situation.

She sighed and lay there for a moment. What an *awesome* date. Would they ever be able to manage even the simple stuff again? If he was King of Annwyn, nothing would be simple again. She shivered and sat up. She couldn't have him unless she became Queen. Maybe it was for the best she'd said no. And she should keep saying no until he found someone else.

But she didn't want that either. She didn't want to spend the rest of her life imagining him with someone else. She gritted her teeth. She was going to have to make a choice: let him go forever or go with him forever. Neither seemed like good options.

The two necklaces brushed against her skin. She touched the familiar one made of iron. It had protected her for so long and yet Felan hadn't seemed bothered. She knew his skin would burn if he touched it. He'd shown her that once to prove he was fairy.

With a flick of her fingers, she removed the small mirror he'd given her. A gift so she could watch him while he was away. Why hadn't he done that the first time around? She held it in her palm, not sure if she wanted to look or not. He'd given her free rein to peek into his life. Did she want to look? Did she want to see what he did when he wasn't with her?

Would he be taking care of himself after being kicked out of her bed? Her cheeks heated at the idea of catching him in such a private moment, yet she couldn't resist taking a look into the life he'd kept hidden from her last time they were together.

She uncurled her fingers and thought of him. The surface of the mirror wobbled and then she saw him, blue blood and dirt was streaked across his cheek. She watched, confused, as the scene widened and he swung what looked like a sword, his clothes—the ones he'd worn to see her—stained with fairy blood and grime. Her heart clenched.

No sex—battle. She didn't want him to die after just remembering why she had once loved him and why it would be so easy to love him again. Did she love him enough to give up everything when she knew he wouldn't do the same for her?

——∿∿——

The moment Felan stepped through the doorway into the mortal world, he was attacked. A Grey armed with fairy silver swung at him. The blow only just glanced off Felan's sword. A fraction to the left and it would have cut his arm. He knew Sulia well enough to know this wasn't the trap—this was just the warm-up.

The Grey attacked again, the silver blade glinting in the moonlight. Felan pressed forward. He wouldn't retreat to Annwyn. If he did, the next time he stepped through, there'd be an army waiting for him. *May she wither*.

He shifted to the left and brought the blade of his sword up underneath the Grey's guard. The sword bit through clothing and into flesh. He pressed harder and twisted. The man cried out and dropped his sword.

"What did she promise you? A return to Court?" Was Sulia making deals with Greys? He hoped so, as then he'd be able to drop her in the river without a second thought.

He shook his head. "My son." He gasped for breath, his skin collapsing as he fought to live. "She has my son."

Fuck. Was there no low Sulia wouldn't drop to? "Who is your son?"

"Darkling child."

Blue blood trickled down Felan's sword. This Grey had fathered a child with a human in the mortal world. A child that would need to kill to live. Most darklings didn't survive past their first year.

"Find him, please. Not his fault."

It wasn't the child's fault that he was darkling or that

Sulia was using him as a pawn. "I can't let you live after attacking me."

The Grey nodded, his strength fading along with what was left of his looks. Haggard and sunken, he'd be dead in moments. "Find him." His hand grabbed Felan's so they both held the sword. "Please."

This was the reason he'd tried to keep Caspian a secret. As much as he didn't want to draw attention to his son, he was going to have to warn him to be on guard.

"I'll do my best."

The Grey's grip tightened. "Find him or she will kill him. She will kill them all."

All? What was Sulia up to? "Where are they?"

"I don't know." The Grey took a shuddering breath.

"You could have sent word instead of attacking. I could have helped sooner." How many children had Sulia taken hostage? Were they all darkling or changeling as well?

"Would you have stopped to help the banished when you are fighting for your own life? Don't let her—" he coughed. Dark, dying blood ran down his chin. He looked up at Felan, then his head lolled back. Dead.

The body became heavy on the sword. Felan pulled it free and wiped it clean on his jeans but didn't bother to sheath it. He had a feeling that wasn't the only Grey he was going to have to kill tonight. Killing fairies was always bad business, banished, exiled, or otherwise.

Worse was Sulia's method of ensuring assistance— blackmail. It was one thing to trick and make deals, but quite another to stoop to coercion. There was no honor or wit in blackmail. She'd take Annwyn over his dead body—and she seemed to be thinking the same thing.

Taryn stepped through the doorway from Annwyn. She must have only been a few paces behind him, but with the time difference across the veil, a life had been lost. She looked at the scene. "Are you sure you don't want to wait while I assemble an army or at least a strike force? I'm not sure I'm going to be much help in an actual battle."

Felan raised one eyebrow. "Doing that will take time I don't have. You have been training with Verden and that will have to do." He glanced at the body of the dead Grey. "He wasn't a properly trained swordsman. I'm hoping most of them won't be."

She gave a small nod. "You told me this job would be mostly a title to see out your father's reign."

"It was supposed be. I didn't expect Sulia to want a war."

Taryn considered this for a moment. "Perhaps she doesn't. Perhaps she hopes to kill you, and me, out here in the middle of nowhere. No one would ever find us."

"I'm harder to kill than you think." He wasn't sure who he was reassuring, Taryn or himself.

"I'm not." She glared at him. "You need Verden here, not me. He should be carrying this sword and the responsibility."

"I can't change that now. You want him un-banished, we best make sure neither of us dies today." He touched her arm. "You've killed a Grey before."

"I got lucky. He wasn't expecting me to put up a fight."

"That's because you are young and were raised across the veil. No one knows what to expect from you, but they respect you. You made a deal with the King and won. Few can say that."

"I got lucky. I know that. You don't need luck; you need experience."

Felan nodded. Taryn was right, but she was all he had. While Verden had worked very hard to get to the position of Hunter, Taryn had gotten the job because no one else wanted it and he'd known she would be on his side. "I guess luck will have to do."

He took a breath. The air was tainted with death and the tang of blood. He'd go alone to the grove and leave Taryn to protect the doorway again. Sulia would either plan to kill him or trap him. He needed more help in Annwyn. Dylis should be here, the woman he would make his Hunter once he was King. He glanced at Taryn, knowing she was right. She wasn't a warrior, and if she died, Verden would be devastated. "Hide the body. Guard the doorway." He looked at his watch. He knew it wasn't showing the correct time, but it would be good enough. "If I'm not back in an hour, you can enter the grove—although I'll probably be dead." He went to take off his watch, but she pulled one out of a pocket.

"I used to wear one all the time in the mortal world. I want to be able to use it again." Her words were pointed and aimed at his heart. She didn't play games like a Court-raised fairy would—at least not unless she absolutely had to.

He looked at her. "You will."

"Not if you die tonight. You need someone to watch your back."

"Sulia won't kill me." But he wasn't as sure of that as he had been. While Sulia may not be holding the sword, she would be there cheering it on and orchestrating the moves like a power-crazy puppeteer.

"You trust her far more than I. Class-A bitch."

He nodded. "She has hostages. She listened to my mother and then perfected her teachings."

"Where do we begin looking for them?"

"I don't know yet. But if she had one to make him fight"—he pointed to the dead Grey—"she will have others."

Taryn frowned. She wasn't used to all of this, even though she was learning fast. "What do you want me to do?"

"One step at a time…maybe this is something Verden and a hound can do." Finding the hostages and breaking Sulia's hold over the Greys she sought to use would be a big battle to win. He knew Verden wouldn't refuse the job.

Felan rolled his shoulders and rotated his wrist. He was guessing there'd be no wild fae protecting the grove, as they wouldn't go anywhere near Sulia. He doubted that she had found a way to corrupt them to her will. If she had, he was in big trouble. Bigger trouble.

"Good luck," Taryn said.

He nodded at his Hunter. He was going to need it.

His heart was bouncing in his chest, but he wouldn't reveal or give into the nerves and fear. He'd spent far too long learning how to play the games of Court to ever give anything away. By the time he reached the edges of the holly grove, he was calm.

Beneath his feet, the ground was almost silent, and above, the stars gleamed as if nothing was wrong with the world. He paused at the grove, now filled with only real trees instead of trapped fairies. In the middle of a small clearing sat Sulia, on a chair that must have been brought from Court.

Around him trees rustled, but there were no wild fae here.

"You made it." She sounded surprised, as if she didn't realize how well he could use a sword.

Felan walked into the clearing, his naked blade clearly visible. But she didn't move, didn't stand. She was acting as though she was already Queen and he was seeking an audience. Everything had been carefully staged, and for that he had to admire her. She was playing a good game, but he wouldn't let her win.

"I was busy. I got your invite, but I had a better offer."

Her face contorted in anger for just a moment before she masked it. He kept his smile hidden. She was worried about this. Good. He walked a little closer. There were people hiding among the trees. He could feel them, the weight of their stares and the peculiar resonance that only a Grey had, as if they were a hollow vessel waiting to be filled.

"Was that before or after you stripped the trees from the sacred grove?"

This time he smiled. "This was no sacred grove. We both know you had planned to kill every fairy here."

Her skin whitened a fraction more. "Oh, don't tell me you are finally taking an interest in politics? Haven't you left it a little late? It's rather more complex than dancing or gambling."

"Yes it is, but it's my birthright." He was quite happy to let her assume that he'd only just decided to pursue the throne.

"You think you are fit to rule simply because of the blood in your veins?" She laughed. "Tell me you're not that gullible?"

"You think you are fit to rule? You've slept your way

to this position, made deals, and taken hostages to force people to support you. Do not mistake bought loyalty for love."

"Love? I don't want love. I want to rule Annwyn and the mortal world. I want power." She stood. Dressed entirely in white, she was ghostly. The only color was her red lips and nails. She was a vampire sucking the life out of the Court. She would turn the Court on itself just to watch the blue blood spill for her entertainment. She tilted her head and looked at him as if he were stupid. "Is that what you want? Love? Someone to warm your heart?"

"I want many things." Staying in Jacqui's bed and hearing her say she loved him was high on the list. Not letting Sulia anywhere near the throne was another.

"I'll make you a deal, Felan." She drifted closer.

He placed the blade between them. Sulia or his mother had tried to poison Taryn, and he wouldn't put it past Sulia to try something underhanded with him. For all he knew her nails were tipped in poison and one scratch would kill him.

"You won't hurt me. I'm unarmed and I'm pregnant." She ran her hand over her stomach. "Do you know how many humans I had to sleep with? I have worked hard to be your rival; already the people are looking at me instead of you. I have an heir and consort, while you have nothing."

"You haven't seen my hand, so don't be so sure."

She laughed. "You bluff. Why not make a move? Come on, surely you want to end this winter?"

"When I am ready, I will."

"When I'm ready." She mimicked. "You will never

be ready. You aren't King material. Let us make a deal. We can save Annwyn and you can be free of the responsibility you shunned for so long."

Was she so blind she still saw him only as a player and no one of substance? However, he saw no reason to disillusion her. What deal would she offer him? "What do you propose?"

She smiled so sweetly he wanted to gag. "People like you. I've seen the way you gather a flock around you. Plus you can dance and keep the Court happy while I do the important part of ruling."

Felan raised his eyebrow.

"You get to continue as you have been. I'll even let you keep your human lover, if you truly have one—she can even have a child—but you marry me."

"And the mortal soul?"

"My consort will happily relinquish his."

Right. Her offer seemed to fit the requirements of saving Annwyn, but more importantly, she wasn't directly ousting him—which told him more about her than she probably realized. She was worried she wouldn't have enough support if it came to outright war. He decided to play along with her game. "So we would rule Annwyn together?"

Sulia nodded. "Perfect, don't you think?"

"But what if I'd rather walk away?"

"And what? Live in the mortal world? As a Brownie, keeping house for some mortal?" She crossed her arms.

He was messing with her plan. He was aware of movement all around the grove. He was surrounded. This could get interesting.

"You'd give up all the glamour of Court for the mortal world? I don't think so, Felan."

Again she didn't use his title; she was being too casual about all of this. But then again, maybe she didn't
expect him to walk out of here at all.

"So I rule with you or not at all?"

"Yes. That is my deal. Take it or die." She stepped
back, and from the trees, a dozen Greys emerged.

"I'd rather live and rule."

"You want war?"

No he didn't. He wanted to spare Annwyn and the
mortal world as much as possible but that option was
drying up faster than a puddle in the middle of summer.
"You want to destroy Annwyn? Force a winter that will
kill tens of thousands of humans?"

"I will do what it takes to win, Felan. You don't have
the balls. You won't even lift your sword to strike me.
You're weak, and you'll be a weak King." She spun
away and walked out of the clearing.

"At the moment, I am the only one in the game. You
haven't declared your intentions at Court."

Sulia glanced back at him. "I intend to…it's a pity
you won't be there to see me claim my birthright."

Her birthright. She grinned as she saw the shock he'd
failed to hide on his face. Edern had no children. She was
lying. She had to be. Otherwise, why had she not made
this proclamation before? It was one thing to challenge,
but it was another to have a legitimate claim. He could almost feel Annwyn sliding through his fingers. She'd being
playing her cards very close to her chest while seeing if
she could gain support without the blood ties. *Cunning*.

"So you have lied about name all this time…for
what purpose?" Lying wouldn't win her friends or
favors at Court.

"I didn't lie. I allowed the Court to believe that the people who raised me were my parents." She smiled. "I too can split the finest points of truth."

"But you cannot prove that Edern is your father either." With Edern long dead, who would vouch for her lineage?

Her lips twisted. "It won't matter, Cousin, as you won't be around to challenge me." She walked out of the clearing, moving like a ghost through the trees.

He took a few steps after her, but an army of Greys had him surrounded. He spun slowly, gauging each one. Some had given up stature and were small, like trolls, but most were taller; some were grotesque, as they'd sacrificed looks for size and power. It was impossible for a Grey to hold on to everything. At some point, they had to choose if they wanted to stretch out their sorry existence.

Were all of them here because Sulia had kidnapped a loved one? What if she got her hands on Jacqui? He knew even as he thought it that he'd do whatever Sulia asked to save Jacqui. He had to find a way to protect her without drawing attention to her.

A few of the Greys carried iron bars, gloves and cloth wrapped around their hands to stop the burn. Even still, holding it for too long would weaken them.

"I know she has your lovers or children captive."

"You can't help us. If your father had lifted the banishment, we'd have been on your side, and our families would have been safe." Then the shortest Grey attacked, swinging the iron like he intended to take out kneecaps.

Felan jumped over the first swing and brought his sword down flat on the troll's arm. Bone shattered and the iron fell to the ground. He didn't want to be killing fairies of any kind. He didn't want to claim his throne with blood.

"I have no feud with you. Walk away and I will do my best to find your families," he said as he defended strikes. A few had been gifted swords—where Sulia had gotten them from, he didn't know. Most had makeshift weapons. Something caught him across the back. Iron. He hissed and dropped to his knees. The Greys moved closer. He pulled the knife free of his boot, twisted around, and threw. It caught the Grey in the chest. He fell back, dead. Felan stood, swinging his sword to make room.

Some of the Greys backed off.

"Last chance, or I spare no one." But that didn't mean he wouldn't try and find the hostages. His back stung from the iron burn. The thin human shirt had done nothing to protect his skin.

For a moment there was hesitation, then they swarmed. He kicked and fought. Iron caught him on the arm. He snagged the knife from the dead Grey and threw it again. With each step, he tried to edge away from the clearing and put a tree at his back.

Metal on metal rang through the night, and it took a moment for him to realize he wasn't the only one fighting the Greys anymore. Taryn was also attacking. The last four Greys ran.

The Hunter went to go after them.

"Let them go." Felan drew in a breath. Adrenaline pumped through his system, his heart was racing and his breathing too shallow. "Where's Sulia?"

"She didn't come to the gate."

"Call the hounds. I want her found."

"You're injured."

"I'll live. I want her found. Now." His voice was harsher than he'd intended.

Taryn stepped back from him and whistled. Two white hounds with red-tipped ears shimmered out of the darkness.

He wiped his hand on his shirt, then realized the blood was his.

"Let me get you back to the gate first." Taryn looked at him, and he saw the worry in her pale orange eyes. He was sure he was hurt worse than he looked.

"Go. I will make it on my own." There was iron in his body. He could feel it burning and sapping his strength, but he needed Sulia captured before she could make her claim to the throne.

Taryn hesitated for a moment, something Verden would never have done, then left, following the hounds as they tracked Sulia.

Even as he seethed, he knew Sulia had broken no laws. She hadn't made any deals with Greys, hadn't actually attacked him herself. There were so many loopholes in fairy law. He straightened carefully, aware of the open wound on his back and a dozen smaller injuries.

That was the last time he played human for Jacqui. She would accept him as Prince or not at all. It was the last time he played the wastrel more concerned with games and dancing too. From here on in, he would be nothing but the rightful heir to Annwyn.

Chapter 10

FELAN WALKED BACK TO COURT. HE'D MADE IT TO the gate, and just being back in Annwyn was making him feel better. The wound on his hand had almost stopped bleeding. His back hurt, and if he stood still too long, the world started spinning and tilting as if determined to throw him off. He needed to rest. But first he needed to let Sulia's supporters see that he was fine and that she didn't have the control or wit that he had. Even though at the moment he barely felt in control of putting one foot in front of the other. He made his way to the hall, where people would be eating and gambling and dancing.

As a shadow servant went past, he helped himself to a goblet of wine and a piece of cake. Both would go a long way to helping Annwyn heal his damaged body and slowing the effect of the iron. If he'd remained in the mortal world, the iron would have had greater and faster effect. Here, he could feel the ebb of strength and the increase of pain, the burning blistering his back and slipping into his blood.

His appearance in the hall almost stopped the music. It certainly halted conversation, which was exactly as he'd hoped. Expressions ranged from shock to carefully arranged concern. With his father's withdrawal to the Hall of Judgment, this chamber was virtually Sulia's. He needed to make a stronger showing and gather his supporters more visibly. His game was too subtle.

Of course, without Jacqui, he had no game.

Felan raised his goblet, the muscles in his back and shoulder protesting, but he didn't let his expression change from mild boredom. "Carry on. Just ran into a bit of trouble." He smiled like it was just a few scratches, but he could feel the iron beneath his skin. The wound on his back wasn't healing. It wouldn't until the iron was removed.

"What kind of trouble?" The man's gaze skimmed over Felan's blood-splattered clothing.

Felan had been counting on curiosity being roused. How many here knew that Sulia had set an ambush? Not enough that word had slipped to him early. He wished he had someone amongst her supports. If Taryn hadn't been forced to become the Hunter of Annwyn, she would have been amongst Sulia's ladies and become a spy for him. Perhaps the people dining were just shocked to see him so disheveled and battle weary.

"The Grey kind. Someone has been coercing them." He looked carefully around the room. Sulia's supporters, the ones he recognized, looked away. Some of them would have known her plan, and he wanted each of them to search their hearts and make sure they were backing the right heir. He wanted them to realize that it wouldn't be simple to best him or remove him. He would fight the whole way.

"Perhaps you should take an escort next time you venture into the mortal world." A man he didn't recognize looked concerned—or he wanted to know where Felan was going.

"It's a sad day when the Crown Prince of Annwyn cannot walk around without fear of attack. Until Sulia declares either her claim to the throne or war, I am the heir. Attacks on me are considered treason."

"So declare war first." The man shrugged.

"I will not pit fairy against fairy. I have no desire to drive Annwyn to snow."

There was some muttered agreement and some argument. Had that point already passed? He glanced around the Court, the pretty people in their finery partying like nothing was wrong despite the mud on the floor and the bare branches on the trees. Would any of them lift a sword, or would they be more content to watch? A formal battle required at least twenty swords on each side. He'd much prefer a formal call than the small skirmishes his father and uncle had indulged in.

Jacqui deserved so much more than this, more than the bitter squabbles and double-edged games. But she would also bring humanity back to the Court, something that had been lacking for too long. She'd make love seem possible to all, instead of just a sign of weakness to be exploited. Annwyn would be better with her…would she be better with Annwyn?

Sulia's offer flitted through his mind. Take Jacqui as his mistress and let Sulia rule while he lived free of the Court. If he did that, she would be accepted without a fight. There would be no winter. It would be over. But the idea made his blood run cold. How long before she would poison him and rule alone? She didn't need him when it was her consort who'd sacrificed his soul. No, once the deal was done, Sulia would ensure she was the only one left standing. She had no honor. Her promises to him weren't worth the breath they took to speak.

He had to act now, before Sulia regained control of the situation.

"I want a full Court meeting tomorrow. Spread the word." His fingers loosened on the goblet, and the room grew darker at the edges. Noise seemed to vanish. He was in serious trouble. He let the goblet slide from his hand, and had turned before it hit the floor. All he could do was hope that it looked as though he'd deliberately dropped the goblet and not that it had simply slid from his fingers because he was too weak to grip it any longer.

He kept the charade together and made it to his chambers, where he collapsed facedown on the bed.

He'd nearly died in that grove. If Taryn hadn't been there, he probably would be dead. He drew in a breath. It seemed like days had passed since Jacqui had kicked him out of bed and he was no closer to securing her affection than he was before. He wanted to remember the taste of her lips and the feel of her skin, but all he felt was the cold burn of iron and the leeching of his strength.

In mortal words, today had been an epic fail.

Felan opened his eyes, aware that someone was in his room. He hadn't even realized he was asleep. His hand closed over his sword, though he wasn't sure he'd be able to swing it.

"Stay your hand. Taryn sent word." Dylis sat on the edge of his bed. She was supposed to be looking after his son. Now more so than ever. If Sulia knew about Caspian...he couldn't even finish the thought.

"You should be across the veil." His voice sounded rough to his own ear.

"Verden is there, guarding the house as you requested, and Bramwel is at the shop, watching over it. You have done all you can to protect what must be protected. Let me clean your wounds and make sure they are free of rusty pieces of iron."

Felan grimaced. He knew it had to be done. That his back still ached and burned around the wound wasn't a good sign. He hoped the wound wasn't as bad as it felt and that it was just the failing of Annwyn making him heal slower than usual. The cold was in his blood, in every fairy's blood. The cold bred corruption, and without the magic flowing thick in their veins, they were little better than Greys holding on to the memory of summer.

"Thank you." There was nothing else he could say. After the power shift, Dylis would be his Hunter. A job she'd be good at. More importantly, she supported his plans to fix the Court and make it something to be proud of again, instead of a place of cruelty and calculations. She didn't want Sulia on the throne—or anywhere near the throne.

"If you don't get up, I will have to cut your clothes off." There was a hint of mischief in her voice. Once he would have laughed, now he just winced.

"Cut them." He wouldn't need his mortal clothes again. "There is iron in the wound."

"I know."

He heard the slide of metal on sheath, then the tearing of his shirt and jeans and cool air on his skin. He was going to miss these clothes and what they meant. Maybe after he was King, he could visit the mortal world again. Jacqui would want to spend some time across the veil.

"Hmm." Dylis's fingertips prodded his back. He gritted his teeth against the pain that raced over his skin and gripped his stomach.

The mattress shifted as Dylis got up. He heard liquid—wine no doubt—and the clinking of glass.

"This is going to hurt, but I'm sure you know that already."

"I have no doubt you will take great—" He hissed in a breath, then all he could do was focus on breathing and staying awake. Gradually, the stinging lessened, and while his back throbbed, it didn't seem to burn.

"A couple of rust flakes were mashed into the wound." She held the cloth out for him to see.

They were tiny. Had Sulia told her Greys to use rusted iron, or was that an accident? That would've been a slow, paralyzing death he wouldn't wish on anyone— even Sulia—if it had been left untreated. Had she been hoping he'd be too injured to make it back to the gate and that he'd slowly die in that grove?

Dylis rustled around. "Think you can sit up?"

"Of course." He did, carefully, noting the ache in his muscles. It had been a while since he'd fought. The last funeral games to honor the wasting of a member of the Court had been over a mortal year ago. He needed to get in some more practice, as he was sure he was going to need it. With a few careful movements, he shed the remains of the clothes. They'd been ruined before Dylis had cut them off him; now they weren't even fit for rags.

"I know you won't need them for long." She placed fresh bandages on the bed, ready to wrap around his chest and back, then glanced at him. "But it would be wise to cover the wound. Although, if you spend as much time as you have been in the mortal world, it will take you longer to heal."

He didn't have any choice about how much time he spent across the veil at the moment. He had to monitor the rips in the veil, and he needed to woo Jacqui. "I know. I'll be careful. I won't let my shirts stick to it."

She pressed her lips together. "Felan, if she'd killed you…"

"We wouldn't be having this conversation." He was aware of the stakes and had been for what felt like his whole life. He felt the weight of his every decision, and he knew how many lives hung in the balance. "Thank you for coming."

"You have done right by me and mine. I will not see you stumble now." She ran the wine-soaked cloth over the abrasion on his arm.

"I will not fall at the last hurdle."

"You must act. Everyone is twitchy. Bram and I are worried the shift will come and we will be on the wrong side."

"I've called a full Court meeting." He wouldn't be rushed into bringing Jacqui here. He wouldn't rush her. He closed his eyes and rubbed his face. His hand still smelled of death, the metallic scent of blood mixed with the sweeter scent of wine. It clung to the back of his throat in a sickening perfume.

"That's not what I mean." She'd lowered her voice to just above a whisper.

Because she didn't want to risk being overheard, or because she didn't want to have this conversation with him?

"I know what you mean." But he couldn't tell her the

truth. "My line is secure." The lie was so easy to say. He just wished it were true that Jacqui was his willing Queen and carried his child. He opened his eyes. Blue crusted his nails. He needed to bathe.

"No one believes that."

He nodded. He knew that too. "Let me handle the Court. Has Taryn found Sulia?"

"She stopped looking to get me. Sulia will come back of her own volition. She won't allow you to capture her and drag her back."

"I'll arrest her the moment she crosses the veil," he snarled.

Dylis grinned. "No you won't; you don't want war. She's watched you and studied you. While you tried to work out who was plotting against you, she has had time to play and plan."

"And I have played into her hands. It was she who called me back seven years ago, I'm sure of it. I just can't prove it." Sulia or his mother, it didn't matter which one when the result was the same. He'd lost Jacqui and his child—except the child had already been lost. How would that have played out differently here?

Would Jacqui have survived? Even if she had, she'd have had no soul; they wouldn't have been able to have more children unless they'd taken other lovers across the veil. If Sulia had attacked while he and Jacqui grieved, Sulia would have won. He shuddered as he realized she'd actually damaged her own chances.

"Look forward, Felan." She squeezed his hand. "I will send a shadow servant with fresh spring water from across the veil. You will send word when the time is close."

"I will let you know the outcome of the meeting. I have business over the veil." He tilted his head and gave her a pointed look, meaning he didn't want to discuss it here. They'd been working together long enough that she got the message. He'd meet her at Caspian's house later.

"I will await your visit." She stood, her orange-and-black outfit looking like something that mixed fairy and mortal fashion. She spun to show off the multilayered skirt and striped stockings. "You like? It came on a doll, but I liked it so I made it bigger."

"It's very you." And not very Annwyn. Not yet anyway.

Dylis left his room for a moment, and he took a breath to center himself. He'd called a Court meeting, but he wasn't entirely sure what he was going to say. Maybe the time for words was over, and as Dylis had said, he needed to act, and make it sharp and decisive.

Two shadow servants carried in a bath. They dropped a piece of fairy silver in it and the water became as still as glass. When the silver didn't discolor, they moved away. If it had discolored or the water had splashed and reared up, someone would have been trying to poison him with river water—his mother had tried that once before on Taryn and had almost succeeded in killing her—but this water had come across the veil, so unlike the river of the damned, it wasn't made of death and disease.

He dismissed the servants. He'd rather be alone with his thoughts so he could plan his speech. Dylis waited, the ever-attentive loyal courtier.

"You can go." She didn't need to stay and guard him.

"Shall I send Taryn?"

He shook his head and eased off the bed. Thrown over a branch was a towel. A mortal one, thick and fluffy. He'd discovered lots of things he liked while courting Jacqui the first time. He went to take his watch off and stopped. The face was smashed. He hadn't noticed when it had happened. His heart stuttered and a lump formed in his throat. For a moment all he did was stare at the broken trinket. While not silver or made of precious gems, the white ceramic watch held true value for him. It had been a gift from the time when Jacqui had loved him and anything had been possible.

"I'll get it repaired." Dylis took it off his wrist. He let her take it without an argument. "If you need anything, let me know. Don't shoulder this alone."

He nodded, not knowing what else to say. She touched his arm, then left him alone. She wouldn't stay in Annwyn. She would go back to Charleston and await his next instruction. He just had to work out what that was. There were too many things circling with no fixed path. He stripped off his underwear and tested the temperature of the water.

Warm. No doubt it had been hot when first brought across the veil by some low-level fairy before being handed over to the shadow servants. His fingers didn't even make a ripple because of the silver bauble in the bottom of the tub. How easy would it have been for someone to put a few drops of the river in here and poison him while he was already weak. Yet no one had even tried. He was surprised. Perhaps Sulia hadn't expected her Grey army to fail.

How many knew that he'd been poisoned by iron, and who would suggest it to exploit it?

Taryn had suspected, but she'd been there.

Dylis knew. But he trusted both. Had one of the Greys reported back to Sulia? Where had she hidden while the hounds had hunted for her? She was too crafty for his liking. A dangerous opponent. He needed to catch her off guard while she was still debating what to do next, after his shocking survival.

He eased into the bath and closed his eyes. The tension didn't leave him and the water chilled too fast around him. He scrubbed at his hands, removing the blue stains. The smaller scratches were already healing. His back stung but no longer with the burn of iron. He rubbed his face.

There were so many things that could go wrong. The fastest solution would be to bring Jacqui here straight away…but she wasn't pregnant. And she didn't want to be pregnant. Hell, she didn't even want to have sex with him.

Was it best to wait until the last day or act sooner? What would Sulia be expecting from him? To wait. Without a doubt, her plans would be fixed around his mother's coming execution. He dunked his head under the water and then stood. Not even the drips from his body stirred the water. He needed to move up his time line and press the slim advantage that he had over Sulia.

As he dried and dressed, he worked out his next few steps but stumbled every time he thought of Jacqui. What would he tell her? Or was this good-bye? He paused for a moment, shirt half-buttoned, then realized it was no longer a choice. Maybe there had never been another choice after what happened seven years ago.

—∿∿—

Jacqui was walking back from her lunch break when she saw it. An imp. A one-foot-tall pile of trouble. She stopped immediately, stunned to be seeing a fairy other than Felan; then she had to pretend as though her phone had buzzed to give her a reason to stop. She fiddled with the screen, never looking directly at the wasted little Grey with the long, spider-leg fingers, then kept walking as if there was nothing there.

However, her heart was hammering. She hadn't seen a Grey for years. And yet here one was, a week after Felan had shown up. Coincidence? She didn't think so. She touched the iron crescent that had hung at her throat for the past four years. It was proving to be more of a balm for her mind than actual protection from fairies. Lower still was the mirror.

She'd seen the battle and seen him live, had watched as a beautiful blond fairy tended his wounds. She couldn't deny the spike of jealousy at their obvious familiarity. Then she'd seen him in a bath, eyes closed as if he were drowning under the weight of what was going on. Even when he should be peaceful, he looked tense and unhappy. Her heart ached for him. If she hadn't told him to stop, if she'd insisted that he stay, he would've never been caught in the battle. Guilt had added its weight to her heart.

From the corner of her eye, she tracked the imp. It was definitely following her. Felan had been attacked by Greys. Was this part of the same plot? She shivered even though it was sunny. No matter how much she tried to ignore it, she was tied up in Felan's race for the throne, and she couldn't say no. She didn't want to lose him forever. She just didn't know if she was ready to commit to forever in Annwyn.

When she walked into the coffee shop, she glimpsed the imp still trailing her. This was not a random Grey that was tagging along. It wasn't trying to make trouble by tripping her—those people who tripped over their own feet were usually tripping over a Grey; she'd seen it happen—or throwing litter in her direction. This one was deliberately watching her and staying out of the way. It must know about her and Felan. Why else would it be here? And if it knew about her and Felan, it would be reporting back to someone, someone who wasn't on Felan's side.

The old fear resurfaced, the one where people would think she was crazy for nervously looking around or deliberately stepping over things that no one else could see. She shrugged off the worry; she hadn't been like that in years. She'd trained herself to act as if she didn't see them, but she hadn't seen any for years, and at the first test, she'd almost failed. She drew in a breath and smiled at Ash, who looked terribly busy restocking the sugars on the tables.

The after-lunch lull. Usually she liked this little pause. Today the shop was too empty. Just her, Ash, and the imp. Its dull skin was stretched tight over delicate bones. It was too thin and too tiny. It was dying, and coming after her was its last throw of the dice, an effort to win favor with the Court.

She busied herself restocking the drink fridge. Maybe it was only attracted by the mirror. But she didn't quite believe that. Too many things were happening too fast. Like her and Felan and the way she'd so easily invited him into her bed. Thoughts of that night were now tainted with what had happened afterward. She should have swallowed her doubts and kept going, let herself drown in the pleasure he offered like she always had. She wanted to be able to close her eyes and let the last seven years vanish as if they were nothing but a bad dream.

It was too easy to let reality slide around Felan. The imp squatted in the corner as if settling in to watch her while still being out of the way. She closed her eyes and sighed. This was reality—her reality that no one else could see. She wasn't crazy; she just saw fairies.

If Felan walked into the shop now, the imp would have something to report, which would mean more Greys or even a visit from a hostile Court fairy. The idea of more fairies arriving to spy on her, or worse, was enough to make her blood run cold.

She closed the fridge door, the chill of the air sweeping over her arms and drawing up gooseflesh. The time for ignoring Greys was over; she'd seen that in the mirror as Felan had cut them down. But could she kill it? Maybe she could just capture it?

And what?

It was dying anyway. She knew she had to kill it and eliminate all threat to her and Felan. She swallowed, not sure how she was going to do it.

This was why she didn't like fairies in her life; she was finding reasons to justify murder. And yet if she didn't do something, there would be worse to deal with.

"I'm going out the back." She wiped her hands on her pants and hoped she didn't look as guilty as she felt just thinking about it. Maybe she could put the imp in the freezer. Wasn't that a kind way to kill snails?

Ash nodded and went back to filling up the napkin holders.

Jacqui opened the door and went out the back into the storeroom, half hoping the imp wouldn't follow, but it did, slipping through the gap just before the door closed.

It wouldn't follow her into the bathroom would it? Did she want to be shut in the restroom with it? No, and if she stood here for much longer, it would get suspicious. She picked up the broom and gave the floor a halfhearted sweep. The little brat kicked her dust pile and laughed. That was more like what she expected from a Grey. If she hadn't been able to see it, she'd have just assumed she'd accidentally trod in the pile. Her fingers tightened on the broom. She had to do it. She could do it.

With a mock sweep she caught the imp against the wall with the broom. "Why are you here?"

It gasped and tried to wriggle free, but Jacqui pressed harder. It wasn't getting away now that she'd revealed she could see them. No good would come of that. While she hated that Felan had given her the fairy wine, she was also glad. It meant she could see the danger instead of being blind.

The imp licked its lips. "You have a fairy mirror."

Jacqui shook her head, refusing to be sidetracked or tricked. "Who sent you?"

"No one."

She pressed a little harder and tried to think of it as a rat and not a fairy. Who was she kidding? She hated using mousetraps. Every time she had caught a mouse, she'd thrown out the whole thing because the idea of dealing with the body made her want to hurl. On cue, her stomach tightened and bucked. The lunch she'd just eaten turned sour.

The imp was probably lying, especially since she was holding a broom to its chest. And now it knew that she could see fairies, which meant that if it was reporting back, they would be more careful about being seen next time. She shuddered. *Creepy.*

"You're lying."

The imp grinned. "If you were going to kill me, you would have by now. Let me go and I'll make sure they go easy on you."

She released a slow breath, closed her eyes, and pushed. Bones cracked and there was a small squeal and a wet squish. Then silence. She gave the broom an extra shove just to be sure, then opened one eye to check. The imp's head was bowed, its arms hanging loosely. She eased the broom away from the wall. The crushed body fell to the floor. Blue blood and guts were smeared over the cream paint.

Her stomach heaved. She dropped the broom and ran for the toilet, only just making it. She threw up until there was nothing left, but every time she thought of it, her stomach went into spasms.

"We have customers and you're taking your sweet time." Ash opened the door and stuck her head through into the storeroom. "Are you okay?"

Jacqui forced herself away from the toilet, wishing she'd shut the door. "I think lunch was bad."

"You don't look so good."

Of course she didn't look good; however, she was doing better than the imp. She tried not to glance in that direction. Her stomach twisted but she swallowed and sucked in a breath. "I'll be fine. Just give me a minute."

She had to dispose of the evidence that Ash couldn't see but other fairies could.

"Okay, I'll manage." The door clicked closed.

Jacqui took another couple slow breaths, steeling herself for the cleanup. She put the broom away first, then, with the dustpan and brush, she swept up the dust and lifeless body. While she gagged a couple times when she glimpsed innards, she survived the trip to the trash. Then she wiped down the wall. No one would know.

Slowly and carefully, she rinsed the cloth and then washed her hands until there was no blue blood to be seen. She dried her hands, glad that they weren't shaking. While she still looked pale, she didn't look as though she'd just killed a fairy spy. The small round mirror that Felan had given her glinted in her reflection.

Don't look. I don't need to check on him.

But she did. What was he doing while she killed?

She pulled the mirror from around her neck, cupped it in her hands, and looked into it one last time.

Felan was wrapped in a dark cloak and around him were thin bare tree branches, as if he were high up. His lips moved, and she knew he was talking to someone. He looked cold and sad and resigned. Alone. She wanted to be able to reach out and hug him. She wanted him to be here to hug her and tell her she'd done the right thing.

He was never here when she needed him. It was always the other way around.

She had to make him realize how unfair it was what he was doing, but when she looked at him in the mirror, she knew he was suffering enough just trying to keep Annwyn together and getting ready to take over.

To take over, he needed her.

What did she need from him?

Once it had been enough just to have him around. Then she'd never wanted to see him again. Now? She didn't know, only that what they had wasn't enough. She smashed the mirror against the sink, then let the shards wash away. Then she dropped the chain in the trash. For a moment she stood there, unable to move. She'd destroyed her only connection to Felan and she wanted it back. She wanted him back. And she hated herself for that weakness.

If Felan never came back, she'd know he was living the rest of his long life with another woman, someone who had agreed to live in Annwyn and be the Queen of the fairies—and she'd have to live with that knowledge for the rest of her life. That she'd kicked him out and forced him to take someone else as his Queen, someone who didn't love him, thus giving him the one thing he didn't want—a loveless marriage.

In that moment, she knew what it was that she wanted.

She'd seen the lust in his eyes, heard him say the words, but she'd never felt loved. Special, yes. Desired, yes. Loved? No. Did he actually know how to love, or was he so caught up in the drama of Annwyn that he'd never let himself risk actually showing it? She believed the loss of the baby had wounded him—she didn't doubt that at all. She didn't even feel like he'd ever lied to her, but he hadn't been completely honest either. He'd always kept part of himself carefully guarded.

When he came back, they would be having words,

because she couldn't live in another world if he was always going to be a little distant. She wanted more than Annwyn. She wanted his heart. Jacqui left the storeroom and went out the front. There were two tables of customers. Nothing Ash couldn't have handled on her own anyway.

"Better?" Ash wiped the coffee machine.

"Yes."

"So…have you heard from him?" Ash said.

Every afternoon at the end of her shift, she'd expected to see Felan walk in, and every day she'd been left staring at the door. Four days and not a word. Some things never changed. And yet, this time she knew what he'd been doing while he was away, and none of it had been pleasant.

"No." How did she explain that this is what he did? The whole time they were together, he'd make her feel like the only woman he desired in the world; then he'd go and leave her desolate for days or weeks. She was a puppet at the end of his string, always dancing to the tune he played. The worst part was she always wanted more, even now when she knew what to expect.

"That must have been one awful date." Ash raised her eyebrow. She was still trying to fish for the details.

"I've had worse." Much worse with humans. Dates with Felan were always something she remembered, even if for all the wrong reasons. She wished she hadn't kicked him out of bed. He was right. What were the odds of her getting pregnant with one ovary and him being a fairy? Slim? Remote? Impossible? She should have taken the chance and saved him from the battle and the wounds. If not for the mirror, she'd have never known. He'd given her a look into his life and not just the good bits. The mirror had been so tightly focused on him that everyone else was blurred as if out of focus. But she'd felt his tension and an all-pervasive chill. The mirror had never warmed against her skin. Yet she missed it already. Missed him.

He would be back. He always came back…even if it did take seven years.

She picked up a cloth and went to wipe down tables, anything to get away from the look in Ash's eyes. If he was a drug, she was addicted. Even when she'd gotten clean, the aftereffects were still there—the memories, the seeing things that didn't exist. Her life would never be fairy-free.

Chapter 11

FELAN CLIMBED THE STAIRS FORMED OUT OF BRANCHES. They spiraled up, around the trunk of a tree. Up here, above the castle, there was more of a bite to the air. Frost gleamed on the bark like silver and the branches were totally bare. Beneath him was castle Annwyn. What had once been the leafy green roof was now dead fingers of twigs reaching skyward. Beyond the castle, the ground was patched brown and white. The snow was spreading. At night, the snow was falling, and it wasn't leaving during the day. Soon it would snow day and night, and winter would have truly arrived in Annwyn. It cut at him to see the place he loved so cold and desolate.

Snatches of music drifted up from the Hall of Flowers. The party continued…but the wine was no longer flowing so freely. There was no fruit. Soon they would have to source food from the mortal world. He grimaced at the thought. No one would want that job when they expected the power shift to happen in days. Annwyn days. He had no idea how many mortal days had passed while he was recovering.

The time difference wasn't going to be helping his cause with Jacqui.

The stairs ended at a door. Silver bars crossed the frame like a spider's web. His mother shifted in the darkness. The spider or the fly?

She stood up and walked over, her skin as white as

snow and her eyes as dark as night. "I didn't expect you to come."

There was no glimmer of the mother he remembered from his childhood. The woman who'd laughed and chased him around the garden. Those vague early memories had stayed with him. The ones where she'd deliberately hurt his father also remained etched in his mind. His parents arguing bitterly and not bothering to hide it, and then the descent into bitterness and scheming. Was it worth it? Was she enjoying the fruits of her efforts?

He pulled his own cloak tighter around him. He longed for summer; already the cold and mud was depressing. Even the Court was giving up on the bright colors and taking on the darker colors of winter, midnight blues and blood reds, black and deep-bruised purples.

"Mother." Now he was here he didn't know what to say. He didn't love her. He didn't trust her. And yet he couldn't walk away without saying something to her before her death.

"Lost for words? Go back to your gambling and dancing. It's what you do best."

He was tempted to bite, but she was just goading him, hoping he'd let something slip, a tidbit for Sulia to devour.

"I'm not sure there are any words left to say, Mother, only that I had to come up here and wish you well on whatever we face after death." He'd love to know why she'd chosen to back Sulia over him, why she couldn't be happy with what she had, and why the love of his father wasn't enough. What had gone wrong? How could he stop his Queen from becoming like her? But he knew he wouldn't get a straight answer. He doubted she knew the truth from her own lies anymore.

And Jacqui?

How would she fare here? Better? Was that the best he could hope for? Or would she be unchanged?

"Do you cede to Sulia?" She gripped the silver web, her eyes bottomless pits of greed.

"Never. But I will trade you one answer to one question if you so wish."

Eyra tilted her head and considered him as if she'd never truly seen him before. She hadn't really looked at him in a long while. "I accept. You may go first."

He nodded. "When my father first took you in his arms, did you love him or was he always a means to power?"

She laughed, her body shaking, before she dissolved into coughing. Being imprisoned and exposed to cold was taking its toll on her, but when he peered into the gloom of her cell, he saw blankets and cushions. Someone had supplied her with a few comforts.

"You speak of love as if it is something to envy, to desire. Power is the only truth. You failed to grasp that young, so I sought out a more suitable successor."

"Sulia."

"The daughter Gwyn denied me. You were required as part of the deal, but she was the child I longed for."

"She's not your child." Had his mother's mind slipped that much?

"She was brought to me as a youth. I taught her the ways of the Court and she blossomed." Someone had protected his cousin, lied about her true lineage to the Court but not his mother. While she'd known all along that Sulia was the daughter of Gwyn's defeated brother, she wasn't stupid enough to be caught in a lie. No doubt the person who had lied had paid for it with their life. His mother didn't like loose ends.

"And look where it has gotten us," he muttered. But if Eyra had never loved Gwyn, then maybe he and Jacqui had a chance—if she loved him the way he loved her.

"My turn." She grinned, all ice and malice.

Was he prepared to lie? Not directly. He'd rather be truthful, but if it endangered Jacqui, he would and damn the consequences. He wasn't going to let his mother anywhere near her—or his mother's minions.

"To rule you need a Queen and heir. Do you have both?"

"Yes." He didn't blink as he spoke. It was a lie that he was getting used to saying. He hoped that no one ever discovered his deception. He didn't like what he was becoming and he couldn't blame it all on Sulia or winter. Desperation brought out the worst in people. Him included.

His mother drew back, her eyes wide with shock. "You kept that quiet."

"While you watched me dance, I was planning. While you rolled the dice and watched me bet, I was putting my plan into action. Now, while we wait for snow to fall, I am ready. Your death with bring in a new era. A new Annwyn."

Her pale lips moved, but for once she had nothing to say.

Felan turned away and was down the first step when she called after him. "I will have my funeral games. Your battle for the throne will honor my death. I will be truly immortal and the stones will sing of me!"

He swallowed and took the next step without looking

back. People would remember her as the woman who'd brought war and winter to Annwyn. A sad legacy.

"Felan, you can't walk away from me. Felan!" The breeze took her words away.

It took all his strength to keep walking and not look back. The woman calling his name wasn't how he wanted to remember his mother. That woman was long gone and now she saw him as the enemy. She would try to trick him into revealing something. All he'd told her was that he was prepared and Sulia would have a harder time than she first thought—something Sulia had discovered yesterday.

He reached the bottom of the tree and glanced up. From the ground he couldn't see her, but she'd be watching everything—and for once she was powerless.

—⁓—

Five days and not a word from Felan. Jacqui walked along the beach, needing to clear her head. She hadn't seen any more imps except in her nightmares. She'd been watching the news and reading the papers ever since Felan had mentioned the plagues. Countries were shutting borders. In some places, the military had assumed control. People were being urged to cancel all nonessential travel, and public gatherings, like concerts and sporting events, were starting to be canceled. People were worrying and stockpiling for what they believed was the coming disease-ridden apocalypse. The world was falling apart, all because she wouldn't be Felan's Queen.

The responsibility almost crushed her.

She took a deep breath laden with salt air and turned

to face the ocean. She was one little cog. A no one. Any woman could save the world. It didn't have to be her. Felan could have anyone. But he wanted her. He'd wanted her from the moment they'd first met in college. Need wasn't love. He'd said the words, but she'd never really felt them, not when he up and left so easily. While she loved him, she didn't need him. It had taken her seven years to learn that and be okay with that.

What was she going to do?

This place was her home. She wasn't fairy and didn't know how to be Queen. She didn't even have the full story about what was expected of her from Felan. She watched the waves roll in against the sand, creeping closer to where she was standing, but even the ocean failed to calm her.

If Felan had asked her the night they'd celebrated her pregnancy, she knew she would have accepted with barely a blink. She'd wanted a life with him at any cost. It shouldn't be different now. How selfish was she, worrying about her tiny life while thousands died because she wouldn't agree?

But that was part of the problem; there was too much pressure on a relationship that had already failed once when tested. What if they failed again? Only this time they'd be stuck together in Annwyn for a very long time. Marrying a fairy took *till death do us part* to a whole new extreme.

She blew out a breath and turned to go home.

Then she saw him, walking toward her along the sand, his long, dark blue coat catching in the breeze. For a moment she thought she was imagining things. He wasn't even dressing like a human this time—not that most humans would notice, as he'd be using a glamour. To her he looked every inch the fairy Prince.

A smile twisted her lips. She liked seeing him as he truly was, instead of him pretending to fit her world. In moments, she was in his arms before she could even think it through. She'd missed him, worried about him. What the mirror had shown wasn't enough and yet too much. He smelled of cold and frost. His clothes were darker too. She was used to seeing him in bright colors or human clothes. This man was different, more was happening than what she'd seen in the mirror or in the newspapers.

Perhaps she shouldn't have destroyed the mirror.

His body tensed. "Gently. I am still healing," he whispered in her ear. His lips brushed her cheek as his arms slid around her waist.

She nodded and eased her embrace, her fingers gliding over the dark blue fabric, soft and thick. He was dressed for winter, not a California summer. She lifted her gaze to look him in the eye. This time there were none of the smiles she was used to. She saw the naked worry and the stress in the set of his lips. "I know. I saw."

He drew away. "I don't have long. Things are moving faster than I had thought."

Only just back and he was brushing her off already— after she'd just flung herself into his arms. She pulled her hand free. "It's been five days."

"I knew it had been days. I wasn't sure how many. I wanted to be back sooner."

She shook her head. "Save it. I know the excuses." *Annwyn came first. It always did.*

"You used the mirror. You saw what it's like."

Jacqui looked away. She had, and she couldn't deny that it had given her a greater understanding of what he was doing while he was away from her. "I'm glad your injuries weren't life threatening."

"They were. The iron could've been fatal." His gaze lowered to where the mirror should hang around her neck. "Where is it?"

She blinked and then met his questioning gaze. "I saw you fight. I saw you with the blond fairy, and I saw you high in the trees talking to someone else. I didn't want to look, as it felt like prying."

"I wanted you to see, to understand my life there."

"Your gift attracted an imp." She couldn't keep the accusation out of her voice.

Felan drew in a breath and cast a quick look around. While there were people on the beach, no one was looking at them and there were no Greys this close to the ocean. "What happened to the imp?"

"I killed it. I killed it so it couldn't report back. I killed for you." She hated that. Her love for him had turned her into a killer—even if it was of small, banished fairies that no one else could see. She saw and she knew and she'd always remember.

"I'm sorry, but you did the right thing." He didn't sound particularly sad.

That was the worst part; she knew she'd done the right thing. She'd protected Felan and herself. "I broke the mirror. I didn't want the connection to Annwyn. I don't want to be killing to be safe."

"You will be safe once I am King."

"Will I? Because what I've seen of Annwyn so far isn't very appealing."

"You are seeing it at its worst." He cupped her cheek and turned her head so she had to look at him. "I have days, Jacqui. I need to know: am I wasting my time?"

"Wasting your time?" She raised one eyebrow and took a step back, edging closer to the ocean. "Am I your first choice or your only choice?"

"Both."

"I'm not ready. I may never be ready for what you want. You come and go and expect me to jump when you appear. Then you leave and I'm left waiting. Nothing has changed. Will anything ever change?"

"You think I like this? That this is how I want things between us?" He let her go and scrubbed his hands over his face. In that unguarded gesture, she glimpsed how hard he was trying to hold it together, hold everything together for two worlds. "Do you love me?"

She looked at him. The man she'd fallen for at eighteen was still there, but he was being swallowed up by the responsibility he had to shoulder. "Do you really need to ask me?"

He nodded.

"Yes. That's why you could always hurt me so badly."

"I don't mean to," he said.

"I know, but you do. You will again." One day he would turn up and he'd take her to Annwyn and that would be that. It didn't matter how much she fought it or tried to deny it. Fate was breathing its icy breath down her neck.

"I have called a Court meeting. I have to strike before Sulia, the woman who also wants the throne, tries to kill me again."

There was an edge to his voice that worried her. "What are you going to do?"

The ocean rolled against the beach and the silence expanded. He didn't want to tell her. Did he not trust her?

"Annwyn needs you. You should come with me today."

The pressure gripped her and sucked her breath away. Did he realize what he was asking, what he wanted? Or was he so focused on the big things that he wasn't looking at the details and the people who were wrapped up in his plans? Then she realized she was his plan. She was how he was going to stop Sulia. He was going to take her to Annwyn sooner rather than later. She took another step back, her shoes sinking into the soft, wet sand. "It's always Annwyn. What about you? What do you want? Do you want me? Do you need me? Do you love me?"

"Of course I do. But what I want doesn't matter."

"And what about what I want?" She took another step back, aware she was moving closer to the ocean; it would be lapping at her heels in a moment. He wasn't taking her to Annwyn today. There were things she had to do. She had to speak to her parents. How long had it been since she last called them?

"It's bigger than us. You've seen my life; you've seen the news. You would condemn two worlds?" He took a couple steps forward, his gaze flicking between the ocean and her.

"No. But this is about us. It has always been about us. You have just refused to see it because you're scared." Cool water slapped against her ankle. She took another step back and it swirled around her legs. "You are either there for me or you aren't. I can't save the world on my own and neither can you. But don't you dare tell me this isn't personal. Don't tell me that it's for the greater good. Tell me you love me, that you need me. That we can do this and everything will be fine." She kept walking backwards, away from Felan and into the ocean, her eyes filled with tears. "Just once, prove that you will do what it takes to have me because you want me, not because I'm a pawn in your game." Tears rolled down her cheeks. If he was going to take her from everything, he had to promise her something.

Felan watched her walk into the ocean, the choppy surface steely gray beneath a cold sky. It might be summer, but he was sure a storm was rolling in. He took a step forward, the edge of the water only a step away from his boots.

Jacqui watched him. "If you want me, you have to come and get me."

It was one thing to admit to needing Jacqui for Annwyn's sake and another to admit that he needed her—that without her it was like living in a permanent winter. In Annwyn, love was seen as a weakness. He had tried for so long to avoid entanglements, or anything that could be construed as a weakness, that he couldn't find the words. He'd told her that he loved her many years ago. That hadn't changed. But when he looked at her, up to her hips in the sea, he knew that wasn't what she was looking for. She was forcing him to prove it. His word was no longer enough.

"I want you. I have always wanted you, and only you, by my side." It was Jacqui who had made him realize what love was, and despite what his mother said, love was more pure than power—and much harder to obtain.

"Seven years ago, you were planning this. You

always knew, yet you didn't tell me." She swiped angrily at the tears on her cheeks.

"I would have."

"When? The day you decided it was time to go?" A wave rose up and hit her back. She gasped and stumbled, but didn't go under. She was almost waist-deep in water, and he wasn't sure what to do. How much further would she go?

"No. I would've done things differently."

"Do you know what it's like to love someone and have them always talking of duty, of always putting something else first?"

"Do you know what it's like to always have the duty, to grow up knowing what is expected? People telling you that you don't have the luxury of love. That a good Queen is the best you can hope for, saying that love means nothing?" He took a step forward, the ocean lapped at his boot. He suppressed the shudder. "That because I wanted more, it somehow made me less worthy of being King?"

Her lips parted and he watched her expression change. She was getting a taste of the expectation he'd lived with for centuries. And it sucked, to use her words.

"I am fighting for my life, my right to rule, for Annwyn and the seven billion people on this side of the veil. If I fuck up, if I let Sulia sink her fingernails any deeper into Annwyn, then what is happening now will be nothing. I'm trying to prevent a war. I'm hoping that you love me enough to understand, enough to share the responsibility. I don't want to fight you too. I don't have that much strength."

"I don't want you to fight me. I want you to fight *for* me."

"I came back. I'm ankle-deep in ocean. What more do you want from me?"

She looked at him. There wasn't that much distance between them, a dozen paces, but it might as well have been half a world.

"I want you. I want to feel loved. Not desired or required. You say you love me but never show it."

He went to argue with her but stopped. She was right. He was so used to moving strategically that he was always thinking ahead. He never let his heart guide him—he didn't trust it. With deliberate movements, he unbuttoned his heavy coat and tossed it onto the sand. He unbuckled his sword and threw it onto his coat. The cup of life he kept on his belt. He couldn't afford to let it out of his sight or have it fall into the wrong hands. She wanted proof? He'd give her proof.

As the water eddied around his ankles, he bottled up the fear and took another step forward. Her eyes widened as she watched. She obviously hadn't expected him to come after her.

"It doesn't matter where you go. I will come after you. Not because of Annwyn, but because I can't live without you. I learned that over the past few years." He braced himself as a wave slapped against his thighs. His heart was beating faster than it had in battle. He'd rather face a dozen Greys again. This was horrible. He wanted to run back to the safety of the beach and the dry sand.

Cold and wet, his trousers clung to his legs. "I love you. I don't know how to prove it so you believe me."

Three more steps until he reached her. He could do this.

"You have never even asked me if this is what I want. You just assumed I would say yes."

"Fine. Will you marry me and rule Annwyn with me?" Another wave hit him. He was sure it was getting choppier. Would it rise up and swallow him? He reached out and clasped her hand. "Please, Jacqui. I have lived for centuries and have only loved you. And even if I'm not good at showing it, believe me when I say only you have ever broken my heart and made me feel like I was dying." He pulled her into his arms, and she cried against his shoulder.

"I never wanted Annwyn—only you." Her breath came in sobs that shook her body.

"I know. You have me. You had me from the moment I first saw you." He began carrying her back to the beach. He wanted to be out of the water as soon as possible. When the water was no longer sucking at his legs as if trying to keep him, he placed Jacqui down. "Is that a yes?"

Please, let it be a yes. He wasn't sure he could stomach taking her across the veil if she really refused. He'd always thought she'd come around and see what needed to be done, that she was more than a waitress, more than just a mortal woman. She was the one who would save both worlds...and make him happy for the rest of his life. He only hoped he could make her happy.

Her arms remained around his neck. In the silence, the ocean mimicked the beating of his heart, a thudding that resonated through the earth that had consequences that reached far beyond the shore and into deeper, darker depths.

She nodded. "Yes."

He kissed her before she could change her mind or add extra clauses or make extra demands he knew he'd

agree to. He just wanted to enjoy the moment, the one
he'd feared for so long.

Her lips were cool and salty, but her mouth was
warm, and she was pressed against him, his arms around
her waist. His tongue dipped and tasted, and he wanted
to sink to the sand with her now and hold on to this for
as long as possible—to pretend that he didn't have a
hundred and one things to do before the Court meeting
he'd called in haste.

But she'd said yes; it would all work out. The iron of
her necklace pressed against him, and heated his flesh,
his shirt not offering enough protection from the metal.
It would start burning him soon.

The breeze chilled his wet clothing. She shivered in
his arms.

"Let's get out of the cold," she murmured against
his lips.

He pulled a glamour and heat surrounded them.
"How's that?"

Warm air danced across his skin. He eased his hold
on her and led her to where he'd thrown down his coat
before going after her. He spread it out on the sand,
moved his sword aside, and then sat. The sun was setting
over the ocean, staining it red.

"You've hidden us."

"Yes. I thought the people who were watching had
seen enough." He pulled her down to join him. She sat
between his legs, her back to his chest, and for the moment he could relax and pretend he had nowhere else to
be and nothing to do. He kissed the side of her neck and
let his hand slide up her thigh, her black pants clinging
to her legs like a second skin.

"It's a public beach." But she tilted her head and didn't stop his hand from sliding under her shirt.

"Not anymore it isn't. This little bit is ours, and only ours."

"I thought you couldn't stay?"

"I can't stay the night." He cupped her breast, her nipple peaking and pressing against his palm. "No matter how much I want to."

"You wanted to last time as well."

He held his breath. Was she saying no again? "I want you, Jacqui. When I'm with you, I can forget about everything else for those moments."

"I want you too." She twisted around and kissed him. Her fingers traced along his jaw. "I shouldn't have kicked you out last time."

"I needed to fight that battle." It would have happened eventually anyway.

Her hand slid to his side where the drinking horn hung. "What's this?"

"Something I am guarding."

She turned and looked at him, one eyebrow raised. He had to stop acting as though he couldn't trust anyone, but old habits were hard to break.

"The cup of life, a fairy artifact used for healing." Amongst other things. In truth, he should have returned it to his father, but Gwyn hadn't asked and Felan hadn't volunteered. His father knew he'd need it and he couldn't risk Sulia getting it.

Jacqui nodded. For a few minutes they watched the sun sink, as if swallowed by the ocean.

"How far would you have waded out?" He kissed the back of her neck.

"I don't know. I didn't plan it. I just didn't want you to take me to Annwyn there and then."

"It will be soon." Too soon and yet not soon enough. He needed to tell her so much more, and yet he didn't want to break the moment.

"I know." She rested her head against his shoulder. "Is there sunset in Annwyn?"

"Yes. But not like this. We can come back here occasionally."

"But I'll have to live there." She traced shapes on his leg, the heat of her fingers warming his skin through his wet pants.

"Yes…you won't age and the people you know will."

"They'll die."

"So will you, eventually, but not for hundreds of years."

"Almost immortal." She drew in a breath. "What if we don't last forever?"

He'd wondered the same thing. Love wasn't common in Annwyn, but he had to put his faith in something and believe that there was more to life than just gambling and deals and games. Love seemed like the best thing. "I guess we have to try. I hope we do. I want you to be happy. I'll do whatever I can to make you happy."

"And what about you?" She half turned, so she could look at him again.

"Being with you makes me happy. Seeing the end of winter will make me happy. Beyond that, I don't know right now." He didn't need to think that far ahead, not when there was so much to do before then. He cupped her face and kissed her slowly. Around Jacqui, he'd never had to be anything more than himself. She made him remember everything that was good and worth saving, and she had found a part of him that was worth holding on to—his heart.

He drew back, knowing that while she'd agreed to marry him, she didn't entirely know what she'd be giving up. It was more than just the mortal world. "Do you remember when I told you fairies have no soul?"

She nodded and watched him closely.

"Did you ever think I was less of a person because of it?"

"No…" She spoke carefully, as if she could sense something was coming.

His hand moved against her hip. For a moment he didn't want to say anything, in case she pushed him away again, but the deal was already made. It was better he tell her now than later. Later, they needed to be worrying about the lack of heir.

"You can't keep your soul in Annwyn. A human with a soul would suffer unbearably and end up being tricked out of it."

"What are you saying?" She was frowning now.

"When you become Queen, you have to give up your soul and become like us."

"But it's part of me. Isn't it? Won't I die without it?"

He shook his head. "Your soul would heal Annwyn, and in exchange, you get the long life of a fairy."

She was quiet for a moment, the sound of the waves filling his ears as he waited for it to sink in. "And what happens when I die?"

"I don't know what kind of afterlife fairies get. Maybe none, as it is the human soul that goes on either in Elysia or the river of the damned."

"I lose my chance at heaven or hell, or whatever the afterlife is."

"You lose your chance at the mortal afterlife."

"You should have told me all of this before. Like years ago—or even yesterday. Ten minutes ago, before I agreed to be your wife."

He looked away; even watching the ocean was better than seeing the accusation in her eyes. "I know. I just didn't know how to say it."

"How about something like: if you want to marry me, you have to give up your soul?"

"I didn't want you to say no. I couldn't bear hearing that. It's why I never asked you before and why I just assumed you would be my wife regardless. I thought our love would be enough."

"You're asking me to give up everything for you." Her fingers pressed against his leg.

"I'm offering you everything—a life beyond the mortal span, two worlds, and my eternal love." He tilted her chin so she had to look at him. "I love you." He didn't want to have to remind her that it was too late to back out, that she'd made the deal and he had to hold her to it. Or would Jacqui make him break his word again?

She closed her eyes. "I love you too, but I am the one making all the sacrifices to be with you."

He bit back the laugh. She saw going to Annwyn and living for centuries as a sacrifice. "What would you have me give up? If I could give up the throne and know we could live in peace, then I would, but it wouldn't last. My lifespan is so much longer than yours."

"How did you ever date me, knowing all of that?"

"At first it was just for fun. I like the mortal world. You

were fun to be around, full of spark and hope. When things started to get more serious between us and I started to wonder how you would fit in Annwyn, I was surprised when I could imagine it so easily. Picturing you by my side wasn't hard at all. I told you what I was because I wanted to see how you'd react. When you became pregnant, I thought that was it. I was making plans to sweep in and take control…my plans fell apart on both sides of the veil."

"So you weren't planning to take me to Annwyn from the first day we met?"

"No. I was planning on taking you to bed though. No games, no deals, just lust. It's very heady to someone who is always watching every move at Court." He drew her closer. "Why didn't you run when you knew what I was?"

"Because I wanted to be more…You made me feel like I could do anything and be anyone. You listened to me and what I wanted."

"I still listen. And you won't be trapped in Annwyn."

"You are assuming we're going to win."

He smiled. "That is the only outcome I want to think about. If I can go into the ocean to get you, I can beat Sulia to the throne."

Jacqui took a deep breath. "And I can give up my soul to be your wife."

The tension Felan had been holding on to released. He'd almost been expecting her to refuse. "Thank you." She had no idea how relieved and happy that made him. That was almost better than hearing her say that she would marry him. He kissed her again.

"Just how private is this magic?" Her breath tickled his lips.

"Very. Humans can't see or hear a thing."

Then she turned around, pushed him onto his back, and straddled him.

He smiled and undid her shirt, smoothing his fingers over her skin. The need to have her was rough in his blood. It may not have been seven years in Annwyn, but it felt like longer since he'd had her in his arms. His fingers traced the cup of her bra, then he hesitated at her necklace. When she said nothing, he removed the iron crescent and dropped it on the sand.

She covered the place where it had rested with her hand and looked at him for a moment. He could see the questions in her eyes, but then she blinked and they were gone. Whatever needed to be said could be said afterward—and she seemed to have reached the same conclusion.

She rolled her hips. He was already hard and resenting all the clothing between them. Her hands slid over his shirt, but he wanted to feel her skin against his. He drew her forward and caught her lips. His fingers freed her hair from its clip, and it tumbled around her shoulders in dark curls. He liked when she wore it down, messy and a little wild. He liked it more when she was naked and her hair was loose and her eyes were half-closed in ecstasy.

He opened the button and zipper on her pants, even though he knew they were never going to come off like this—and nor were his. She smiled and kept moving her hips as if she knew exactly what he was thinking.

"Are you sure no one can see us?" She lifted her hips, and he slid his hand into her pants.

"Totally." He eased his fingers over her panties and caressed her, taking his time to rediscover her body instead of rushing like he wanted to.

She drew in a breath, but this time she moved her hips against his fingers, trying to find her own pleasure. Her eyes closed, and he wondered what she was thinking. He wanted to slide his fingers under the fabric of her panties and feel that slickness on his skin, but he didn't want to disturb her; he wanted to see her come.

Little moans caught in the back of her throat. He knew those sounds. Music he'd never thought he'd hear again.

"That's it, come for me." He claimed her mouth, his tongue flicking against hers. Her body tensed against him; then a shudder ran through her as she gasped. Her hips kept moving, only slower this time, as if she was trying to catch her breath.

He pulled his hand free and rolled her onto her back. His coat was going to be ruined by the sand, but he didn't care. He worked her pants and underwear down, the sodden fabric clinging to her legs as she tried to kick off her shoes. After a little bit of wriggling, she was almost naked. Her shirt was open, and she still wore her bra, but it was close enough. He kissed her belly and up her stomach while her hands undid his trousers and pushed them down.

Reluctantly he drew away to shed his boots and trousers, neither of which were really wet anymore, just damp, thanks to the magic keeping them warm. He placed one knee between her legs and moved over her. The thought that she'd still turn him away lingered even as he eased closer. She didn't realize how much power she had over him.

Her hands skimmed up his sides, pausing at the bandage wrapped around his ribs to protect the wound on his back. He kissed her throat, tasting the salt on her skin—and a little sand. Her fingers pressed against his hips as her legs moved apart to allow him closer. The head of his shaft brushed her inner thigh, then her hand was there, wrapping around him and guiding him to her slick core.

As he sank into her, he closed his eyes. He'd missed her so much, and now that he was in her arms again, he was afraid it would all be taken away. He held his breath, almost expecting her to change her mind, but instead she lifted her hips.

With Jacqui, it was always different. It was never simply the sealing of a deal or scratching an itch. She was able to reach in and tear down his defenses because she never wanted anything else but him. He was always the one dragging all the baggage and making it hard for them to move forward, always worrying about what it would mean.

Now he knew. Jacqui was his.

She drew him down for a kiss, her fingers tangling in his hair and her legs wrapping around his hips as if she planned on never letting him go. Need burned hot in his blood. He opened his eyes to watch her. Her eyes were almost closed, her lips parted as she panted.

A shimmer of desire traced down his spine; no fairy would ever let themselves sink into such abandon. He placed his lips to hers in the softest kiss. Her core clenched around him as she came, her cry of pleasure on his lips.

He thrust twice more and gave in to desire. For a moment he didn't move, just let the sensations wash over him—the sound of her heart, her breath on his skin, the waves along the shoreline. Maybe the ocean wasn't so bad after all.

Jacqui opened her eyes, so dark in the dusk. Her fingers stroked down his neck.

"I love you." He meant it with all the power he could put into the words. He felt the magic in them. Would she?

She smiled. "I know. You went into the ocean for me."

"I would do anything for you." Without her, he might as well be banished.

———~~~———

Before she was ready, Felan pulled away. Her body missed the weight and warmth of his immediately. That was some engagement celebration. It was also apparently going to be a very short engagement. How much longer did she have with her soul? Her soul for the safety of two worlds and the lives of billions. Was anyone really that important?

He passed over her pants, now dry but covered in sand. She shook them out as best she could, well aware that compared to the coat she was sitting on, they were really cheap—but he didn't seem bothered. She pulled on her panties, and he distracted her by kissing her again. For a moment, she almost expected her underwear to come straight off again. She melted into his arms. How had she gone seven years without him? Had she not noticed how empty her heart was and how cold her bed was?

He smiled at her. "I don't want to leave you now."

"Well, I guess we won't have long to wait." How long did she have left in the mortal world? She needed to eat chocolate and ice cream, to walk on the beach and do other things that she couldn't do in Annwyn. She didn't even know what she could do in Annwyn. She'd agreed to live in a place she'd never seen, rule people she knew only a little about, and become one of them. She swallowed down the rising panic. That was the only way she could have Felan, and it would be worth it. She had to believe that.

He nodded. "After the Court meeting…a few mortal days maybe?" He glanced at the ocean, and she knew he was thinking of what needed to be done. Their time was over. When he looked back at her though, this time his focus was on her. "Will you be ready?"

No, never. What have I agreed to?

"Yes." As she said it, she knew that she would be. This is what they'd started seven years ago. If things had gone to his plan, millions of people wouldn't be dead. She could save them, not that anyone would ever know. She'd once told her mother that there had to be more to life than just working, living, and dying. Her mother had laughed and told her not to be silly. Perhaps even then, years before she met Felan, she'd been marked for this, her destiny.

He sat on the coat next to her and put his boots on. The embossed leather would be ruined from the ocean, but he didn't seem concerned. Was it really that easy for him to replace his clothing?

"So what now?" She glanced at him. He was watching her, half reclining on the coat as if they were at a picnic.

He stared at the ocean but didn't seem to be seeing it. "Where there was one Grey, there would've been another."

Her stomach rolled at the memory. Would she ever get over that peculiar scent of fairy blood and the feeling of breaking bones? "You mean there's another watching me, us, now?" Had it watched as they'd had sex?

"It would have left when it saw me meet you."

"It could have overheard everything."

Felan shook his head. "After you killed the first one, I suspect they will stay well back. Which is good. It's safer. But now Sulia knows who you are and where you live." He lips formed a thin line. Gone were the easy smiles she usually saw. This was the grim Felan she'd glimpsed in the mirror—the one trying to save his world and hers. "I can't keep you safe here."

"What do you mean? I can't go to Annwyn now." She had to say good-bye to people. That realization caused a little lump to form in her throat. Would they think she was dead?

"No, not now, not yet." He frowned. "Have you ever been to Charleston?"

"What's in Charleston?" How was South Carolina any safer than California?

"My son and his guardians."

She felt her jaw drop open. "You have a son?"

He gave a single nod. "I had an affair with a married woman over thirty years ago, but when I saw her with her husband, I realized all we had was lust, not love. She loved her husband. I walked away. Caspian was born here. He is a changeling."

He had a son who was older than she was. "Were you planning on making her your Queen?" He'd said she was his only choice.

"Annwyn has been in trouble for a while. I liked her a lot, but not enough. When I saw the way she looked at her husband, I wanted someone to look at me like that. So I waited. I was selfish." He shook his head, old regrets written in his features. "I could have

spared both worlds a lot of grief if I hadn't reached
so high."

For how many decades had he been balancing what
he wanted with what Annwyn needed?

She placed her hand on his thigh. "I don't think wanting love is too much to ask."

He laughed. "You don't think like a fairy. I hope you
never do." His finger traced the curve of her cheek. "So
you'll go to Charleston?"

"Do you have any other children I should know about?"

"No others. I never wanted them to be used to get to
me. It hasn't been easy keeping Caspian safe." His lips
turned down as if the memories still hurt.

"How do you know I'll be safe there?"

"Because I trust his guardian, and I trust Caspian."

She nodded. She didn't know these people and yet
she was going to have to trust them with her life since
staying here was no longer an option. Did Felan realize
he was asking her to cross the country? "It's not as simple as driving there. It's the other side of the country."

"I know my geography. Are the airports still open?"

"Internal flights only and all nonessential travel is
supposed to be canceled." She licked her lower lip and
tasted salt. "What if I get sick? There are so many outbreaks at the moment." And the idea of being stuck in
a plane with people who could be harboring anything
from TB to the bubonic plague really didn't appeal.

His eyebrows lowered, and she knew he was running
through options she couldn't think of.

"What if a Grey gets on the plane with me?" Now
that she'd started thinking of all the bad things that could
happen, she couldn't stop. If it was a big Grey, it would

be much harder to kill, and some Greys still had magic. She glanced around the dark and almost deserted beach as if expecting to see something moving in the shadows.

"Taking you via Annwyn is also a risk. We could step through the doorway and be attacked. It's happened in the past, and I don't trust Sulia."

"She'd be that bold?" Would this fairy woman really try to kill her just to claim the throne? Of course Sulia would. She'd already tried to kill Felan, and he was the Prince.

"Desperate." He sighed and was silent again. "Private charter."

"What?"

"I'll hire a private plane."

"Now, at this time of night?"

When he smiled this time, she saw the fairy, the cool, calculating smile of a man who knew exactly how to play dirty. "In this situation, I think a few little enchant-ments are required and necessary."

"You won't hurt anyone?"

"No one will be hurt, I swear. But I can't let Sulia capture you. Where I refuse to kill her consort, she would not hesitate to kill you."

The sound of the waves was drowned out by the beat-ing of her heart. This really was life and death. "You swear I'll be safe?"

"Yes." He didn't even hesitate. She knew how much he valued keeping his word.

She took one last look at the ocean, then turned to Felan. Her fiancé. "Then I'd better get home and pack."

Chapter 12

WHILE JACQUI HAD PACKED, HE'D PLANNED THE REST of his day in detail. Great detail. From whom he needed to speak with to what he needed done. There was no ambush waiting on the Annwyn side of the doorway when he'd left California, which was a welcome surprise, but also a reminder of how confident Sulia felt. She didn't expect him to act until the last moment. And he wouldn't, but he was going to choose when that moment was, not her. The tension in his shoulders and the way his hand rested on the hilt of his sword just in case as he passed through the veil made him realize what a good defense the doorway was. If he were Sulia, one of the first things he would have done was secure the doorway, thus forcing his opponent to use the old doorways that only went to a fixed location. It was a pity the Window had been broken; it had been a useful—albeit dangerous in the wrong hands—portal that could be carried in a pocket.

The time difference between Annwyn and the mortal world was working against him. Dawn was lightening the sky over Charleston already. Those few moments in Annwyn had chewed through the night. He glanced up. How close was Jacqui to arriving? A few more hours?

Had he done the right thing in leaving her to travel alone?

Maybe taking her to Annwyn would have been better,

but he didn't want her there for the Court meeting—he
didn't want her there until the last moment. Couldn't
have her there until she was pregnant. Was she already
carrying their child? Probably not. He was going to
have to resort to magic or he would lose at the final
hurdle and both their lives would be forfeit. Given her
fear of pregnancy when she'd kicked him out of bed
the first time, he didn't know how he was going to convince her that he needed an heir. His fingers brushed the
old-fashioned drinking horn hanging from his belt. He
should have told her while he had the chance, but even
now the moment on the beach was a precious gem he'd
never let go of.

He could always have the Court meeting without
bringing forward the execution, but it would be an
empty threat and that time had passed. He needed to
cut Sulia, and cut her deep. Catch her off guard and put
her on the back foot. Sulia didn't think he had the heart
to bring forward his mother's death. His father had set
these events in motion and had made peace with the
decision. Felan had already spoken his last words to the
woman who had let the loss of her soul steal her humanity. It was up to him to carry out the sentence for treason.
While he knew he had to, it still didn't sit well, ending
his mother's life. If it all went wrong, he'd only have
himself to blame, but at least he would no longer be
following; he would be leading the dance to the throne.

He walked up the road from the cemetery toward the
old house where Caspian and his lover, Lydia, lived. He
had barely entered the property when Verden appeared
in the garden still cloaked in shadows left over from
the night.

"You know you give off a resonance of Annwyn that attracts banished fairies?" He leaned against one of the oaks.

In the dull light, Felan didn't see a change in the old Hunter of Annwyn, temporarily banished from Annwyn. A Grey. However, it had only been just over one week, and if Verden was careful and didn't use magic, he could last for quite a while. Once Felan was King, Verden's sentence would be reduced to exile.

"Your heart longs for Annwyn." Like all Greys, he just wanted to go home. Verden understood the risk that if Sulia took over, there would be no reduction in his sentence. For that reason alone, and his love of Taryn, he was loyal to Felan.

"My heart longs for Taryn. I don't particularly care where we are."

"I know she has been across the veil to see you." The Lady of the Hunt was virtually living on this side of the veil.

Verden gave him a lazy smile. "You aren't here to discuss what she does when not running around for you."

Felan shook his head. "She does it for you, not me." He didn't care that Taryn acted out of love for Verden and not duty to the throne. She'd do what was needed to put him on the throne and lift her lover's banishment. "But you are right. I have important matters to discuss. I'm assuming Taryn is already here?"

Verden nodded. "Dylis and Bram too. They are living here at the moment."

Good. And bad. The people he trusted most were all in one location. If Sulia was smart, she'd wait for them to leave the protected house and attack. Maybe her support wasn't as strong as she claimed and her allies refused to participate in an outright attack on the rightful heir. That didn't mean they wouldn't agree to a declaration of war.

He looked at Verden again, closer this time. He'd expected him to shrink and make a small dwelling in the garden, but obviously Verden was determined to hold on to stature in his banishment. "Where are you living?"

"Not in a burrow or in the scrub. I will not live like a criminal fairy."

Felan didn't point out that he technically was a criminal, but his only crime had been wounding the King's ego publicly. If Annwyn hadn't been on knife-edge, he probably would've gotten away with a simple demotion and lost the rank of Hunter.

Verden pointed behind him. "There are old workers' cabins on the property. I've been fixing them up. Caspian was quite happy to acquire the materials and for me to do the labor. It is quite comfortable. Of course, if you took the tea set home, I could just live in the house."

Felan smiled. He'd given Caspian an enchanted silver tea set to keep his house free from Greys. Another precaution Felan had taken to protect his son. "Has there been any Grey activity here?"

"You're looking at it. No one else will come near while I am here."

The tension he'd been holding on to eased a little. Verden's word was as good as his swordsmanship. This property was as secure as it could be. "Get Taryn up and choose a place for the meeting, outside. I'll go wake up everyone else."

Without waiting for an answer, Felan went and knocked on the door. He didn't have to wait too long for footsteps to move quickly down the hallway. The lock clicked and the door swung open. Caspian stood there in jeans and a T-shirt. Both looked crumpled, but Felan still smiled. He'd seen his son more in the last three months than he had in the last thirty-five years. He hoped it would continue after he was King.

"I'm sorry for the early visit, but we need to talk."

"Is it time for the power shift?" Caspian stood aside to let him in.

"Almost. How did you know?"

"The Brownies have left the house and Dylis is acting like she's walking on hot coals." He shut the door. "I'll get the others and meet you in the kitchen."

Taryn's parents had been Caspian's Brownies and had kept the house for him, but with the power shift coming, they had gone back to Annwyn. That was part of the reason for his visit; he didn't want anyone to be caught on the wrong side, where death would be instant.

"Outside, so Verden can be present." Most fairies wouldn't make that concession for a banished fairy, but Felan and Verden had made deals, and in his heart, Felan knew that he would have done the same thing as Verden for the woman he loved.

Felan walked through the old house and into the kitchen. It had changed since he'd last seen it. For one, there was a fairy-made tea set sitting on the kitchen counter; secondly the house looked lived in. There were coffee cups by the sink, fruit in a bowl, and notes stuck to the fridge. His son was making himself a good life with the mortal Lydia.

Voices filtered down from upstairs.

He didn't want Verden to think there was a brief

secret meeting happening inside, so he went out the back door and down the path. On the grass was a table and six chairs—not enough for everyone. Taryn and Verden were already there. He nodded at Taryn. A few minutes later, Lydia, Caspian, Dylis, and Bramwel came out. Despite the early hour, everyone seemed alert.

Verden stood on the other side of the table, his gaze skimming over the chairs, and for a moment Felan wondered what he'd do. Verden stepped back, allowing everyone to sit except him. It was the right thing to do, given that he was the lowest-ranked fairy, but at this point in time, Felan was willing to throw out rank and go for the survival of everyone here—and Jacqui.

He would stand while he talked. He preferred to be moving anyway. "Everyone sit. You too, Verden."

They did, turning their chairs to face him. All of them looked grim, although getting woken up at dawn by the Prince of Annwyn probably wasn't the best start to a day.

"The next few days will determine all our fates. I will speak to those I trust at Court separately, but there are things I'm not ready to share even with them." He swallowed and looked around the table—three happy couples who were risking everything by being associated with him. Caspian didn't even have the luxury of choice. He was guilty by blood. "I trust you with my life and Jacqui's."

Dylis sat up straighter. "She has a name."

"And she will be arriving in Charleston this morning." He pulled a carefully folded piece of paper out of his pocket and handed it to Caspian. "Can you please go to the airport and collect her?"

Caspian nodded. "What does she look like?"

"Dark curls, blue eyes." He paused for a moment and thought of all things he'd once tried to forget and yet never would. She had engraved her name on his heart, and some wounds never faded. "I doubt she will have a problem spotting you." There was a family resemblance even though Caspian was mortal.

"Am I to assume she will be staying here?" Dylis said.

"Sulia's Greys found her in California. I had no other choice."

"It's fine. There are plenty of rooms." Lydia smiled, but it looked forced. Because she didn't want someone else staying or because was afraid of Greys after her last encounter?

"Hang on. Sulia is working with Greys?" Caspian looked directly at him. "Isn't that against the rules?"

"As far as I know, she hasn't made a deal with them; she has taken their families hostage, some of them are mortal." Usually trusting the word of an unknown Grey wasn't wise, but he'd seen the fear in the man's gaze as he'd faced his last moment and begged not for his own life, but his son's.

Everyone was silent for several heartbeats as the meaning sunk in.

Verden spoke first. "I'd heard whispers but didn't believe it."

"That gang of Greys was willing to kill for her because she's threatening their families?" Taryn leaned forward and put her elbows on the table. "How did she arrange that?"

"I can only assume she has supporters willing to resort to kidnapping." Which made him worry even more about Jacqui. Perhaps he should have sent Dylis or Taryn to travel with her. It was too late now, and at the time the best plan had been to get her on a plane as fast as possible.

"We killed most of those Greys." Taryn paused. "You think there's more? You think they will come here?"

"I think it's a possibility you should all be aware of." He looked at Verden, the person most as risk, as he wouldn't be protected by the tea set in the house.

Lydia glanced around the garden as if expecting a Grey to melt out of the shadows. "And you are bringing Jacqui here. We will be a beacon to every Grey and fairy loyal to Sulia. We'll be trapped in the house."

"Lucky you." Verden crossed his arms.

"It's only for a few days…which is my next point of business." Felan took a few paces, then turned back to face them. Everyone was watching, waiting for him to say he had a solution. It was less of a solution and more of a gamble. But what fairy didn't like to gamble? It was a hell of a lot more fun when lives weren't at stake. "Tomorrow in Annwyn is a full Court meeting. You must attend." Felan paused and waited for the inevitable *why*?

When it didn't come he was surprised.

"And me?" Caspian crossed his arms.

This was the part of the conversation Felan had been dreading. "If you go to Annwyn, you will be safe from the power shift, however, being there will bring its own dangers. People know your face; they will know you are there for me. Sulia is out to hurt me regardless of the bloodshed." He would rather Caspian stay on this side of the veil, trapped in the house, as Lydia had put it.

"And if I stay here?"

"You are mortal; the power shift won't kill you, but

it will be unpleasant for a time because of your fairy blood." Unfortunately, he wasn't sure how unpleasant or for how long. No one had ever bothered about change-lings too much, as they were born on the wrong side of the veil to start with. Although one changeling had recently arrived in Annwyn on the arm of a fairy and had willingly given up his soul—making him fairy—and sworn to fight on Felan's side. He couldn't ask Caspian to do that. Caspian's life was here.

His son frowned as if considering, then glanced at Lydia. "Will Jacqui be attending the Court meeting?"

"No. I will come for her soon after."

Dylis slapped the table. "Why not take her in for the meeting?"

"I can't risk her murder." If he lost her, he'd walk away from Annwyn so he could die in the power shift when Sulia took over. And if he took her back without a child growing in her belly, all was lost anyway.

Verden tilted his head slightly, his gaze carefully neutral. "What are you planning?"

"I'm going to bring forward my mother's execution and close the doorways." No one in and no one out. He was hoping to spoil whatever Sulia had planned.

"You need someone to bring Jacqui to Annwyn be-fore that." Verden leaned forward. "I'd offer, but..." He smiled, knowing that he couldn't set foot in Annwyn at the moment.

Verden was right. He couldn't leave Annwyn once he went back for the Court meeting. Which meant he wouldn't be the one holding Jacqui's hand for her first glimpse of Annwyn.

He could only give Jacqui full Court protection once

he was either accepted as heir or the formal call to war had been issued, and he could only do that once she was by his side in Annwyn—proof that he had everything he needed to take the throne. Almost. Could he tell anyone here the truth, that Jacqui wasn't pregnant yet?

He still had time. He hoped he had time. He glanced at Taryn, but she had to be by his side as Lady of the Hunt. That left Bramwel or Dylis.

Dylis inclined her head. "I will do it. I've protected Caspian and will protect Jacqui as my last act as guardian."

Bramwel kissed her on the cheek. "Don't be late."

"I won't." Dylis placed her hand on Bramwel's thigh.

Felan hoped this wouldn't all unravel, but he'd listened to the stones singing of his father's battles. He knew how many consorts had been killed before they even set foot in Annwyn, and then those who had been poisoned or stabbed before the formal protection could be given. Until the formal protection was given, it was consort hunting season. Unfortunately for him, Sulia only needed a willing man, not even the father of her child. His consort needed to be pregnant with his child, a fairy child.

One of the first things he was going to do was issue a law protecting all consorts on both sides of the veil. The killing for political gain had to stop.

"We'll meet again this evening, then cross to Annwyn—except Dylis and Jacqui. After the Queen is executed, I will only have one mortal day to produce my consort." The trick being, if he left, Sulia might take the doorway to prevent him from getting through, or follow and attack him in the mortal world. All of which had been done before, which was why he had to stay and make sure Jacqui could get through.

"How will you gauge the time difference?" Caspian glanced between Felan and Dylis.

"That I can help with." Verden pulled out Felan's ceramic watch. The watch Jacqui had given him all those years ago. "I found a man who owed me a favor."

"We have fairy watchmakers?"

"I've discovered there's a lot that happens here that we don't acknowledge in Annwyn."

"Banished?" Felan asked.

"Exiled." Verden raised his hands. "He knows his time is up."

Damn it. He didn't want fairies to die because they were in exile. It was one thing to condemn them to a social death beyond the veil but another to kill them. Not even banishment was a direct death sentence—but most used too much magic and suffered the rapid effects. Unlike Verden.

Felan held the watch. At first glance, it looked the same, but as the light shifted on the glass face, he saw the Castle in darkness. Not a clock, but enough that the wearer could gauge the time at Court. "Will it work in Annwyn?"

"I hope so. I cleared a debt for it," Verden said. "He wanted to die knowing he had left no promises unfulfilled."

"Thank you for getting it repaired." For a moment he just held it and watched the second hand tick happily around the face. He doubted anyone here knew how much it meant to him. Then he handed the watch to Dylis so she could have a look. "Bring Jacqui through during the execution. Take her directly to my chamber and do not leave her unattended for any reason."

Dylis peered at the watch, tilting it to catch a glimpse of the Court. "Will you set guards on the doorway?"

"No, I want Sulia to think I'm planning on coming back to claim my bride." He'd even reference that clause when announcing the new execution date. Let Sulia make assumptions about his plans. "Verden, I want you to find out what you can about the kidnapping, track down the whispers."

Verden nodded once. "I'll see what I can do."

"Good." Felan looked at everyone at the table. Dylis handed the watch back to him and he put it on. "I'll be back this evening."

⸺·⸺

Jacqui held her breath as the plane touched down, bounced, and then settled on the runway. The small craft shuddered as the pilot slowed. She had no idea how much Felan had paid, but the plane had taken off from the small airport and was landing at an equally small one in South Carolina. She'd never been this far south before. Hell, she'd never been on a tiny little plane before. Or forced to flee across the country because Greys were after her. A day for firsts really. And none of them were good.

Except for the bit where Felan had actually asked her to marry him...although it wasn't what she'd hoped the proposal would be. She'd hoped for more romance and less drama. But every time she thought of him wading into the ocean to get her, her heart gave a patter of excitement.

The plane came to a stop, and after a couple minutes, the pilot got out of his seat. "Here we are." He gave her a weak smile. "I hope your family stays safe with all the trouble happening."

"Thank you." Her stomach tightened. She was partly responsible for all that trouble. The escalating death toll, the grinding to a halt of all travel and tourism, and increasing fear. Was this how the end began, with fairies going to war over who should rule? Had people thought that the end was coming thousands of years ago when Felan's father had fought to keep Annwyn from his brother?

She shivered, even though the plane was warm. The pilot opened up the door and she climbed out, her one bag thrown over her shoulder. She still felt bad about lying to Ash, and for telling her she was going home before all the planes stopped flying. She still didn't know what to say to her parents, only that she had to say something before she went to Annwyn. But she could do that over the phone.

Jacqui walked across the tarmac, hoping that Caspian would be there as Felan had promised. And if he wasn't? She wouldn't let herself think of that.

Airport might have been glorifying this place. It was more like hangars and a small building for passengers to pass through. As soon as she stepped into the building, she saw him and she relaxed a little. Her lips curved in a smile, but even as it formed it froze. Something was wrong. The man was using a glamour. He walked toward her. For half a second, she considered running, but where was she going to run to? Instead, she forced herself to take a breath and keep moving toward him. He didn't know that she could see through glamours.

He already had dark hair, but he was too young to be Caspian. His eyes were brown, not green like Felan's, and he was trying to dress like a fairy but without pulling off the style or elegance. Human then? Not changeling, as they always had pale eyes that gave away their parentage. Felan had told her what Caspian looked like as she'd packed for the flight. This man wasn't Caspian, but he was hoping she'd think he was. Not a good sign.

The man smiled at her, but it was too sickly and she could see the cunning in his eyes. This was a man who'd do anything to ingratiate himself with powerful people. "Glad you arrived safely."

He offered his arm, but she didn't actually want to touch him, so she shifted her bag to the other shoulder. "Yep, good flight."

Where was Caspian?

She walked toward the doors as quickly as she could, trying to work out a way to avoid getting in a vehicle with this man. He followed a few paces behind—that made her worried. She could turn around and speak to the one person at the desk, but what would she say? That this man was trying to kidnap her when he'd done nothing wrong? Yet.

The doors swished open and sunlight bounced off the footpath. A silver sedan was parked against the curb; a dark-haired man leaned against it. He lifted off his sunglasses and revealed eyes of the palest green. Exactly like Felan's. That was his son.

His gaze flicked to the man following her, but he didn't move. "I thought you were traveling alone?"

"I did." She turned to face the other man and did her best to look confused. "You aren't both here to pick me up, are you?"

The man looked at Caspian, then Jacqui. "You'd

best come with me if you want to be safe. He's a glamoured Grey."

"He's a glamoured human. Why would a human need a glamour?" Caspian moved toward them both.

She really wanted to run to his car. But since he was treading carefully, she decided to follow in his footsteps and be safe. "What's going on?" She turned to be able to see both men.

The fake Caspian grabbed her arm. "Stop being silly. I wouldn't want you getting hurt."

Jacqui stomped on his foot and yanked her arm free. "Don't touch me."

As he reached for her again, she gave up on playing it safe and ran for the silver car. She was yanked back by the man grabbing her backpack, and she couldn't shrug out of it fast enough. Her butt hit the footpath. The man lifted his foot to stomp on her belly, and she punched him in the groin. He doubled over and she scrambled up.

Caspian grabbed the man by the collar of his burgundy waistcoat and hauled him upright. "Who sent you?"

"Your future Queen," the man gasped out.

"And you are?"

"Stuart, her consort."

"You're an idiot. Run while you still have the chance."

"I will be King." He struggled to get out of Caspian's grip and failed.

Caspian saw the ring on Stuart's finger and tugged it off. "We'll see." The glamour ended as soon as the ring was off his hand. "Don't wear my face again." Then he dropped it on the ground and stood on it. The ring crunched, and for a moment the scent of cold and pine trees filled the air. He released Stuart with a shove in the opposite direction.

Stuart stumbled and turned, determined to have the last word. "I'll do what I want and answer to none. Especially you, changeling." He spat and walked away as if he'd won. From a safe distance he turned around. "You won't live to see the execution." He mimed shooting her and then laughed.

Jacqui watched him. He was Sulia's lover. Sulia knew she was here. She'd crossed the country for no reason. Her blood chilled and seemed to stop moving. Her wrist started hurting and her legs felt weak.

"Are you okay?" Caspian picked up her bag,

She nodded. No she wasn't. She'd just been attacked by a man wearing magic, her butt hurt, and her wrist ached. She shook her head. She should've been safe here.

"Come on. The quicker I get you back to the house, the better." But Caspian wasn't watching her; he was watching Stuart's back. Stuart seemed to be the kind of man that you never took your eyes off. Not even for a second.

"I'm not safe anywhere."

"I won't let anything happen to you." He opened the car door and held it for her. "There's too much riding on this."

She was getting tired of hearing that. Like it was her responsibility to save the world. *Worlds*. "So why did you wait out here if my safety is so vital?"

"I saw him go in and thought it best to wait."

"He could have killed me."

"Not in there he wouldn't have. He would've hoped you'd get in the car with him." Caspian placed her bag on the backseat. "You saw through the glamour."

"Don't make that public knowledge." While she'd hated the ability for so many years, it was becoming quite handy when the enemy didn't expect it.

"You aren't a changeling."

"Nope, I unwittingly drank fairy wine." There was no need for Caspian to know his father had given it to her without telling her what it was or what the side effects would be.

He shut the car door after her, then walked around and got in. "Have you ever been to Court before?"

She shook her head; she was trying to concentrate on getting through the next few days. One thing at a time for the moment.

Chapter 13

TWENTY MINUTES LATER, SHE WAS SITTING IN A GRAND old plantation house at the kitchen table with one fairy and one human. Caspian and another male fairy had left to put a note up that his shop would be closed for the next few days. Most people would think it was because of the disease outbreaks. She knew better. It was all about staying safe from those working for Sulia.

Lydia was the human at the table and Dylis was the fairy—the one who'd she seen with Felan in the mirror—and they both looked concerned.

"Really, I'm fine. I just landed on my butt." She'd said it three times already. She wasn't made of glass.

"You sure?" Lydia glanced at Dylis and a shiver of warning traced down Jacqui's back. What weren't they saying?

Dylis rolled her eyes as if humans were dense. "And the baby?"

"What baby?" Had she missed part of conversation somewhere?

"You aren't pregnant?" Dylis leaned forward, her eyes wide. "That lying bastard." She stood up. "He told me that his line was secure."

Was that what the attack had been about? They all thought she was pregnant and Stuart had wanted to make her miscarry? The image of his raised leg ready to stomp down on her stomach filled her mind.

"He told you I was pregnant?"

"Not in so many words." Her eyes narrowed. "You have to be pregnant for him to take the throne. He needs an heir, and you won't conceive once you've given your soul to Annwyn." Dylis almost glittered with annoyance. She would've been beautiful in her anger if she'd been angry at someone else.

"Pregnant?" Jacqui leaned back. Felan had failed to mention that as well. If he'd been here, it was entirely possible that she would have killed him. How could he leave that bit out? It was so typical of him. She closed her eyes and saw him wading out to get her, remembered the heat of his kisses as they'd made love on the beach. He'd known and said nothing—surely he could have slipped that in while telling her she'd have to give up her soul?

Dylis laughed. "You agreed to be his wife without examining the fine print? Never make deals with fairies without understanding the terms."

"Enough." Lydia got up and put her arm around Jacqui. "Dylis is honest, in the brutal fairy way, which I'm sure you're used to. And I'm sure Felan had a good reason to lie about the baby." There was an edge to her voice that couldn't be hidden.

But Jacqui didn't want to be coddled. She'd ask Felan about the lie later—although he would deny that it was a lie and more of an omission of the truth. To her, an omission was still a lie, but to Felan they were completely different, as a lie was a deliberate and misleading act.

Did slimy Stuart know that he'd have to give up his soul to rule? Even if he didn't, he'd probably sell his own mother for the power. It wasn't just Felan versus Sulia. It was Jacqui against Stuart. The downside being Stuart didn't need to be pregnant.

She wasn't sure she wanted to be pregnant after last time…

Had the sex on the beach been simply because he needed to get her pregnant, or had he actually wanted her? She drew in breath loaded with suspicion. Is that why he'd tried to sleep with her after their first date? No, she'd invited him back. He'd simply accepted.

And if she needed to be pregnant before going to Annwyn, hadn't he left his run a little late? These things could take months, and they had days.

"Felan is coming here this evening?"

"Then he goes to Annwyn. I will smuggle you in later so Sulia doesn't try and kill you." Dylis smiled as if what they were talking about was perfectly normal.

"So if I don't get pregnant tonight, what happens?" The silence was complete and unnerving. "I mean, there has to be a backup. These things don't just happen. Fairies aren't known for their swimmers." And she only had one ovary. Surely there was another plan.

Dylis looked at her fingernails as if they were the most fascinating thing in the world.

Lydia shrugged. "I don't know. He needs an heir…do the rules say the Queen has to be the mother?"

When Dylis looked up she didn't need to speak. Jacqui could see it in her eyes "There has been more than one heir before. While the Queen is usually the mother of the first child, the others are fairy through their father's line."

"So he could have an heir already." She felt sick. The room was too hot. Her throat prickled and sweat beaded down her back. He could've been having sex with half a dozen different women in the hopes of getting one pregnant. No, he'd said he had no other children except Caspian. Could Caspian be his heir, or was that not allowed because he was changeling?

Dylis shook her head. "He doesn't. It's why we were hoping to see you walk in with a rounded stomach."

"And you know this how?" Just what was Dylis's relationship with Felan? They were obviously close from what she had glimpsed in the mirror.

"Because I've occasionally been his lover over the last seven years."

Right. Of course. She hadn't expected him to be celibate. She hadn't been single. They'd separated, so there was no need to be faithful. Yet when she looked at the delicate blond with icy-blue eyes, Jacqui wondered how he could see anything special in her—aside from her soul and womb. Today was getting steadily worse with each passing hour—just maybe she was starting to regret saying yes to him.

"I know you humans think sex is everything; it's not. It's love and power that count. When Bram and I want a child, I will find a suitable human male. If he wants one for his line, he will find a suitable female. The children will be raised by us. They will be our children. Our love will be unchanged. In Annwyn, to let your husband or wife go and create a child is seen as a great gift, not only to them but for all of Annwyn." The snark was gone from her voice. Dylis actually believed what she was saying.

"But he would be having sex with someone else." Even the thought was too much. She wanted to be the mother of his child.

"It's just sex. Fairies aren't fertile with each other; if we didn't sleep with humans, we'd have all died out years ago." Dylis was frowning, as if she couldn't understand the fuss. "His heart is yours and has been for years. I knew it when I was with him."

"Then why sleep with him?" Jacqui snapped.

"It was convenient. It stopped others from hassling him for a place in his bed and gave me someone to do while Bram was trapped as a tree. It was an arrangement that suited us both at the time."

Lydia gave Dylis a glare, then looked at Jacqui. "This is a lot to take in, and you've been up most of the night. Why don't you go upstairs, have a shower and rest, and when Felan gets here, you can talk to him?"

"She'd better do more than talk. If the Court knew he was bluffing…" Dylis made a slicing gesture across her neck.

If the Court knew, Felan would lose all support. Sulia would win by default and Felan's life would be forfeit. The crushing weight was back—the same weight that Felan must have been carrying alone for decades. She didn't know how to deal with all of this. She needed time that no longer existed. "You're not going to tell anyone, are you?" Jacqui asked.

"Of course not. That won't help get him on the throne, and I will do whatever it takes to make that happen." Dylis stood and walked out the kitchen door. The door swung closed behind her.

Lydia inhaled. "She's been Caspian's guardian since he was born. You can trust her. She won't do anything that harms Felan or Caspian."

"But I'm expendable." As she'd once said to Felan,

any woman could be Queen. She'd just been the one dumb enough to agree. She wasn't sure their love was enough to conquer Annwyn.

––––––∿∿∿––––––

The second floor of Callaway House was all bedrooms and one bathroom. Lydia had given her a room with a four-poster bed, complete with sheer curtains. If it was meant to make her feel like a princess, it wasn't working. After a shower and some food, she'd slept a little. Now she was watching the sunset, knowing Felan would be here soon and wondering what to say to him. She didn't want to argue, but she wanted answers…or reasons, since she already knew the answers.

She fiddled with her cell phone. If she didn't ring her parents soon, it would be too late. With the death toll climbing by the hour and hospitals overflowing, maybe she was already too late. She found her mother's cell phone number and pressed dial.

It rang a few times, and just when she thought it was going to go to voice mail, it connected.

"Hello?" Her mother's voice was still rather prim, as if she were blaming the unknown caller for interrupting.

Jacqui bit her lip. What did she say?

"Hello?" her mother said again. She'd hang up in a moment.

"Hi, Mom. It's Jacqui."

"Jacqui? Oh my God! Are you all right? You're not sick?"

"I'm fine." *About to leave this world but fine.* She swallowed to keep her throat from closing up. "I was just ringing to see if you and Dad are okay."

"We are. Your father made sure we stocked up on water and canned food, so we are going to stay inside for as long as possible. I hope it doesn't get any worse. Your brother can't get home."

"I think the airlines are just about grounded." She sniffed. She wasn't going to cry. She would see her parents again. She'd make sure Felan gave her that. "I saw his last game on TV." There would be no football this week, as large gatherings were banned and the teams couldn't fly. The whole country was grinding to a halt.

"You're safe?" her mother asked again.

"I am."

"Did you want to talk to your father?"

Jacqui closed her eyes as a tear trickled down her cheek. *I'm not going to cry and blubber all over the place.* "No."

She didn't want to listen to him tell her how much of a waste of space she was for getting pregnant, for dropping out of college, for breaking down, for stopping her meds. Her mother had wanted her to stay on the meds and stay at home, so she could be easily controlled. They were both as bad as each other, but they were still her parents.

"He loves you. He just wanted what's best for you."

He wanted what was least embarrassing for him. "Just tell him I'm happy. That I'm engaged to Felan and we're expecting a baby." Now who was lying about the baby?

Jacqui could almost hear the shockwave hitting her mother in the seconds of silence that passed before she spoke. "What?"

"Yeah. It took seven years, but we found each other again. And this time you and Dad won't get between us." It was because of their hatred of Felan that she'd kept the baby a secret the first time, a secret that had almost cost her life. She hadn't meant to tell her mother that, but she wanted her father to know that he was wrong. Wrong about everything. She was strong and capable and smart. And she could save the world.

"Are you sure that's what you want? He was so bad for you."

"Mom, he was the good part of my life. You let him believe I'd terminated our baby. But I forgive you, and I forgive Dad." They didn't see the world the way she could. They didn't know that fairies and Greys walked among them, and that it wasn't human governments causing the plagues.

"Honey, you're scaring me. What's going on? Are you sure he's not hurting you?"

"He never hurt me." She drew in a breath. "I just wanted you to know I'm fine. I'm glad you and Dad are holed up in the house. When this is over, I might come and see you if Dad can be civil."

"What about a wedding?"

"It will be overseas." Which was about as close to the truth as she could say.

"I thought you were in California?"

"Not anymore, Mom."

"Where are you?"

"It doesn't matter." The bedroom door handle turned. She knew before the door opened it was Felan. "I have to go." Felan stood in the doorway, hesitating as if he wasn't sure he was welcome. Perhaps Dylis had told him about their conversation.

"Jacqui, please. I miss you. I love you."

"I love you too, Mom. I will see you soon. I promise." She was looking at Felan as she said it. She hung up as he closed the door and then leaned against it as if for support. She'd never seen him look so tired. He was still in the same clothes. His dark blue coat was crumpled. His hair looked like he'd raked his fingers through it many times.

"Tough day at the office?" She tried to sound like she was joking and failed. There was too much going on for her to find anything funny. She just wanted it all over. The deaths, the anguish, the uncertainty of if they would survive until morning.

"I heard you were attacked."

"I survived. So did the imaginary baby." She patted her stomach.

He closed his eyes. "Jacqui."

"Don't. Whatever you are going to offer as an apology, I don't want to hear it. I don't want sorry. I want to know why you didn't tell me what you needed."

Felan looked up. "I did. I said I need you. I love you and I can't live without you."

"The fine print, Prince Felan."

He winced and glanced away at the use of his title. When he looked at her, his face was unreadable—the mask of the Prince who wouldn't let anything slip. "I thought you wanted to know what I wanted, not what Annwyn needed?"

She threw a pillow at him. Damn him for tossing her words back at her. He caught it and let it fall to the floor.

"Don't split hairs. This is my life too. Dylis said you need a pregnant Queen and if I can't give it to you, you will go elsewhere. Is that true?"

"No." He pulled something from beneath his coat and tossed it on the bed.

It was the drinking horn that had been on his belt at the beach. Even though she wasn't fairy, she could feel the magic lifting the hairs along her arm. She glanced from the horn back to Felan.

"I never planned to have a child with anyone but you. The cup of life ensures that happens."

"You said it heals."

He nodded. "It heals the sick, creates life, and is the opposite of Annwyn."

"Where did you get it?" Had he been carrying it around so he could use it with her? Would he have told her first? He'd have had to, as there was no way she'd have drunk anything out of a magic horn without noticing—although she had drunk fairy wine without noticing.

"My father."

Did everyone know they had to make a baby tonight?

Felan gave her a half smile as if he knew exactly what she was thinking. "I borrowed it a while ago. He never asked for it back. I suspect he knew I'd need it."

"Why didn't you tell me?"

"I had so many things I wanted to tell you last night, but you didn't want to listen to me. You wanted me to prove that I love you. I did. And have again. I want only you as the mother of my child."

Jacqui raised one eyebrow. "That's not as sexy as you think it sounds."

"I'm not trying to be sexy. You would know if I was.

We need to close this deal. This is business. I need a pregnant Queen."

She wrinkled her nose. "I'm not having sex for business."

"Then have sex with me because I'm going into a full Court meeting as the unpopular choice. Because if it all goes bad, this could be it. But if it goes well, then plan A is covered and you become Queen of Annwyn with me, and our child will be the future ruler—in a millennia or so."

"And if I say no?" She wasn't ready to get pregnant.

He shook his head as if he didn't want to answer, then set his jaw and looked at her. "I don't want to take that option, but I will if you don't want my child."

"I do." That lump was back in her throat. "But I'm worried it will happen again. I've had less than a day to get used to the idea of having a child with you now…as opposed to in five years or so. What if it doesn't grow in the right place? What hospital will you take me to in Annwyn? What happens to me then?"

"You don't think I've thought of that every second of every day since you told me what happened? I don't want to lose you. I will take you to the best mortal hospitals. Tell me what you need to make this happen and I will give you everything in my power."

"I want more time to accept all of this. I want time for us." They'd only just got back together. It was all happening too fast. She hadn't planned on having children in the near future, not when she'd only just got her life sorted. But then she hadn't planned on Felan coming back into her life in such a dramatic fashion either.

"That is the only thing I can't give you. I believe in us.

I never stopped loving you, I just didn't know what it was or how to get it back and keep it safe. How to keep you safe." He pressed his lips together and frowned. "Perhaps you can use the time difference between the mortal world and Annwyn in your favor, so the baby grows slower. Nine months in Annwyn is far longer than nine months in the mortal world. Traditionally, the Queen would spend time in the mortal world, so the baby would be born sooner and summer would return to Court."

She nodded. That was better than nothing. She'd just be pregnant for a very long time…in mortal time anyway. No wonder Felan lost track of time between the two worlds so easily; it was already hurting her head. "I also want ultrasounds, early ones to make sure it is growing in the right place, that the baby is okay this time."

Felan's eyebrows pinched together as his frown deepened. "I don't know what an ultrasound is."

"It's a scan. You can see the baby as it grows."

"Really? You have technology that lets you see the baby inside you?" He seemed almost excited by the idea.

She risked a smile. "Yes."

"Annwyn should have that magic."

She nodded again. Annwyn *should* have that magic. She was sure there'd be plenty of fairies who'd love to be able to see their baby growing. "I also want to see my family again—not now, but after you are King."

"You may come and go between worlds as you wish. But you won't age, so we will need to think ahead, maybe glamours. I want you to be happy, Jacqui. I don't want you to regret this choice, now or in two hundred years' time or even two millennia."

"What if I wanted a second child, like the Queen did?"

"Then we would have to talk."

"We're talking now."

"If there are two heirs, then there will always be war for the throne."

"That's different than now because?"

"Neither of us has declared war. I might have to once you are in Annwyn if she won't step down, but I see your point." He studied her for a moment. "If you want a second child, you would have to have sex with a mortal." He gritted his teeth. "I would let you, but I think I would want to be there. And what if I want a second child and you do not?"

She hesitated and realized that she couldn't avoid the question when she had expected him to answer. "Then I am present." Although the idea of seeing him with someone else would be gut wrenching, she was still thinking in human terms. Perhaps in a few centuries she'd think differently.

The corner of his lips curved. "You weren't serious."

"I wanted to know what your answer would be. A thousand years is a long time."

"You're thinking in mortal years. Time is different. In my mind, we weren't apart for years. It doesn't feel that long and yet I know that much time has passed. Even watching Caspian grow up through the mirrors, it was hard to see him change so much in what felt like a short amount of time."

"It's a good thing you didn't wait too much longer, or I would have been old."

He laughed. "After I'd gotten over the initial hurt, I checked on you in the mirrors. I needed to know you were all right. Any other requests?"

"You need to honest with me from here on. Tell

me what you plan, what you want and need. I may not grasp the complexities of Court life at first, but give me a chance and I will."

"I've tried to protect you."

"Yet you gave me a mirror so I could see what you were dealing with."

He sighed. "If I'd thrown all of this at you, you would have run. I remember you freaking out when I first told you that I wasn't human."

She smiled, remembering. "But I got over it. You need to trust me."

"I do."

"Do you? Do you really trust anyone?"

He hesitated. "No. Not completely." He ran his fingers through his hair. "I want to. I want to be able to tell someone everything and see if they have any better ideas, but in that same breath, I fear they will turn on me and betray me for a better deal."

"But everyone in this house is here for you."

"Because of deals or blood. Dylis guarded my son because I could free her lover, Bram. He owes me his freedom, so he's on my side. Verden supports me because I will overturn his penalty. Taryn only helps because she wants to be free of Court to be with Verden. No one is here because they want to be."

"Caspian?"

"Is marked by blood. Sulia would use him against me if she could."

"And what about me?"

"You are here because I didn't tell you the whole truth before getting you to agree to be my wife." His lips twisted into a bitter smile.

Jacqui slid off the bed. "I'm here because I love you…that doesn't mean I'm letting you off the hook though." She stood in front of him so he had to look her in the eye. "I want you to swear that you will tell me the truth and not hide the small print."

"You want to make a deal with me?" Both his dark eyebrows lifted in surprise. "Most people don't willingly make deals with fairies."

"I'm not most people. I'm going to be your wife, mother of your child, and apparently savior of two worlds." Most people didn't wake up one day and find that they had to shrug off their soul for the greater good.

He looked at her for a moment. "You know most deals mortals make turn sour. You might hear truths you wish you could ignore."

"Like what?" What nasty secrets was he hiding?

"Like I'm bringing forward my mother's execution. If I wasn't, we would've had more than just tonight. We would have had a few more days."

"I need months, not days."

"You have hours."

"I know, and we are letting them slide by." However, she wasn't going to do anything until he agreed to stop giving her half-truths.

He was silent for several heartbeats. "I don't want to bind you in a deal that will last for more time than you can imagine. I trust you with my heart; I will learn to trust you with Annwyn. Can you trust me?"

"I can." She hoped he wouldn't fail. Forever was a long time in Annwyn.

He swept her into his embrace, as if he couldn't resist touching her any longer. She turned her head to catch his lips. His tongue flicked against her mouth and she opened to him, her body pressing against his. His hand slid down her back to cup her butt and keep her there. While heat flared, she was aware of the seriousness this time. It was more than fun. It was deliberate.

"You're thinking," he whispered.

"I can't help it. It feels so premeditated." They were going to have sex and make a baby with magic—tonight. Now. It was supposed to be fun and easy, not calculated like political strategy.

"The result is, but the rest isn't." He released her and shrugged out of his coat, letting it fall on the floor. Then he undid his belt and sword, and added them to the pile of clothes. "I think I still have sand in my boots."

"You haven't stopped to bathe?" He was in the same clothes, not just the same coat.

"I haven't had time—in either world." Then he was undoing his shirt and pulling off his boots.

She couldn't do this that fast; she needed a moment to catch her breath. But she knew she only had a moment, and everything was racing ahead whether or not she was holding on or ready.

"Why don't you go run a bath?" There was no way he'd have a quick shower. The ocean was one thing, but actual running water was another. The whole time she'd known him she'd never seen him have a shower. He'd wash his hands in a sink of water rather than under a running tap.

Felan looked at her, his shirt open, revealing the hard planes of his stomach and the narrow line of hair that disappeared into his trousers. He looked good, fit and lean, and in his prime, and he always would. As she would. She wouldn't age anymore.

"Will you join me in the bath?"

"Yes." That was an invitation she couldn't refuse. She'd never been able to say no to him, which is what had gotten her into this situation in the first place. When she was around him, she stopped thinking with her head and used her heart instead. "I'll bring some wine in."

She needed a glass, or two, so she could stop thinking. Tomorrow she could think and worry. Tonight she just had to breathe and enjoy…and make a baby. No pressure. She was sure her one ovary just stopped working out of shock.

He wrapped his hand around the back of her neck and kissed her. "Don't take too long. I wouldn't want the water to get cold."

"Remember you have to turn the taps on for the bath to fill." She smiled against his lips, knowing that he hated even watching water run.

He flinched. "Are you sure you don't want to get the bath going while I get the wine?" he said between kisses.

"You survived the ocean; you can turn on a tap." She pulled away. "I'll be back in a minute." Her stomach was already a mass of tumbling knots, a mix of excitement and nerves.

She opened the bedroom door and slipped out. As much as she'd like to just stand in the hallway and gather up her courage before going downstairs, that wasn't going to happen either. She didn't want him to catch her in the hallway. She wanted it to look like she was cool and together, even though she knew he was pulling exactly the same trick. She'd seen the shadows in his eyes and the tension. He just wanted to get the next few days over with and move on, and she felt the same way. They would be together; they just had to push through.

With a smile on her face, she went downstairs, hoping she could slip into the kitchen, grab a bottle of wine, and run back upstairs before anyone saw her, but she never got that lucky.

Lydia and Caspian were sitting at the kitchen table along with Taryn and Dylis. They all looked up from their card game as she walked in. Did they all know what she was supposed to be doing? She swallowed and forced her smile a little wider. Did they even think she was Queen material?

"I just came down to get a bottle of wine." She pointed at the pantry. "Is that okay?"

"Help yourself." Lydia gave her a genuine smile that was betrayed by the sympathy in her eyes.

Great. They all know.

Dylis rested her chin on her hands. "Remind Felan that mortal wine is alcoholic."

Taryn elbowed her. "Would you like candles or something else?"

That was when Jacqui felt the heat creep up her neck and burst on her cheeks. "No." Would she ever have any privacy again? "Just some space." Time, extra time. Another week, a month. A year would be better. She wasn't ready to be someone's mother.

She busied herself pretending to choose a bottle of wine. There was plenty to choose from. In the end, she went with a merlot, a soft red, mellow…it also had a screw top. She took two glasses out of the cupboard.

"You won't need them," Taryn said.

"I'm not swigging out of the bottle." She wasn't eighteen anymore.

"You need to drink from the horn."

Oh. She placed the glasses down. So much for normal and relaxing. They were still all looking at her. "I'll just be going back upstairs." Could this be more awkward?

Taryn got up and hugged her. "Good luck."

That would be it.

"Thank you. I think." *Now please let me escape.* Her nerves had wound up even tighter, and she couldn't be feeling less in the mood if she tried. Maybe a swig from the bottle on the way up wouldn't be so bad.

She got to the kitchen door and glanced back. They had resumed their card game, but even that looked tense, as if they were trying to pass the time. Everyone was waiting. Everything was riding on the next few hours. She unscrewed the bottle and started up the stairs, but she didn't take a drink. No, she'd do this right, and if that meant drinking from the old horn, she would.

By the time she reached the bathroom door, her heart was thumping like she'd run up and down the stairs a dozen times. The taps went off; she could picture him stripping off the last few items of clothing and waiting for the water to still before getting in. He was waiting for her. He needed her and wanted her. She could do this— after all, it really wasn't anything she hadn't done before.

It was almost like setting the clock back seven years.

After tonight, they would be back to where they were before everything went wrong. Instead of moving on and forgetting, perhaps going back and redoing and fixing things was exactly what was needed. Her lips curved. There wasn't any place she'd rather be than with Felan.

She opened the door and slipped into the bathroom.

Two candles flickered on the bathroom vanity, the horn between them. Felan was already in the bath.

"I thought you might have changed your mind."

She shook her head, unable to find any words. She placed the bottle down and began undressing, aware he was watching her every move. She fumbled buttons and tried not to look at herself in the mirror.

Maybe it was the scent of the candles, or maybe there was magic in the air, but when she stepped out of her panties, she was feeling more settled—more aware of the naked man in the bath and the way his attention was warming her in all the right places.

She didn't need him to tell her what to do. She picked up the ancient silver-tipped horn and filled it full of wine, then stepped into the bath. Felan ran his hands up her calves and drew her down, so she knelt over his thighs. He wrapped his hand over hers around the horn and took a drink before offering it to her. The metal was cold against her lips, but the wine was warm on her tongue. She took a long drink. The alcohol hit her stomach and spread, warming her blood and making the room fade away until it was just her and Felan. He took the cup from her and drained it, then let it fall into the water.

Around her the water went completely still, so not even a ripple broke the surface. Her skin prickled with anticipation that she couldn't blame entirely on the wine. The magic was in her. She could feel it sliding around in her blood, washing away the anxiety and replacing it with desire.

His hands caressed her breasts, circling her nipples and raising them into tight peaks. He leaned forward and took one into his mouth, flicking his tongue over her skin. She moved closer, her hands sliding over his arms to rest on his shoulders. As his teeth raked her nipple, she moaned and let her head fall back. Desire consumed her. She smelled it, tasted it—reveled in it. As she lowered her hips, she felt him hard and ready. She moved, letting him slid against her without entering. She wanted him—the heat was in her blood.

She opened her eyes and looked into his. They were pale and bottomless, and in them she saw his endless love and lust for her. His hand slid down her back and cupped her butt, working her over his length. It wasn't enough; she needed to feel him inside her. She slid her hand between their bodies and angled his shaft so she could take him into her core.

His breath caught as she sunk onto him, and he filled her. She leaned forward to kiss him, her nipples brushing his chest with every movement. Her skin was sensitive to every touch, her body awake in a way it hadn't been before. *Spring. Life. Fertility. Magic.*

The magic was working; she was sure of it.

He kept his hand on her hip, keeping a slow rhythm when all she wanted to do was go faster and feel the rush that was building to release. His tongue traced her lip and slipped into her mouth, their moans echoing around them. She rode him harder, the edge growing sharper, the heat in her blood burning hotter, like she was a sun, expanding and consuming everything she touched.

Her back arched, and she shuddered, unable to hold on any longer. For a moment she was sure she died and saw everything. She saw Felan gasp and hold her hips hard against him as she came. She felt the heat of his seed in her body, and her body accepting the offering as the magic swept through her, taking over for biology. She wanted to watch more, but she felt rather than saw a snap, and she was back in her skin, leaning against his chest, trying to catch her breath. His hand smoothed down her back. His heart echoed in her ear, racing as fast as hers. When she closed her eyes, the image was there. She'd been out of her body for a moment, she was sure of it, and yet she hadn't been scared—only amazed at what she was seeing and feeling.

But now in the cooling water, she didn't feel any different. Maybe she'd imagined something magical happening because it needed to happen so badly. It would be a few weeks before she could be sure. And by then if it hadn't worked, it would be too late. She bit her lip.

His hand stilled as if sensing the change in her. "Are you all right?"

She nodded. She had to trust the magic and Felan. Trust a fairy. But he was more than that. He was the man she'd fallen for, the one who always came back for her, regardless of how long he'd been away. Of all the women in the world, he'd fallen for her.

She lifted her head and kissed his cheek. He turned to catch her lips, his fingers tracing her jaw.

"I think it worked," he murmured.

"What makes you say that?" If they had both felt something, then surely it had?

"There was a moment when I felt magic run through me, like electricity."

That made her smile. "You've been electrocuted?"

"Lightning…long story, stupid dare when I was a lot younger." He moved beneath her and adjusted her weight on his thighs. "Did you feel anything?"

"Yeah." But she didn't know how to explain it.

"I guess we cross our fingers now."

"And our toes."

His lips twitched as if he were about to smile, but it never formed. "I love you." He cupped her cheek and placed a simple kiss on her lips.

"I love you too." Her legs began to ache from being cramped in the bath. The candles were flickering and reality pulled apart the small moment they'd shared where nothing else had mattered.

She wanted that back, if only to pretend for a little longer that the fates of two worlds didn't rest on them. Using his shoulder as leverage, she stood up. It was only as she stepped out of the bath she realized the water had been perfectly still the whole time. It had never once lapped at her skin or sloshed around. She watched for ripples as he got out, but there wasn't a single one. When he pulled the plug, the water slid down the plug instead of gurgling.

"Fairy silver keeps the water calm." Then he picked up the horn, washed it in the sink, refilled it with wine, and offered it to her. "Once more before I leave?" He smiled, his eyes glittering in the candlelight.

She took the horn from him, and heat and lust tumbled through her body. She wasn't pregnant yet, as it hadn't implanted and taken hold—would the drinking from the cup guarantee that? What if it didn't? What if it only got the whole process kick-started? There was still a big chance it wouldn't happen. Once more wouldn't hurt.

"In bed this time."

Chapter 14

HE'D LEFT HER SLEEPING, CURLED UP UNDER THE quilt, her hair tangled around her face. She hadn't stirred as he'd eased out of bed, and he didn't want to wake her. He'd paused for a moment to watch her sleep before quietly closing the door. In the hallway he put on his boots and shrugged into his coat, the cup of life and his sword hanging from his belt. The house was quiet, but he knew people weren't sleeping. He would like to sleep peacefully again. For too many months, maybe years, he'd been waiting for this moment. Now it was here, he still wasn't ready.

He hoped the magic had worked.

He thought it had, but until he'd seen the proof in her human technology—the ultrasound she wanted, that he now wanted to see—he wouldn't believe it. The stairs creaked as he walked down them. The TV was on, so he went into the front room.

Dylis, Bram, Lydia, and Caspian were watching the news. He was aware that their attention quickly turned to him, but he was looking at the numbers scrolling across the bottom of the screen. The death toll listed by country. He should have acted sooner. At least he wasn't waiting another week.

"It's been called a global state of emergency, an unprecedented catastrophe," Caspian said.

"It's not unprecedented. It's just that no one alive has

experienced it before. At least it hasn't reached a billion yet." He knew that it wasn't uncommon for up to a third of the human population to die in a power shift. He'd read human history and compared it to the stones singing. He'd made it his job to learn everything he could about both worlds. He was willing to bet Sulia knew very little beyond how to get her own way at Court.

"No one has mentioned fairies. It's a toss-up between climate change and biological warfare. Although there are a few now calling it end of days and waiting for the other signs." Bram leaned forward, his elbows on his knees. "Are you ready to leave?"

Felan looked at the hopeful faces, then back at the TV. At least even if he failed, the death would stop in the mortal world. However, he'd be condemning Annwyn to the rule of a scheming monarch who'd toy with mortal lives for her own amusement. He had to win for the fairies. He had to win for Jacqui and his child being created, for his son, Caspian. He checked his watch. Dawn was coming to Annwyn, gray over the skeletal, winter-clad trees.

"Let's do this." He handed the watch to Dylis. "The execution will be at noon."

She took the watch and put it on even though it was too loose around her wrist.

"The next time you see me, I'll either be King or banished." He didn't mention the other possibility—that war was declared and he was killed in battle.

Caspian stood and hugged him. "Good luck."

He patted his son's back. "I'm sorry for any pain this will cause you."

"I'll live."

"Yes, you will." Felan drew back, the heaviness

growing in his heart. As much as he'd rather spare Caspian any pain, he didn't want him caught. If Sulia won, he had a better chance here than in Annwyn.

Lydia gave him a quick hug too. "We'll be thinking of you."

Dylis and Bram had a quick kiss, then Bram gathered up his things from the floor. They'd all been waiting for him to come downstairs. "Taryn is outside with Verden."

He'd already guessed that. No one was saying good-bye, but it was on the tip of everyone's tongue. In silence, Bram and Felan walked out the back. Taryn and Verden were sitting at the table. She was on his lap, her back to his chest as they stared up at the sky. They were talking softly but stopped at the sound of boots scuffing on the paving stones.

Taryn got up. "It's time then."

Verden stood with her, his hand on the small of her back. For a moment Felan wished he had woken Jacqui, so they could have one last kiss, one last touch. *No*. This way he had to survive to get that reward.

Taryn walked over, her lips pressed into a thin line. She'd grown up so much since the moment she'd first come to Annwyn a few short months ago. When he'd asked for her to attend, he'd never expected she'd end up as Hunter, helping him win the crown.

Verden didn't move. He crossed his arms, his sword glinting in the starlight. "I'll make sure Dylis and Jacqui get to the doorway."

"Thank you." But Felan knew Verden was doing it for Taryn. Once Felan was King, Taryn would be free to return to Verden's side. "The first thing I do will be to lift your banishment."

The previous Lord of the Hunt nodded. "You'd better." Then he released a sigh. "I have people looking for Sulia's hostages. We will find them and free them no matter the outcome."

Would it matter if he lost? If he won, he would have to keep a better eye on the fairies in the mortal world and remind them that they still must abide by Annwyn's rules. He was also going to close some of the loopholes that Sulia was exploiting.

Felan took a final look around. Jacqui hadn't woken to come running down to say farewell. This was it.

He turned and walked through the garden and out the front gate, toward the cemetery where they would cross to Annwyn. Taryn and Bram walked behind him. He listened for any sign of a Grey, watching and waiting. There were a small number of Greys all over the world in various states of wasting. How quickly would Sulia be able to rally another group? He was guessing not fast. She'd planned the attack at the grove for a while—that he'd already saved the trapped fairies had annoyed her, but not spoiled her plan for his death.

He stopped at the doorway and glanced back at the house. It would be a long walk for Verden, Dylis, and Jacqui if they came under attack, but there was nothing he could do except trust they would get to Annwyn before he shut the border.

"Before I risk my life, I'd like to know if congratulations are in order?" Bram kept his hand on the hilt of his sword.

"Everything is in place." He sounded so cold. But he couldn't let himself celebrate, not until afterward. He looked at Bram. "I will not celebrate until I am on the throne and stability is assured." Then he would let himself be distracted by the joy of having another child and what that meant. He had to be a better father this time around.

Bram nodded. "Shall I go first then?"

Felan nodded. They all drew their swords, expecting the worst when they stepped through but hoping those loyal to Felan would have kept the doorway clear.

The air shimmered and the temperature dropped. The smell of frost and decay hit him as he inhaled. Snow drifted down from the heavy, gray sky and landed like stars on his dark blue coat. No one was at the doorway, but someone had been watching and was now running toward Castle Annwyn.

Felan turned to the gate and thrust his sword into the side of the tree. It hummed for a moment. When Taryn put hers in the tree opposite, the doorway would be completely sealed, but that wouldn't happen until after his mother's execution, as Jacqui and Dylis still needed to get through. This was just a partial seal to stop people from leaving. It would make it much harder for Sulia to implement her plans if she couldn't get messages across the veil. A partial seal hadn't been done since...since his great-grandfather had been on the throne. Sealing the border was a forgotten trick, one which he was counting on.

"Test it," he ordered Bram.

Bram gave the sword a tug, but it remained firmly lodged. He looked at the hilt. "That's the King's sword."

"I swapped with my father." Two swords were needed to close the doorway: the King's and the Hunter's. He'd been hoping it didn't have to be the King who activated it, and for the moment, luck was on his side. So far, so good. Except he was now unarmed. "Let's move."

Felan didn't want to give the watcher of the doorway time to make a full report and for Sulia to make alternate plans. If the watcher was on his side, well, the sooner he acted, the better.

The powdery snow coated the ground, covering the dead grass and mud, giving Annwyn an eerie stillness. In the castle he heard music, but it had lost the lilt of summer and was more raucous, harsher and harder.

Someone, one the fairy servants who had been loyal to Gwyn, ran up to him with a clean coat and shirt.

"Get me a sword," he said without looking up.

He stripped in the hallway and redressed in the black. They had really reached the bottom of winter if black was in fashion. The cuffs of the coat glittered with obsidian beads, and gold thread spread from the buttons across his chest and over his shoulders. The collar jutted under his jaw, and the hem swept the ground. At least if he was going to die today, he looked good. A silver sword was placed in his hands. His sword. What was his father wearing?

"Ring the bell." The fairy nodded, gathered the old clothes, and disappeared.

Felan pushed open the doors to the Hall of Flowers and stopped. Sulia was having a party. Food, half-eaten, and drink lay on the tables. A couple cavorted against the wall.

Gone was the glamour of the Court—this was a shallow mockery. Sulia and her human consort sat at the table where the King usually sat. They raised blood-red glass goblets and then laughed.

"Come to join in the revelry?" She grinned, her pink eyes and pointed smile making her look like an angel hell-bent on revenge.

"There is a Court meeting today."

"We know, but you are here without a human. Stuart has seen her, claims she isn't pregnant."

"Stuart does realize that up until about three mortal months, there is no outward sign of pregnancy. My fiancée is safe in the mortal world. I will not bring her for you to attack, again."

Stuart had the grace to fidget and look away. He'd simply been telling Sulia what she wanted to hear. Did he realize what he'd signed up for?

"Oh, it was hardly an attack. We just wanted to know who she was and knock that baby out of her." She laughed as if were a joke.

Felan's fingers curled. He couldn't leap onto the table and kill her. He had no good reason to, and the laws still stood. He could get himself banished. On the other hand, there was no rule to say he couldn't kill Stuart. He glanced at the smug-looking human, not pretty by fairy standards—probably not by human standards either. And certainly not smart enough to finish the job, fortunately. Stuart wasn't worth his time. "The child is fine."

The bell began to chime, calling the fairies to the Hall of Judgment.

"If you don't mind, I have a meeting to preside over. Party if you wish, but some of us have the serious business of ruling to attend to."

Sulia threw down her glass, which shattered over the table. The party stopped as people turned to look. "You aren't King. You will never be King. The people like me; they come to my parties, play my games. I will win."

"Are you willing to declare war when you haven't even declared yourself as a contender? I think you are all talk, Sulia. Stop wasting my time and stop playing games."

Her mouth opened.

Felan spun on his heel and left before she could form a reply. This time there was more than Bram and Taryn at his side. He nodded to familiar faces, including those that had returned from the mortal world to avoid the power shift. Just because they didn't live at Court didn't mean they didn't have a stake in what happened here. What happened in Annwyn rippled across the veil and into the mortal world. And the effects amplified and came back to Annwyn, swelling the river, and back and forth it went until something changed.

Smart fairies understood that.

Dumb ones partied with Sulia and hoped to pretend it would all be fine when she became Queen. It would, but the kind of Court she led would touch the mortal world, and not in a good way. Open debauchery, sneaky games… it would be worse than his father's Court that had allowed scheming and backstabbing to become commonplace.

His would be different. He wanted it to be better for everyone. As he walked into the chamber, now empty and hollow, snow falling through the bare branches and his father sitting on the throne, he wondered if he was aiming too far and the distance was too great. One step at a time and he could cover the ground he needed to.

"Father." He bowed and kissed his father's hand. His skin was cold and dry. And when he looked him in the eye, the wasting was there, turning pale blue eyes cloudy. He doubted his father even had the strength to leave the throne anymore. There was no silver buckled at his waist, as there was no point in wearing a weapon when there was no strength left to wield it.

"I hope you plan to do more than talk today, Son. Annwyn is draining me." His words were soft, like the rustle of summer leaves now long forgotten.

Felan leaned close and whispered in his father's ear. "It ends today." He almost choked on the words. He was going to lose his mother and his father not long afterward. It wasn't supposed to be like this. There were so many things he should have spoken to his father about, things he should have said.

His father sighed. "Thank you." Then his father gripped his wrist. "Do not let that bitch take my throne. If I wanted her to have it, I'd have given up waiting for you."

"I have a plan. I won't let her take it."

His father released him and eased back against the throne.

Fairies filed into the hall. Some were obviously Court fairies, dressed up in black and shades of red and blue so dark they were almost black. Their faces seemed sharper, impossibly pretty yet cruel. Winter was affecting everyone, even if they didn't realize it. Even those from the fringes of Annwyn were dressed in darker clothes. Those that had been in the mortal world looked different; their features were still angular, but their beauty was still there, luminescent instead of deadly. Some wore mortal clothing; others had changed for the occasion. A few still wore the bright colors of summer, as if to remind everyone what they were missing.

The changeling, Isaac, was there with his fairy lover,

the woman who had his soul. Felan recognized her as the daughter of the man who'd been Lord of the Hunt before Verden. A powerful family to have on his side. Felan knew Sulia had tried to win them over to her side, but it seemed they had chosen long before crossing the veil. Felan hoped he didn't disappoint them.

They flooded in until Felan wasn't sure if the room would hold anymore. As he stood and waited by his father's side, he scanned the faces, trying to gauge how many clearly supported him, how many supported Sulia, and who was undecided. It was hard to tell. Who had been offered deals by Sulia while he was on the other side of the veil? More importantly, who had taken the deal?

The doors to the hall remained open, and fairies gathered on the outside when no more could fit inside. Was this every fairy in Annwyn and across the veil, bar those who were banished or exiled? Quite possibly. His word must have spread far and wide. He bit back the smile and lifted his hands for silence.

"I called this meeting, not my father, the King. Annwyn is weakening. Winter is settling. Death has bled to the mortal world."

"And yet you do nothing but talk. I have an heir and consort." Sulia walked through the crowd, arriving late for maximum impact, Stuart at her side.

He was going to kill them both—with iron.

"You transgress, Sulia. Crown Prince Felan called the meeting; he gets to speak first. You may speak second. Show some respect for the laws." The King leaned forward. His words resonated with power that would drain him further.

Sulia looked away, a smile still on her lips as if she

didn't care. Her rudeness wouldn't sit well with those who respected the old laws.

"I didn't come here to make a speech. I came to tell you that the Queen will be executed at noon, and the borders will be closed." For a moment there was absolute silence. One snowflake fell and landed with a splat on his black boot.

Then sound erupted all around the room—shock that it was happening today, relief that it was nearly over. Sulia turned paler.

Felan raised his hands again. "I have one mortal day to present my pregnant consort. Then the coronation will take place and spring will return to Annwyn." He nodded and smiled as if it were all in the bag. Unless Sulia stepped up to contest him officially—or something happened to Jacqui—it was. He had to believe everything was happening according to plan.

Some fairies clapped at that news.

"You cannot bring forward the execution." Sulia stepped forward. "You do not have that power."

Taryn moved from her place on the other side of the King's throne. "As Hunter of Annwyn, I can, and I freely give him that right. Sire?" Taryn inclined her head at Gwyn.

He gave a single nod. "Let this bitter business be done. To delay any longer means letting winter settle more deeply. I do not wish a long, hard winter on anyone."

"Thank you for attending." Felan gave a nod to the crowd and then acted as though he planned to leave, thus ending the meeting. He didn't even glance at Sulia. She was about to miss her window to challenge him.

"Wait. I want my chance to speak." She moved toward

the front, but didn't dare step up and place herself on the same level as the King in a formal meeting. "How do we even know you have a pregnant wife-to-be?" Sulia patted her swollen stomach, drawing attention to the fact she was more than ready to take the throne.

"By your own admission, in the Hall of Flowers in front of many, you attacked her with the intent on harming the baby, and you also arranged an attack on me." He looked at the crowd. "Do you want Sulia and her consort as your rulers? Or me and the woman I've been seeing for over seven mortal years?" He paused to let the words sink in. That was a half-truth at best, but he had been watching her in the mirrors all that time. "She has been preparing for that long."

Not a total lie, but as close as he was going to tell. He needed to be clean, for his words to be true, where Sulia was all about deception. He hoped that his honesty wouldn't come back to bite him.

"I will not step aside when Sulia has not formally declared herself a contender. If she wants the throne, she will have to fight me for it." He stared directly at her. How far would she go?

Her face hardened, and her mouth pulled tight into a thin line, as though she hadn't expected this from him. Was Sulia's only plan to get rid of Jacqui, so she could step in and claim the throne by default?

"I back my son. I do not agree with Sulia's methods, which she learned from the damned Queen." The King's words were designed to remind people that Sulia had once been a favorite of the Queen and that she was most likely tainted by the Queen's corruption. The King looked at Sulia. "Step aside and do what is right."

"No. I have every right to contest the succession, as does every fairy here." She looked around as if expecting others to step forward. No one did. Succession was rarely challenged by those without a blood claim, yet Sulia had a claim, and she wasn't using it to her advantage.

That gave Felan a moment of concern. He glanced at his father. Did he know that Sulia was related by blood?

"Then do it and stop dancing around the edges. Make your announcement." Felan stared at her, hoping she'd blink first and step back. Had she hoped to win through underhanded trickery? That wasn't the way fairies worked. The games and deals were honest; words were kept. Did Sulia plan on destroying even those simple values?

She hesitated. "Very well. I, Sulia merch Edern ap Nudd ap Beli, state my claim to the throne. I have a consort and heir, and I have royal blood that I have kept hidden for fear of attack from the current King."

Gwyn didn't flinch. He'd known. Damn him. Why had he kept it to himself?

"How can we be sure that you are speaking the truth now about your lineage?" Felan raised an eyebrow. Now that he'd forced her into declaring, the game had changed.

"I made sure all of Edern's children were born across the veil," Gwyn said.

"You failed, and now your brother, my father, will get the last laugh with his heir on the throne you fought so bitterly for." Sulia smiled at the King.

"You never knew your father. He never spoke an honest word in his life." Gwyn gave her a slow appraisal. "I am not surprised you followed in his steps and lied about your own name."

"I had to, or you would've arranged my

execution." She stepped closer to the King and Felan drew in a breath.

Taryn moved closer to Gwyn, her hand on the hilt of her sword. "Step back and remember who is your King."

Sulia looked as though she'd just been forced to cut her own wrist as she took a step back and lowered her gaze.

"I never killed any of my brother's children. That is not our way. Children are valued. They were, however, all born in the mortal world as changelings. Perhaps he had one woman hidden here in Annwyn, protected by someone loyal to him." Gwyn blinked and sighed as if not believing it was possible.

Felan realized that his father's plan had been to deny that Sulia was related by blood. There would always be a shadow of doubt over her lineage, even if she won. While it was true that those without a blood claim could throw their hand in and try to take the throne, few ever gained enough support for war to happen. Sulia, on the other hand, already had supporters. So why mention her connection now?

Gwyn turned his head and looked at Felan. "Is the border secure, Son?"

Felan nodded. He had to stop thinking about Sulia and worry about his own plans. As heir, his job was to monitor the veil, something which he had turned to his advantage. He smiled, forcing his lips to turn. He could play this game for a little longer and win. He just had to keep going. "I have closed the border to outgoing travel in preparation for the execution and power shift. No one can leave, but those on the other side of the veil still have time to get home." Felan's smile widened, cool and calculating, and he met Sulia's gaze.

She gave a small, almost unperceivable flinch at the news. "How is that possible?"

"I listened and I learned from the singing stones in the castle. I know how Annwyn works. I know the loopholes and technicalities." He'd spent time listening to the stones as a youth and more recently to learn more about the last few power shifts. The knowledge was there for anyone willing to listen. When things had gotten out of control or he was licking his wounds, or just needed some peace away from Court and the endless expectations, he'd lie on the grass, close his eyes, and listen as the stones sung and spoke over each other, their conversations blending and changing. "I have been preparing to rule Annwyn my whole life."

Sulia's eyes brightened in anger. "You still need to get your Queen here. Good luck getting her across."

Gwyn raised his hand. "Enough. You can formally introduce your consorts and make your pledges after Eyra is executed for treason."

If Jacqui failed to arrive, his quest for the throne was over, and everyone knew it. Felan kept his expression fixed and regarded the Court as confidently as he dared. If Jacqui did arrive, there was a good chance he'd have to declare a formal battle for the throne. Now that Sulia had gone this far, he doubted she'd back down without blood.

Chapter 15

JACQUI OPENED HER EYES AND STRETCHED. SHE KNEW immediately that Felan wasn't in bed beside her, but she didn't remember him leaving. She glanced around the room, looking for a clue as to what time it was. Was she late? No, someone would have woken her.

She got up, her body aching in all the right places. Her hand strayed to her stomach, but there was nothing there that she could feel and nothing else that she could do. She opened the curtains to full daylight streaming in. For a moment she stood, staring out the window at the summer sky and the trees gently moving in a sultry breeze. She'd be back. Maybe not to live but she'd visit. She stood there, not wanting to move; moving would mean admitting she was ready to go.

After several breaths, she realized she had to get moving. She still had things to do. With a sigh, she turned away and began pulling clothes out of her back-pack. It was a little late for doubts, but not too late for a healthy dose of fear about what was going to happen between now and Felan becoming King. She'd brought a dress, but she wouldn't be able to run if she had to, so she settled on jeans, a long sleeved T-shirt, and a cream jacket. Not particularly regal or fairy, but more practical. She finished off her outfit with low-heeled boots—far too overdressed for summer in Charleston but probably underdressed for winter in Annwyn.

Butterflies rioted in her stomach, but she was as ready as she was ever going to be. In the bathroom, she brushed her teeth and hair. When she closed her eyes, she saw her and Felan in the bath and felt the magic tremble across her skin like the softest brush of silk. She hoped it had worked and this wasn't all in vain.

"It's almost time." Dylis leaned against the door frame. The watch she'd given Felan all those years ago was too big on Dylis's wrist. She was touched he'd kept it and had eventually found a way to make it work in both time zones.

"I'm ready." She hoped she sounded more certain than she felt. Dylis looked her over and Jacqui shifted uncomfortably under the scrutiny. "What is it?"

"Do you want something to eat?"

She didn't think she could eat anything even if she tried. She shook her head.

Dylis shrugged. "Let's go."

Jacqui followed her downstairs, the fairy gliding quietly through the house. No one was waiting to say good-bye. Was she really going to leave the mortal world without anyone noticing? Apparently so. Where was everyone?

She clamped her teeth together and refused to let either sadness or nerves get the better of her. They went out the front door and it clicked closed after her. Verden was sitting on the steps, waiting.

"Anything amiss?" Dylis rested her hand on her sword.

"Nothing, not a whisper." Verden almost sounded like he was hoping for an attack.

Dylis scowled. "That's suspicious on its own."

He looked up, a crooked a smile on his face. "That's

what I was thinking. I know you can't swing a sword,
Jacqui, but there's a handful of iron bolts over there and
a pitchfork—just don't take them through the doorway."
He stood and drew his sword. "I know there's a handful
of Greys who live in Charleston, and I'm willing to bet
they are all between here and the cemetery. Does anyone
want to bet on a peaceful walk?"

Jacqui did. She didn't want to have to fight off fairies.
Killing one had been bad enough. However, she picked
up the rusted bolts and the pitchfork. This was so dumb.
She was carrying a pitchfork into a battle while they had
swords. "Wouldn't I be better just running?"

"You won't be able to open the doorway, but we are
all going to move as fast as possible." Dylis glanced at
Jacqui's shoes.

"No quarter given." Verden turned his wrist and the
sword sparkled in the sun. "Ready?"

Jacqui nodded. She could see why he had been the
Hunter. There was a look in his eyes and the way he
moved—when he set his mind on something, he would
have it—which is probably why he'd ended up banished
for pursuing Taryn. She'd never met a Grey so at ease,
and until today had never trusted one with her life either.

In response, Dylis drew her sword. With Verden leading the way, they walked down the path and away from
the protection of the silver tea set and Callaway House.

It was too still—not even the old oaks rustled—and
too hot. She should have carried her jacket, but it would
have just gotten in the way. Her fingers gripped the
pitchfork a little tighter. Would she be able to kill another Grey? Her stomach turned. If she didn't, the Grey
would kill her.

Ahead, a shadow moved in the trees. Or was it a trick of her eyes?

"Trolls by the cemetery fence," Verden whispered.

"There's something up in the trees." Dylis sniffed as if she could smell banished fairies in the area.

Verden nodded and walked a little faster. He let his sword drop as if he wasn't worried. They were past the halfway mark now; if anything happened, they had to make a run for doorway. Her heart was already racing as if she was running. She really hoped there wasn't an army on the other side waiting to grab her. Had anyone thought of that? Of course Felan had. He'd make sure she could get through. She took a deep breath, then the shadows lunged forward. Five foot and ugly, wielding clubs dotted with nails, these Greys had chosen to give up looks and stature to remain strong and had become the trolls of human myth.

"Whatever you do, do not stop. Get her through the damn door." Verden kept walking forward.

"I'll come back and help," Dylis said.

"No, you won't. If anything happens to you, Bram will have me in the river as quick as the banishment lifts." Then he started the fight by taking the hand off a Grey. Screams and the scent of blood filled the air. Then the trolls were all around them. For a moment, Jacqui froze. She didn't know what to do or how to help. She didn't know how to fight.

"Move." Dylis nudged her.

It was enough to snap her out of the waking nightmare. She was holding iron. Dylis blocked a troll's attack and Jacqui saw an opening and stabbed. The prongs connected and sunk through flesh. She yanked the tool back and struck again. This time it got stuck and the troll fell back howling, blue blood weeping from the wounds. Dylis pulled her forward. Now she had nothing except the bolts.

Verden was trying to stay at the back, but the gap was widening.

The doorway wasn't far now. Something screeched and then there was a Grey, clinging to her head and shoulders. Tiny fingers dug into her eyes. She squeezed them closed and tried to pull it off her. The hand still holding a bolt connected with a little leg, but it held fast to her hair. Dylis was still trying to drag her forward, but she couldn't see a thing.

She smacked it again with the bolt and pressed. There was the smell of burning skin and an inhuman howl; then it was gone. Jacqui looked up. Verden had it on the end of his sword. Behind him were three dead trolls. His face was pulled into a grimace, but she couldn't tell if the blood was his or the trolls'. He used his boot to pull the body free and wiped his blade on the dead Grey's clothing.

"Are you okay?" Jacqui said.

He nodded, lines forming around his mouth and eyes as though he was holding back the pain, and she knew he was lying.

"Verden can take care of his own wounds. Caspian or Lydia will help him." But even Dylis looked concerned. "If you don't come with me now, it will be worse for everyone involved." She had her hand around Jacqui's arm, her grip tight.

"Thank you." She called to Verden as Dylis dragged her forward. She hoped whatever injury he had would heal. Then the air shimmered and an icy breeze hit her skin. She was sure she felt snow, but when she looked, there was nothing in front of her except the cemetery. She took a last look at Verden, surrounded by death. It was all for her. Dylis gave her arm a tug and Jacqui took a step. The cemetery vanished, replaced by bare trees and snow.

She'd expected a jolt or something to delineate the mortal world from Annwyn, but there was nothing. One step she was in Charleston, the next she was here. Snow drifted down in lazy spirals, settling on her clothes and catching in her hair. This wasn't what she'd been expecting. It was more winter wonderland than endless summer. And it was wintrier than when she'd seen it through the mirror. The trees were nothing more than silver branches reaching for a heavy purple-gray sky. She released a breath and it clouded in front of her. She was in Annwyn. She turned to wave to Verden, but there were only more trees behind her.

"How do we leave?"

"We don't." Dylis pointed to the sword sticking out of a tree. "No one leaves until Felan reopens the doorway."

—◆◆◆—

Fairies, and the one soulless changeling, gathered like crows near the bank of the river of the damned—but not too close, lest the water rise up and drag them in. The once-flat river was choppy. Waves slapped the shore of Annwyn. The other side was shrouded in heavy mist; not even fairies could see past life and into death. Felan stood motionless watching the procession.

Taryn led the Queen forward. No longer dressed in

finery, she was in a plain black dress. Her hair was loose and her wrists were bound in silver. Felan wanted to look away, but he had to stand fast. No weakness, not now. Opposite him stood Sulia and Stuart.

The Court had walked from the castle to the river to witness the execution of the Queen; now they stood like a guard of honor for her last walk. In fact, it was so she had nowhere to run to. Behind her was the Hunter, before her the river, and on each side were fairies.

His mother kept her chin up. She didn't look at him; she looked at Sulia. Their hands touched briefly before Taryn nudged her forward. The King was absent. He couldn't have made the walk, weakened as he was, plus Felan doubted Gwyn had the heart to watch his wife die, even though he had been the one to sentence her to death for treason.

Felan glanced up. It was almost noon. He hoped Jacqui was close and that this served as a big enough distraction to get her into the castle safely.

Taryn stopped and so did Eyra.

"Do you have any final words?" Taryn's voice didn't quaver, but Felan knew she hadn't been looking forward to this moment. Verden would have marched the Queen to the water's edge at the end of his sword without breaking stride, but then, Verden was used to Court life and knew that the Queen had been poisoning Annwyn against the King for a very long time.

The Queen turned and faced the assembled fairies. More than just the Court, most of Annwyn was here. "I have lived longer than any mortal. I have become one of you, learned your ways, ruled your Court, and celebrated your festivals. My death will not go unnoticed or unrecorded. I will have my funeral games."

There was a flash of silver as she brought a small knife to her neck and slashed. Red blood welled in the wound, a reminder that she had once been human no matter how fairy she behaved.

Curse it. He looked across for Sulia, but she'd melted back into the crowd. Sulia had slid the knife into the Queen's hands so she could avoid the river. His mother started choking on her blood. He grabbed one arm. Taryn took the other one and together they dragged Eyra closer to the water.

"Watch your feet," Felan said.

Taryn didn't glance up. "I am."

A wave reared up, faces pressed against the water, watery hands pushing through the surface, reaching and grasping.

"Push," Felan ordered.

Together he and Taryn gave the Queen a push, and she stumbled forward as they scrambled back. He watched as the water lunged and grabbed Eyra. She cried out and was then dragged under.

His hands started to shake. They were coated in bright red human blood. His mother's blood. "It is done. The doorway will now be sealed until coronation." He hoped that Jacqui was here. "Hunter, close the doorway."

Someone handed him a cloth and he wiped his hands. He wished the memory were as easy to erase. What had he done that had turned his mother's heart against him? Why had she felt the need to tear apart Annwyn? He was doing the right thing in stopping Sulia. He had to believe that this was bigger than his life and his wants. Yet every time he thought of Jacqui, he knew he'd pushed her into this too fast. It was all happening too fast, and he couldn't stop now that he'd started.

Taryn nodded and led the way from the river and back toward the castle, then across what had once been lush lawn in front of the two trees that marked the main doorway to Annwyn.

Footprints marked the snow-covered ground between doorway and castle, but there were too many to tell if one set was Jacqui's or not. Felan wanted to run to the castle and search every room, but he had to trust Dylis.

Please let Jacqui be here and be okay.

As they reached the doorway, he saw a white watch hanging from his father's sword. He moved through the crowd to claim it. Relief washed through him as he touched it and lifted it free. *She was here.* He slipped it into his pocket as Taryn drove her sword into the opposite tree. Annwyn was sealed by the silver of King and Hunter, and would only be reopened when there was a new Hunter and a new King...or Queen.

Chapter 16

THE CASTLE WAS LIKE NOTHING SHE'D EVER SEEN. COLD and silvery, it was made out of trees. Because there wasn't a leaf to be seen, there was also no roof. Snow carpeted the ground, footprints the only reminder that people actually lived here—that she would be living here.

In front of her, Dylis moved cautiously, as if expecting an attack. Human-shaped shadows drifted past, but they didn't worry Dylis, so Jacqui kept going, too scared to speak in case she drew attention to herself. They walked down corridors formed by trunks and arching branches. Gems gleamed in the bark. She wanted to stop and look, but now wasn't the time.

"There's no one here. Felan said to wait in the chamber," Dylis said.

Jacqui nodded. She didn't know where else they could wait. She was here. Felan could say she was his and claim the throne, and it would be over. Everyone could get back to living instead of dying. She could find a new way to live, one where she didn't have to pretend that she didn't see fairies.

They slid through the castle to a cavernous room that twinkled and chimed with every breeze. Mirrors hung from branches and larger ones seemed to be part of the trees. Dylis stopped and looked into one.

For a moment Jacqui saw only Dylis's reflection; then it shimmered and shifted and she saw Verden. He was lying on the outside table at the house she'd just left with his shirt off. Lydia and Caspian were both there, and there seemed to be a lot of cloths stained blue with blood. Was it her imagination or did his skin seem more ashen? Lydia and Caspian appeared to be arguing about a knife. Then Caspian held Verden down and Lydia slashed one of Verden's wounds with a knife. Jacqui looked away.

"They're getting the iron out of the wound. Must be a broken nail in there. If they don't get it out, he will die. Felan needs to hurry up and take over." Dylis watched for a moment longer, then let the image dissolve.

"Is this where Felan would watch me in the mirror?" Her voice echoed, too loud in the silent castle.

"This is the Hall of Mirrors, where we can watch anyone as long as we have seen them in the flesh. Some mirrors are more specific." Dylis lifted her head as if hearing a noise, then turned.

Jacqui spun. Felan stood at the other end of the Hall of Mirrors, looking every inch the Prince in black with gold trim. He also looked tired and hurt. She knew it wasn't a physical wound. His mother was dead.

His lips turned up at the corners as if he was attempting to smile for her benefit, but he failed. "You made it."

"Of course I did." Now wasn't the time to mention the attack or Verden's brush with iron poisoning.

He walked toward her, his boots crunching on the snow. She threw herself into his arms. She had never been so glad to see him. All the waiting, the worry, and now she was here. He was here and they were together. He kissed her cheek, his lips cool, and released her.

"Come, I need to present you to my father and the Court." He took her hand and again she followed.

Her stomach flip-flopped at the idea of being pre-sented. Surely it was a formality. "Then you can claim the throne and everything will be okay?"

"It's not going to be that simple."

Behind her, Dylis muttered something about Sulia and the Queen that Felan also chose to ignore. She gave his hand a squeeze, but he didn't look at her. His gaze was straight ahead, as if he were already thinking of the things he needed to do. After another set of twisting corridors, Jacqui was sure she was lost and would never find her way out again. Then it opened up into a room that could only be the Hall of Judgment.

A gaunt young man sat on a throne. It took a moment for it to register that she was looking at the King. It was the clothing that gave it away. While he looked youthful and the halo of beauty was there, he also seemed fragile, as if just sitting and breathing was costing him energy.

"Is it done?" The King leaned forward a fraction.

"It is." Felan nodded, his gaze on the floor instead of straight ahead.

The King leaned back and closed his eyes. "Then take the crown and finish this, so I can rest."

"The bell will ring soon...I expect Sulia to declare."

Declare what? But the fairies gave no hint—they all knew what they were talking about and she was still the outsider.

The King nodded slightly. "Then do you gamble on that assumption and declare first, or do you let her strike first?"

The huge chamber was silent. Jacqui watched snow land on the King. How long would he sit there before the snow covered him entirely? She glanced at Felan, but he was equally as still. Even Dylis was silent.

That was when she realized they were talking about war. Felan expected Sulia to declare war. After all this, she still wasn't safe and Felan's rule wasn't secure. Her heart beat too loudly and seemed to echo around the chamber.

"I will declare first. Annwyn is sealed. Both consorts are here. There will be only one battle."

"Good. That was my mistake with my brother. We let it spill into the mortal world, killing each other's lovers in the fight to be King." The King opened his eyes and looked at Jacqui. "Bring her forward."

Jacqui swallowed and hoped she didn't look as nervous as she felt. Sweat on her palms was making her grip on Felan's hand slick. He had enough to deal with without worrying that she was going to freak out. She had to keep the panic on the inside. That little part of her that was running around, flapping her arms and pinching herself, needed to be shut down. But maybe that was a normal human reaction to being in Annwyn and greeting the King.

Should she curtsy or bow or something?

Felan stepped up onto the dais and she had to follow. She settled for bowing her head and hoping he didn't think she was rude and unworthy.

The King looked her up and down. "You know what you are giving up and what you are gaining?"

She nodded, glad that she could answer honestly, yet wondering what would've happened if she'd said no.

"I hope you have chosen well, Son."

A bell began chiming.

"My last time presiding over a meeting. I should stand."

"Are you sure, Father?" Felan went to help the King up.

Jacqui's heart broke a little for him. He'd lost his mother and now he was losing his father. Jacqui doubted the King would live much longer. She could almost see him fading away every time he spoke.

"What a touching scene."

Jacqui turned. A woman in black and red with an obvious pregnant stomach walked through the doorway. The man who'd attacked Jacqui at the airport was at the woman's side—Sulia and Stuart.

Stuart grinned at her and took another step forward. "How nice to see you again, Jacqui. I'm so glad you will get a chance to see Annwyn before we get to judge your soul."

It took a moment for the death threat to sink in.

Dylis planted herself between the dais and Sulia. She may not be the Hunter, but she had no intention of letting anything happen. "If you take one more step toward the Crown Prince's chosen consort, I will have no choice but to attack."

"I will banish you along with the rest of his supporters," Sulia hissed.

"Then you will have very few fairies left at Court," said the King. He leaned on Felan's arm before being offered a walking stick. His lip curled, as if he hated this weakness, and yet it was clear he had nothing left. He stood still as more fairies filled the room.

All those pale eyes and pretty faces were on her. She felt plain and scruffy. Her clothing was dirty and smeared with blue blood after the attack. She was sure they were all noticing and judging her. After all, that's what this place was for. Was she unworthy? Did they not like her already after a quick glance?

The bundle of knots in her stomach tightened. Felan had been so sure he'd win, but she realized they could both die today. She didn't want to die. Her hand slid to her stomach, a move that was followed by many sets of eyes. She was under the microscope and she didn't like it. She just wanted this to be over, and for Sulia and smug Stuart to be gone.

The King waited for the murmurs to settle. "My wife is dead. I can no longer rule." He took the crown off his head. "My successor is Felan ap Gwyn ap Nudd ap Beli. He is here with consort and heir; however, Sulia merch Edern challenges my son's right to claim the throne." He paused as if gathering his strength. "Bring your consort forward so we may see him, Sulia."

Sulia and Stuart stepped onto the dais looking like they already ruled Annwyn and like this was just a formality. *Oh, please let it be a formality before Felan was declared King.* However, they both wore supercilious expressions, and she knew that Sulia would do whatever it took to claim the throne.

"You both have consorts and you both have heirs. You both have the right to claim the throne. I command you, Court, think hard about who you want to rule. Felan, Sulia, think hard about what a declaration of war would mean both for Annwyn and the mortal world. This can be resolved today if one of you concedes." The King tapped the walking stick on the dais and scanned the crowd of dark-clad, grim-looking fairies. After a few moments of silence, he turned to Felan. "What have you to say?"

"I am the rightful heir to the throne of Annwyn." Felan paused and looked at Sulia. "My father supports my succession, as does the Lady of the Hunt, so I would like to extend Sulia this one opportunity to back down from her quest to rule. Should she accept my generous offer, there will be no repercussions."

Jacqui's heart bounced against her ribs. She'd never heard him speak so formally or with so much power behind his words. This was him in full fairy Prince mode. It was kind of exciting to see him truly for the first time. But she'd thought he was going to declare war first. What was he doing?

Sulia laughed. "Step down, and I will let your lover live if you jump in the river."

Nice. She was a bit too much like the popular bitch at school, having to cut everyone down to stay at the top, only Sulia took cutting down literally. The little bit of panic grew bigger, but instead of running around, it was sitting in a corner and trying to hide, praying this whole situation would go away.

"Never. Hunter, step forward," Felan said.

Taryn stood in front of the dais with Dylis. She looked grim. Did she know about Verden? If she were in Taryn's place, she'd want to get through the doorway and to his side. But no one was leaving Annwyn until this was settled. Not her, not Taryn. They were all stuck here like a big deadly game of *Survivor Annwyn*.

Getting voted off the island meant death.

Felan took a moment to look at her, then the gathered fairies. "I declare war. Hunter, set the battleground. Set the rules. This will be decided at dawn."

"I didn't think you had it in you, Felan." Sulia tilted her head. "However, I won't be fighting in my condition."

Taryn's face lit up in a smile. "Actually, according to

the law, both the challengers must fight. No fairy may harm a human consort. No iron and no other poison is allowed on blade. All the weapons will be checked by me and my assistant." Taryn indicated Dylis. "The winner takes the throne and the loser, if they survive, is taken to the river. Do you both agree?"

Felan nodded. "I agree."

Sulia lifted her chin. "Very well. I agree."

But Jacqui saw a chink in her composure. Was Sulia worried that Felan might win this? That doubt made hope swell. Felan must believe he could win. She had to believe in him, even if she didn't know all the rules and regulations. For the moment, all she had to do was follow along and stay safe. That fairies were forbidden from harming her eased the tension, but not by much. There was still a battle to win.

Taryn took the crown from the King. "Until the battle is fought, none may wear the crown or sit on the throne. If you attack me or my assistant, you forfeit all rights you have in Annwyn." She looked at Sulia specifically. "Each contender may choose nineteen warriors to stand with them. Choose wisely. I have ribbons to mark those who fight. Everyone else may watch from the sidelines. Felan, as the son of the King and natural successor, I give you the royal purple in its summer shade." She held twenty bright purple ribbons to him.

Felan accepted them and stepped back, handing them to Jacqui. They were cool and silky between her fingers. Like it or not, she was a part of this. But protected. No fairy could harm her—unless Felan lost. She hoped he had some good fighters on his side.

Taryn held up another set of ribbons. "I wasn't sure

what color to give you, and yet I had to choose some-thing appropriate. Something that wouldn't get lost in the snow and blood of the battle. I chose yellow."

She offered them to Sulia, but Sulia hesitated. "Why yellow?"

"Because I want you to think of the summer you have denied Annwyn with your challenge."

"Bitch," Sulia snarled.

Taryn narrowed her eyes. "Hunter to you." She thrust the ribbons at Sulia, then addressed the crowd once more. "Gather your warriors and arms, and present them at the table stationed in the center of the field at dawn." Taryn and Dylis turned and walked out of the hall.

In that moment, Jacqui knew exactly who the next Hunter of Annwyn would be. That was the deal. That was why Dylis was fighting so hard for Felan. Had that been negotiated before or after they'd slept together?

Felan watched the fairies for a moment. He already knew who he was going to select. As his supporters gathered around him, he took ribbons from Jacqui and handed them out. Isaac, the changeling, who had been a soldier across the veil. Bram, of course. He wished he could chose Dylis, but Taryn was allowed to choose an assistant for the battle, and it was better one of his most loyal was not fighting.

Most volunteered their sword, but he had to turn some away. He needed those he could trust with his back in battle, those who knew how to fight. Most got very little practice except for at the funeral games. He nodded as people murmured their support, and Jacqui smiled as though she was happy to be here. Fairies bowed to her and expressed congratulations as if their child was a sure thing. He hoped it was, and that the cup had worked its magic. Then Jacqui was holding the last ribbon. His.

She turned and tied it around his arm and kissed his cheek.

People clapped. Were they actually happy or just glad this would finally be decided?

He would be glad when it was over.

He glanced over at Sulia on the other side of the chamber. It looked as though Sulia had a slight advantage in numbers. *Damn her to the river and drown her twice*. The only reason she had more supporters was because the heir in her stomach was a sure thing. At least the formal battle took away those odds. Tomorrow they would be equal.

Sulia met his gaze, turned her head away, and swept out of the hall, no doubt to start planning and preparations. He had hoped Sulia would back down when she realized he wasn't going to. If she had really expected him to tuck tail and run, she'd underestimated him. Maybe that would help with the coming battle. He looked at his father. He seemed more at ease. Perhaps the knowledge that one way or another this would be over had settled his heart.

"Would you like to go to the great hall or your chambers?"

"No. I'm going to stay here. This is where I have ruled from and this is where I shall remain. Have the shadows bring us food and wine."

Felan closed his eyes for a moment, but they felt gritty and they stung. He should've acted sooner. He should've noticed his father's strength waning, but

Gwyn had hidden it well, right up until his wife's imprisonment. He wouldn't make the same mistake. He'd rather hand the throne over early and live out the rest of his days in exile. He would make sure his child knew that, so there would be no winter next time.

"I'm sorry." This wasn't how his father's life should end. More snow was falling now. By morning they would be wading through it, not just leaving footprints. How fast could he pull Annwyn out of this winter? Even if he stopped winter from lingering, how did he explain to the Court that he'd promised Jacqui a long spring before they had their child?

"No. You don't have time for regrets and nor do I. I knew it would end like this. I should have warned you that Sulia was your cousin instead of keeping it secret."

"I don't blame you." No matter what his father had done, Sulia and Eyra would've created trouble. He should've realized earlier that there would be a fight for the throne.

"But you want to know why I didn't have her banished. For many years I wasn't sure myself if you could rule. I doubted you, and it created the distance that is here now. I should've told you to bring Caspian's mother here and forced your hand." The King drew a breath and eased himself to the cushions on the floor. He had no right to sit on the throne anymore. "But I never wanted you to end up like me." He looked at Jacqui.

How long had Gwyn known about Caspian? Obviously for far longer than Felan had thought. So much for keeping things secret…what else did his father know and hadn't revealed?

"I'm glad you are here. I hope your heart is better

than my wife's." He turned his icy gaze to Felan. "I hope for everyone's sake you win tomorrow." The King paused and sighed. "Verden should've been here."

"Even if you lifted the banishment, he is stuck on the other side of the veil."

"I don't have the strength to lift banishments or exiles. Tell him I am sorry. My pride was all I had left."

"He understands and holds no ill will." Verden knew how the Court worked and knew he'd screwed up in pursuing Taryn publicly.

"Tell him I valued his council while he served me."

"You will see him after the battle."

His father just looked at him. No words needed to be spoken. He wasn't expecting to live that long and was regretting sending one of his friends away from Court.

A shadow servant placed food and drink next to Gwyn. There was very little. Whatever supplies they had would dwindle fast with no access to the mortal world.

"Don't linger here, Son. Do what you need to and make me proud." Gwyn gave him a single nod and a smile. He was dismissed. It was the same way he'd been dismissed so many times before, but this time it felt like the last time.

He couldn't breathe. "I will come back before the battle."

His father grabbed his hand. "Don't torment yourself over my passing. Think to the future."

Felan nodded, even though he knew he couldn't do as his father asked. For so long he'd been wary of him, afraid that his every move would be considered treason and an attempt to take the throne. Now he saw his father would have welcomed the reprieve. It was just his mother who would have fought tooth and nail to hold on to the power.

She would be well pleased with Sulia.

"You will get cold sitting here."

"I'm already cold. I have been part of Annwyn for so long that the winter is within me."

"Father—"

The King lifted his hand. "The shadows can bring me what I need. Go."

He couldn't disobey his father's last order. He turned around to face Jacqui; she was making a point of not looking at the exchange between him and his father. Felan blinked a few times to clear his vision. "Come on. Let's eat and rest. Tomorrow will be a long day, even by Annwyn standards."

Chapter 17

FOR A MOMENT JACQUI JUST LOOKED AT FELAN, NOT sure what to say to him or his father. Or even if she should say anything. She glanced at both men, but neither held her gaze. Maybe there was nothing to say when everything hinged on the tomorrow's battle. How many days were passing in the mortal world while she was here? How many humans were dying?

"Don't think about what you can't change," Felan said, but it seemed he was saying it more for his own benefit than hers.

There was nothing she could do to help or hinder the battle…she couldn't even flee if she changed her mind and decided this was all too much. Then she looked at Felan and realized that he didn't even have that option. He had to make the best of what he had, which meant he had to rule.

He took her hand and led her out of the chamber, snow now dusting his coat and hair, his skin cold to touch. She turned back to look at the King. Shadow servants were setting up a canopy to protect the old fairy, and bringing more cushions and food.

"Won't he get cold?"

Felan shook his head and kept walking as if he couldn't bear to turn around and see what his father had become. "Fairies are part of Annwyn. It feels cool but not cold."

"You feel cold to touch."

He glanced at her. "No, my body is colder because of Annwyn. If a new King or Queen isn't crowned, Annwyn will eventually die and so will all fairies."

"And my world?" Did none of them ever really stop and think of the billions of humans?

"There will be death and disease, but after a time things will settle and it will be as it was before we took over the in-between and called it Annwyn."

Jacqui stopped walking. There had been a time before Annwyn. She'd imagined the fairies had always been here. "What happened before Annwyn?"

"This place still existed and souls still came here…" He grimaced. "When we took over, instead of just visiting, we upset the balance. Instead of souls finding their own way to where they needed to go, they remained. We had to start sending them and it became the King's job."

"And the river?"

"Has always been and always will be. There will always be breaches in the veil."

"So all fairies came from my world, then moved here, and now humans are dependent on fairies to get to the afterlife?" Wow, had humans got it wrong or what? The old religions were closer to the truth than most realized.

"I don't think that was what my predecessors had in mind. They were fleeing from humans who'd developed iron weapons. Wild fae still exist in your world, in the wilds and untouched places, but their numbers dwindle." He had that look in his eyes, the one where he was thinking big. At least that was better than the barely restrained sorrow.

"You have plans."

He drew in a breath. "I do. There is a lot here that needs fixing that has become corrupt and shallow. But it will take time, centuries in your time." He placed his hand on her stomach. "I want a better Annwyn than what I had for our child."

She smiled. He might be fairy, but he still wanted what every father wanted—something better for their child. A brighter future, an easier life. Her heart swelled with love. She had made the right choice in Felan, and she'd known that his heart was true all those years ago.

He put his arm around her and kissed her forehead. "I will take you to the singing stones so you can hear the stories, but not tonight."

"What happens tomorrow?" She didn't want to think about it, but she knew she couldn't hide. That time was over.

"Weapons are checked, everyone forms up, and we fight until one side surrenders or there is only one side left standing."

"Your only options are win or death." Her fingers curled against the soft fabric of his coat. She didn't want to lose him after only just finding him again.

"If I am killed, she will not let you live."

She'd already had that unsettling thought. "Is there no secret exit?"

"It got destroyed, and none of the old doorways will work while Annwyn is sealed. If she wins, she won't open the borders until you are found. I'm sorry." He traced her cheek. "That was my gamble in sealing Annwyn off. It shortens the battle, but also traps everyone here until the end."

She nodded, understanding that he was doing what was best for both worlds. "What can I do to help?"

"You cannot fight. For two reasons: you don't know how and because consorts don't fight."

"What do I do? I can't sit around and wait." She wasn't sure she'd even be able to watch.

He didn't answer. Did he think she could do nothing useful?

She drew back from his embrace. "I can help the wounded."

"I want you to be safe—Sulia would break the rules and shoot you with an arrow just so I lose by default."

"What will Stuart be doing?"

"Probably licking his balls like the cur he is. Come on, let's go to my chamber. I'll need to talk to Dylis and Bramwel anyway, and I don't want to do it in public."

She stiffened at the mention of Dylis's name. While the fairy had been nothing but helpful, and hadn't even looked at Felan with a glint in her eye, she needed to know more about Dylis even though she wasn't sure she wanted to.

They walked down the corridor, shadow servants clinging to the walls, ready to obey immediately. She didn't think she'd ever get used to them.

"Did you dump Dylis because you came back for me?"

"No. Bramwel was freed, and we both knew it was nothing but…what's the phrase? Friends with benefits."

"So we were apart for what felt like months, but you still managed to hook up." There was more bite to her words than she'd planned.

"It wasn't like that. The first time cemented a deal we'd made on top of what we'd already agreed to. Then it became convenient. I didn't have to pretend I was interested in any other woman at Court when my heart wasn't in it. She became my excuse." He stopped and pushed a key into a door. The lock turned with a click. "Besides, I wasn't expecting you to have been celibate."

And she hadn't been. It was just that she'd had seven years to fill. "I had longer to get over you."

"Sex here doesn't have the same emotion attached to it. For the most part, it's an itch to scratch, a deal, a power play. Few fairies get their hearts involved. However, once the heart is traded, few fairies go elsewhere until they want a child." He cupped her cheek. "You need not fear I'll stray or make new deals." He kissed her lips. "I won't."

She lifted her chin to claim his mouth better, her tongue gliding over his lip before darting inside and dancing with his.

When they paused for breath, she whispered, "I just needed to be sure."

Her life was now riding on what Felan did. If they survived tomorrow, they had a long life ahead of them and Dylis was always going to be around.

"Bramwel would call me out if he thought anything was still happening. He's more dangerous than he looks."

Jacqui laughed. That could be said for all fairies. They looked like they belonged on the cover of an expensive fashion magazine. She placed her hand on Felan's chest. "War council first?"

He shook his head, heat burning in his eyes. "No, I want a few moments alone with you, to remember why I'm fighting and what I have to lose." He kissed her again as he brought her into his chamber and closed the door.

Her back was against the cool trunk of a tree. His

body pressed to hers. She could easily forget how cold it was as her body warmed to his touch. He opened the buttons on her coat and slid his hands beneath her shirt. His skin was cool, but his touch left ribbons of heat on her flesh. She shivered with anticipation.

He paused. "Cold?"

"No." How could she be when she was with him, his fingers sliding over her bra and teasing her nipple into a hard peak?

She opened his jacket and pushed it off his shoulders. He shrugged his arms free, his purple ribbon falling on the floor, before tackling the button on her jeans and dragging them down her legs. She wriggled out of her jeans and boots, while he made things more difficult by kissing her inner thigh and running his finger over her panties so her breath hitched with every touch. She wanted his hand on her skin; she wanted him inside her.

He drew her panties aside and flicked his tongue over her clit. She arched back against the wall and dug her fingers into his shoulders as his tongue traced her slick folds. Her eyes closed as she waited for the next touch, for his fingers to ease into her, to touch and tease. Heat pooled in her belly and drew her nerves tight. His tongue circling and dipping, and just when she didn't think she could take it anymore and her legs were beginning to shake, he stopped.

She drew in a shaky breath as he pulled her panties down, and she stepped out of them. As he stood, he undid his pants. He lifted her, and her legs wrapped around his hips as he sank into her. She moaned as he pushed her higher up the wall, his breath on her skin, her arms around his neck, locked together.

Each thrust brought her closer. She gasped as pleasure rushed through her body. He groaned and pressed deep a couple more times before stilling. Leaning against the wall, they rested together until their breathing returned to normal and she became aware of the cool touch of his skin against hers.

Annwyn needed to return to summer so he would be warm again, the way she remembered him being.

He eased her down so her feet touched the ground. As she redressed, she glanced around his chamber for the first time. The bed was formed from tree limbs, swathes of fabric hung from branches like curtains for privacy. There was a nook full of clothing, but there was more clothing scattered and hanging from branches as if he hadn't gotten around to putting things away or sending them to get cleaned—she assumed they got cleaned somehow. Not all of the furniture was part of the castle, there were also some freestanding items that he must have brought across from her world. A dressing table covered in trinkets and things, a chair, and a mirror that was cradled by branches.

Soft light filled the chamber through the openings in the walls, where the tree trunks didn't quite meet. Unlike the big public chambers, his room had a ceiling made of branches, so there was no snow. She tried to imagine it green and covered in leaves, instead of bare and cold, but failed. Her imagination didn't seem to stretch that far.

Felan dropped his coat on a chair and sat. He smiled at her, but it didn't wipe the worry from his face. She was sure that he'd changed since they'd been here, his looks becoming sharper, like a hungry wolf. Winter was in all the fairies, not just the old King.

"I'd offer you a bath, but there will be no spare water. The privy is behind that curtain and down a ways—but it is private. The benefit of being the Prince." But the way he said it didn't make it sound like being Prince was worth the private bathroom.

"No spare water?"

"We are effectively trapped, besieged."

"But you did it." How much spare food and water did Annwyn have?

"To stop Sulia from getting fresh supplies. It is a double-edged sword." He raked his fingers through his hair. "I'm going to get Dylis and Bramwel in here—are you all right with that, or did you want to sleep?"

Sleep would be good, but she wasn't sure it would come. The anxiety was building again. The doubt—that they would fail or that they would win and she wouldn't be pregnant. Her hand slid over her stomach. No, not fail to be pregnant, fail to stay pregnant, because she knew something was happening, could feel it at the edges of her mind as if the magic was still humming in her blood and taking effect.

Felan watched the movement. Was he as worried as her?

They could worry if they won.

"It's fine. I don't know how well I'd sleep anyway." She ducked behind the curtain and down the narrow corridor to see what passed for a bathroom in Annwyn.

—◦◦◦—

After talking with the only people he knew he could trust one hundred percent about tactic and strategy, Felan had managed to sleep. He was sure Jacqui had also, though he wasn't sure either of them had slept particularly well. He lay still for a few moments longer, his chamber gray and dull in the early morning light. In summer it would be bathed in gold and the leaves would rustle softly. He longed for the warmth that had vanished so quickly, autumn but a few days of orange and gold before it was gone.

That was what was wrong. Annwyn was too quiet, too eerie, as if it were a shadow of its former self—a ghost waiting to fade away or be given new life. He eased out of bed, not wanting to wake Jacqui. Beneath his feet, the floor was cold. He missed the tickle of the grass against his soles and the sweet smell as it was crushed with each step and the flowers that trailed from the ceiling and perfumed the air.

He washed in the small bowl of water in the bathroom, the ball of silver keeping it ripple free. For a moment he was tempted to lift it out just to see what would happen. Stepping into the vast ocean hadn't killed him...but that had been in the mortal world, not here. And today he wasn't willing to try.

Jacqui was awake when he walked back into the bedroom. "I thought you'd left already."

"I wouldn't go without a kiss for luck." Or farewell. He knew the thought shouldn't even be in his mind, but only a fool failed to look at all possible outcomes. He'd set the dice in motion, now he was waiting for them to land—hopefully in his favor.

Her lips curved, but it was forced. He knew exactly how she felt.

He picked up his clothing and started dressing. Plain, dark purple clothes—the winter purple that was almost black—the padded shirt, and then the silver chainmail. He didn't bother with a cloak that could tangle around him. However, he put on two knives, one on his waist and one in his boot, plus his sword.

"What is Annwyn like in summer?"

Felan stopped and turned. "Like the most perfect day." If he closed his eyes, he knew he could summon up the memory, even if he couldn't feel the sun and heat on his skin. "Remember when we went hiking and had the picnic, how the place had felt deserted and yet full of life?" Birds and chipmunks and butterflies had been all around them, and even though the track had been less than twenty yards away it had felt as though they were the only people for miles. It hadn't been too hot or cold but sunny and with a light breeze. It was as close to perfect as he could ever remember experiencing in the mortal world. That had been the day he'd told Jacqui what he was. They'd spent hours talking about what that had meant, and he'd seen the wariness in her eyes fade to acceptance and understanding. He hoped she'd have that same chance here. "It's a lot like that. Magical and yet ordinary. And it will last until we cease to rule."

She frowned as if remembering, then nodded slowly. "And spring?"

"Spring will allow the leaves to grow, for flowers to bud, and the grass to return…but it won't reach its full lushness and summer until our child is born. I am okay with that. There is no need to just live in summer. Perhaps a long spring is what the Court needs to remember not to take summer for granted." They needed the long spring to adjust to their new roles and reformed relationship. He drew her into an embrace. "We can do this."

"I know. I just…I just need to know what I am hoping for. What you are fighting for."

"I'm fighting for everyone—you, the baby, me, Annwyn, and all of the mortal world."

Jacqui drew back. "Just fight to live, Felan. Let the rest fall into place."

"You're right. One thing at a time." He touched her cheek and hoped that this wouldn't be the last time he held her in his arms. Then he let her go so he could finish dressing. Showing up late to the battle he'd called would be very bad form.

Jacqui began dressing, again in her jeans and boots, but this time she put on one of his shirts, a bright blue one that fell to mid-thigh on her. Over that, she put on a cloak of bright, summer green that he hadn't worn for a very long time—seven mortal years to be exact. She looked like a spring Queen. For a moment he considered changing their plans and letting everyone see her. She was life, vital and beautiful in the gaudy colors of the summer Court. Without her, there would be no summer worth seeing in Annwyn.

Sulia would bring summer, but it wouldn't be one filled with joy. It would be hard and crackling with tension, like a thunderstorm waiting to burst. Corruption would grow and Annwyn itself would change to match. He'd seen thorns on the flowers where once there had been none and knew they were his mother's doing as she fed the deal making and scheming.

He picked up the cup of life from the dressing table and handed it to Jacqui. "Hide this, so Sulia can't use it. I think she still believes my father has it, but I want to be sure it is safe."

If Sulia had it, she would use it to heal her supporters and he would lose simply by injury.

She nodded. "I'll only get it out if things are going badly."

With Dylis and Bramwel, they had agreed she would watch from one of the upper chambers—that way only a few would know where she was—and that she would only assist if things were going really badly. The definition of *really badly* had been debated, but if Sulia outnumbered them two to one or Dylis and Bramwel were both out or Felan was injured, that was bad.

Then he handed her a silver knife with a blade no longer than his fingers. "Only if you have to defend yourself." He didn't want her to start her rule with blood the way he was.

She took it carefully and slipped the sheathed blade into her back pocket. The cup disappeared beneath the shirt, hidden. While he really wanted to leave a guard with her, he couldn't afford to lose a single sword and couldn't be sure he trusted anyone else.

"Good luck." She pressed her lips to his for a moment.

It was enough to take away anything he might have said to her. There were no words of comfort or pretty lies. This was it. She bent down and picked up the ribbon from where it had been forgotten last night. She carefully threaded it through a ring on the sleeve of his armor and tied it in double bow. He held her hand for a moment, then led her out of his chamber.

They walked upstairs and through the castle. He could hear preparations being made, people talking, but he didn't know if they were on his side or Sulia's. Maybe some had rethought overnight, and there would be a few last-minute changes…maybe, but he didn't trust them if they were that fickle.

He opened up a door and checked inside. Dylis had found this room. There were so many in the castle that didn't get used or that had been forgotten about. This one was a hollow in a trunk, the window a split that wasn't wide enough for him to pass through. Below was the battleground, the area between the castle and the sealed doorway. From here, Jacqui could watch, but most importantly she would be hidden and safe.

Already the armies were gathering. Dylis and Taryn were checking weapons and making sure none were poisoned with the river water. The hounds darted around, their red-tipped ears and tails the only parts visible against the snow. There was definitely a thicker covering this morning; people were sinking up to their shins in it. That would make the fighting harder.

He needed to get down there, but his hand was still around Jacqui's as if he couldn't bear to let her go. What if this was it? He closed his eyes for a moment and tried to imagine the victory, the first buds of spring and her stomach large with his child. He tried to see himself on the throne, but it all seemed so far away. He opened his eyes and looked at her.

"I love you. Whatever happens, I love you." He embraced her, drawing her closer, but unable to feel her body because of the stupid chainmail.

"I know. I love you too. No matter what, I'm glad we got a second chance." She was smiling, but her eyes were glistening.

He couldn't be here if she was going to cry. Instead, he kissed her cheek and pressed a key into her hand.

"Lock the door after me and open it for no one except me, Dylis, or Bramwel."

She nodded, her teeth worrying at her lip. Then he turned and left. He paused to listen to the snick of the lock, then made his way down to the battlefield.

Chapter 18

IN THE LITTLE ROOM SHE WAS WARM, BUT THAT WAS about all that was good about being locked in the sparsely furnished hollow in the tree. She didn't feel safe. She didn't want to watch out the window, yet not watching and not knowing what was going on was worse.

The two sides had taken their places at opposite ends of the field. A brown-haired woman without a ribbon on her arm—Taryn, the supposedly neutral Hunter—stood in the middle. While noise drifted up, Jacqui couldn't make out the words. Last-minute rules? A reminder to play fair?

Purple and yellow ribbons fluttered on the warriors' clothing. Sulia wore black with just the yellow ribbon on her arm. Both sides had archers and swordsmen. Could all fairies fight? Is that what they learned as children? She knew Felan was unusual in that he could read and write, but then he'd made a point of learning about humanity in preparation for becoming King. Now none of that mattered. It all came down to a formal battle fought with just twenty people per side.

She held her breath as Taryn moved off the field. There was a tent set up—for the wounded or was the King watching? She couldn't see anything more than the green, patterned roof. Were people really willing to die today, or would first blood be enough? She remembered everything Felan had said about Sulia and knew that she wouldn't stop until every last supporter of Felan's was on the ground.

For a moment, neither side moved. Her heart pulsed, counting off the time. Then everything happened at once. Sulia's side started running forward and Felan's loosed arrows. This wasn't a fairy game or a mock battle; people were actually going to die. Her hand strayed to the cup. They didn't have to. She could save them if she filled the cup with wine and they drank from it. But they'd gone through all of this last night. Everyone knew the risks, even though it had been centuries since the last real battle. The last one had been between Verden and the old Hunter. Verden had won and claimed the title while the old Hunter had been sent to the river. Which was exactly where today's loser would end up. She closed her eyes but couldn't move away from the window.

The ring of metal on metal filled the room. She paced, she sat, she leaned against the edge of the window, always looking for Felan and finding him too close to the front for her heart to rest. Sulia stayed near the back, giving orders, but surrounded by three soldiers just in case Felan's warriors broke through. The snow turned gray as it was churned up beneath feet, then it became spotted with blue as blood was spilled.

For a moment she lost sight of Felan, then he re-emerged out of a pack. He was trying to cut his way through to Sulia. Arrows arced overhead and sliced anyone below. Felan and the small group around him had crossed into the enemy side. The rest of his army was pushing through, but not as fast. What if he got cut off, surrounded, and killed? Her stomach flipped and dived. It had seemed like a good plan last night. Her gaze scanned the field. Sulia was using her squad to try and surround Felan. Her archers had stopped firing. Felan's were still picking off yellow-ribbon wearers on the edges, leaving the center melee unhindered.

A scrape behind her tore her attention from the field. She listened again, trying to block out the cries and noise of battle. A clicking kind of sound, like metal on metal, as if…as if someone were trying to open the door.

For a moment her heart stopped and she heard nothing. It was as if the whole of Annwyn stood still as she realized she was screwed. Trapped and probably about to die, because if it were Dylis or Bram, they would have called out. She had to hide the cup. Above her, the ceiling was a tangle of branches. It would have to do; there was nowhere else. She stood on the chair, hoping it wouldn't collapse beneath her weight, and shoved the cup up into the ceiling, then jumped clear. There was no point in pushing the chair against the door, as it opened out into the hallway, and it was too cumbersome for her to use as a weapon, so she put the chair between her and whoever was coming for her.

It was another couple of heartbeats before the door clicked and swung open.

Stuart.

He stepped back, as if surprised he'd actually found her, but quickly recovered. He pocketed the tools he'd used to pick the lock, then stepped into the room. "I've been looking for you all morning."

"Why would you do that when your lover is on the battlefield, fighting for your life as well as hers?"

He snorted. "Do you really think she won't win?"

Jacqui didn't bother answering. Her fingers were brushing the hilt of the small knife in her back pocket while she tried to look casual. He stepped around the chair, and she mirrored him, keeping the chair between them. If she could reach the door, she could make a run for it. He obviously had the same thought, as he moved back, putting himself closer to the door. There was no way she would have time to squeeze herself out the window, assuming she'd fit, and even then, tree climbing had never been her specialty. She was the kid who got halfway up and got stuck—or fell. And the ground was a long way down.

"What do you want?"

He grinned as cold as any fairy, and she knew exactly what he wanted.

"I thought the rules said no human was to be harmed." She'd been there when they were spoken, and so had he.

"No *fairy* was to harm a consort. There was nothing about us having our own little fight. We can decide the winner, not them. It's us who has the power. Do you not realize that? Without us, there is no Annwyn." His eye took on a gleam usually reserved for fevered fanatics.

Did she play along or strike first?

Stuart took a couple steps back and snagged the door. He closed it with a thud. While not locked, if she did make a break for it, it would take her longer to get the door open and he'd be on her. She scanned his black clothing looking for a weapon, but saw none. But that didn't mean he wasn't going to try and finish what he'd started at the airport. He'd be hoping to make her miscarry or kill her outright.

"You realize if you'd just lost the baby or run away,

none of this would be happening. No one would be dying. This is your fault; you gave Felan hope."

"Sulia isn't the rightful heir. I think the blame lies with you and her." She forced a smile and tried to look relaxed. "If you care to look out the window, you'll see that Felan is carving his way to her as we speak. When she is dead, you will have to plead for his mercy."

"Never. He will not win. No one even believes you are pregnant." He leered at her. "Maybe that's his game. You are the distraction, the Queen, but his child is in someone else's stomach. Either way, once you are dead, he loses." He moved closer and she stepped back. Fear made her heart beat hard and her breath catch. He was going to corner her.

Whichever way she ran, he would catch her. Her heart hammered, the singing of metal and the screaming of people filled her ears. He stepped onto the chair as if he planned to jump and knock her down.

Stuart glared at her. "You are mine now." His lips were curled into a sneer as if he thought she was useless and trapped. A toy for him to break at his leisure.

She pulled the knife free but kept it hidden beneath the folds of the cloak. If she screwed this up, Stuart would take it off her and use it to kill her. If she gave him the chance, he'd jump on her and pin her to the ground, and that was much worse. Her gaze scanned his body as she pretended to dither about which way to run, as if she were seriously considering making a break for the door. He mirrored her every move. "Come on, pick a direction and let's get to this. One." He held up one finger.

Where could she stab him that would be fatal? Not

the ribs, too many bones. The neck? On the chair he was too tall. Her gaze lowered.

"You're going to die anyway, so I might as well have some fun first. Two." Two fingers.

The groin—which was almost eye level. Yes, that would work.

"Give up and I'll make it quick. Beg me for mercy. Three." He flexed his fingers as if preparing to leap down and grab her.

She exhaled and took one more breath. "Never."

He lunged, and she swung the knife up. The blade bit into fabric and flesh, his body weight as he fell toward her driving it deeper. They stumbled backward, locked together, her hand now slippery on the hilt, but she held on and twisted like Felan had said, then tried to drag it upward. Stuart was yelling and pushing her away. She tore the knife free, determined not to let him have it. Her hand was painted crimson. He clutched at his thigh. Blood coated his hands and splattered on the floor in hot, pulsing spurts. She'd hit the artery.

"You fucking bitch." He lunged again but fell over, slipping in his own blood.

Jacqui took that second to open the door and run.

———

Felan couldn't feel his toes. His muscles had stopped aching a while ago, now he just slogged on because quitting was death. The main part of his force was somewhere behind him. Around him fluttered a few purple ribbons in a sea of yellow that was pressing closer and closer with every breath.

He was not going down.

Jacqui was waiting for him. He wouldn't fail her—or Annwyn or the mortal world.

He couldn't. This was what he'd been born for. What he'd prepared for—in his own way. He tried not to kill, just wound, cutting at his opponent's legs or hands, using the sword as a club so they fell into the now blue-stained snow unconscious. So much blood and still the battle went on. Who'd have thought forty fairies could bleed so much without dying? He knew logically some would be dead, but he tried not to think about it. The people who were trying to keep him from getting killed were as much a hindrance as they were help.

Above the noise sounded a bell, the clear chime calling for the ceasing of hostilities. People faltered. Had the battle been won? Was Sulia dead? Surrendered? He didn't believe it. It had to be a trick. Taryn rode through the mess on a white horse with a bell in her hand, ringing for a halt to the battle. What was she doing?

"Felan ap Gwyn ap Nudd ap Beli, step forward." Taryn cast her gaze over the field.

The fairies around him, friend and foe, stepped aside so he could make his way to the Hunter.

"Sulia merch Edern ap Nudd ap Beli, step forward."

Felan watched as her army parted and then formed alongside her like an honor guard as if they expected foul play. If there was any, it would be coming from her.

"The rest of you, stay back." Taryn raised her hand and Sulia was forced to walk up to Taryn alone, like he had. "Remove your ribbons. The battle is over."

Sulia grinned and clapped her hands as if she'd been expecting this outcome. What evil had she executed while he'd been fighting? Where was Jacqui?

Felan's heart stopped and the exhaustion from fighting claimed him. He wanted to crumple to the ground and never get up. The only reason the battle would be over was if one of the consorts was dead.

Not Jacqui. No, she couldn't be dead.

But Sulia's smile didn't falter.

He stood only because he refused to die on his knees. Without Jacqui, he would willingly walk into the river. He couldn't live without her again.

A procession of shadow servants came out of the castle bearing a body. He glanced away, not wanting to see, but a flicker of color near the back of the procession caught his eye. He looked over; it wasn't Jacqui they were carrying. She was walking behind, her light green cloak splattered in red.

Sulia drew in a breath. "No."

The horse stamped its feet, as if eager for this to be done. Taryn waited until the shadows drew close, then placed the body on the ground before her. She slid down from the horse and drew back the cloak so everyone could see who lay there. Even in death, Stuart didn't look peaceful. He looked annoyed, as if he'd been cheated.

Felan looked at Jacqui—she was pale. Was she hurt? It was hard to tell. It was also hard to tell how Stuart had died, even though Jacqui wore his blood. But he was dead, which meant Sulia had no consort and no soul to give to Annwyn. Annwyn was his. Jacqui was his. A smile formed on his lips. This was the first time in weeks he had reason to let the worry go and be truly happy.

"The consort of Sulia is dead, killed by the consort of Felan."

Around him swords were being sheathed.

"No, I can get another consort. The battle must be finished." Sulia's voice took on an edge of desperation.

"Only the King and the Hunter can remove the swords closing the veil. Without a consort, you are not eligible to fight for the throne. Therefore, you lose. Felan wins." She paused, then said it again. "A new King is made. Long live Felan!"

A cheer went up, but he wasn't listening anymore. He was moving toward Jacqui and she toward him.

He hugged her close, kissed her lips, aware he was covered in blood as well. "Are you okay?"

"Yes. Except I killed a man." She looked a little pale, as if she might faint.

"It would have been you if you hadn't." Had Sulia sent Stuart to find Jacqui and kill her? Or had that been his own plan, one which had unraveled fast?

"I know." She closed her eyes for a moment and drew a couple breaths. "All I can smell is blood. I'm going to be sick." She stepped away from him, her hand on her chest as she sucked in several deep breaths and swallowed a couple times. After a few moments, she seemed to get control of herself and turned back to face him. "Are you okay?"

"Yes." He knew he was cut and bruised, but it was nothing that wouldn't heal in a few days.

People were calling his name. He took Jacqui's hand and turned to face the Hunter. Taryn held the crown in one hand and a knife in the other.

"Do you accept the responsibilities as well as the privileges of King? Do you promise to judge all souls fairly and condemn none who might redeem themselves?

Do you promise to keep Annwyn stable for as long as you can before passing on the crown?"

"I do." How much time had she spent memorizing these words and learning what to do? Verden had done a good job coaching her. He should be here to see her. To see that in such a short amount of time, she had risen from a daughter of Brownies to the Hunter who saw the change of Kings.

Taryn faced Jacqui. "Do you willingly give your soul to Annwyn? Do you promise to serve with the King as best you can and to uphold his laws?"

There was a slight pause. Felan squeezed her hand.

"I do."

He could almost hear the sigh of relief…even from those who hadn't supported him. At least winter was over. Spring could start. They could all start again.

"Your hands."

Felan released Jacqui's hand and held out his hand, palm up. She copied. He risked a glance over. Her lower lip was pinched between her teeth. It was going to sting; getting cut was never fun. He could imagine losing one's soul wasn't fun either. He hoped for her sake it wouldn't hurt.

Taryn made a slow slice on his palm, but he welcomed the sharpness of the blade and the spilling of his blood this time. Taryn repeated the process on Jacqui's hand. Blue and red blood dripped on the ground, coloring the snow.

Felan clasped Jacqui's hand so the bloods mingled.

Jacqui's eye's widened, and a moment later he felt the jolt rush through him, as if Annwyn was racing through him all at once—every tree and rock, he knew them all in that instant. Then it was gone…mostly, except for a kind of pressure. Souls waiting to be moved on realized.

The snow stopped, one last flake landing on their joined hands and melting on Jacqui's skin.

Taryn squatted down, peering into the mushy snow where their mixed blood had fallen. He knew what she was waiting for. His toes curled in his boots. What if it hadn't worked? Was Jacqui really without a soul now? Would this fail if she wasn't pregnant? He resisted the urge to get down and stare at the dirt, and tried to breathe calmly, as if everything would be all right.

People were moving, stepping closer. Anxiously waiting. Planning what they'd do if it failed? What would he do?

His heart thudded as if he were still fighting. Jacqui gripped his hand tighter, blood still oozing between their palms and dripping on the dirt. Did something just move? He held his breath and stared harder at the tiny patch of brown, willing something to happen.

A single blade of green broke through the dirt and slush of snow and blood. Brilliant, spring green. It had worked! Jacqui was pregnant and Annwyn had accepted her soul.

Taryn stood. "Spring is here."

But Felan wasn't listening to the official announcements anymore. He picked Jacqui up and swung her around. They'd done it. Annwyn was safe, the river would calm, and the mortal world would stabilize.

He set her down gently and kissed her on the lips, not caring that everyone was watching. He no longer had to hide her to keep her safe. She was the Queen; she was his love, his heart.

Epilogue

FIVE MORTAL MONTHS HAD BEEN ONLY WEEKS IN Annwyn. His father had died with the autumn equinox, and there had been a mock battle to celebrate his passing before laying him out and letting Annwyn reclaim him. As a result, there had been no festival.

This time Felan knew he was going to have to put on a show, his first as King. It was almost midwinter in the mortal world, and he wanted to be able to show proof of his heir. There were still whispers that nothing was happening fast enough, that Jacqui should be spending more time in the mortal world to bring on summer. But Felan intended to keep his word and let spring develop slowly while he and Jacqui settled into ruling.

However, none of that time had prepared him for ultrasound day. He was more nervous than he had been going into battle or walking into the coffee shop that first time after seven years and speaking to her. He was sure his palms were sweaty. Yet she didn't release her grip on his hand as he sat next to her waiting for the sonographer to get started. He wondered what the woman would do if she realized the King and Queen of Annwyn were anxiously waiting to see if everything was all right with their baby. The doctor hadn't wanted to do the early scan at first, but when Jacqui had mentioned her previous ectopic pregnancy, she'd agreed.

Now they were here almost holding their breath, waiting

for the results. He wasn't letting himself think ahead. He didn't want to. He just kept repeating to himself that everything would work out. Jacqui gave his hand a squeeze and closed her eyes, as if she couldn't bear to watch. The woman made a few clicks and a few notes. Felan watched, but the blobby black and white picture looked like…well, fuzzy black and gray and white shapes that made no sense. He couldn't imagine anyone in Annwyn getting excited over these images. And he had no idea how he was going to create an enchanted object that showed what was going on inside the way this machine did.

"Okay, everything is as it should be. I know you weren't sure about your dates, but it looks like you're about seven weeks pregnant."

Jacqui sighed and opened her eyes. Her grip on his hand loosened and he let the tension he'd been holding ease a little. However, he'd heard the "but" in the woman's voice and was waiting for the rest of the news.

The woman moved the pointer on the screen to a kind of a blob. "Here's baby number one and here's baby number two."

"Two?" Jacqui lifted her head.

"Multiple births can be a bit of a shock. They're fraternal twins; you can see that they have separate placentas."

The woman was talking, but he was staring at the screen as the two little blobs suddenly became real. She did something and he heard their rapid little heartbeats. Two tiny babies because they'd used the cup of life twice. It had worked almost too well. Had there ever been fairy twins before?

"Would you like a picture to take home?" the woman asked.

He nodded. "Yes, thank you." Would the Court believe him when he explained what the little smudges represented, or would they be just amazed at the technology?

It had been a long time since anyone had put the time and effort into making artifacts, but maybe this would excite someone enough to try. Now that they weren't all jostling for position, there was time to experiment again and develop the deeper magic that had been lost over the last millennia.

The sonographer handed the print to him, and he tucked it into his jacket pocket. They were both dressed as mortals today. Even the fairies that had remained in Annwyn were dressing in simpler styles, copying Jacqui. He'd even seen a few men in jeans—although the artwork that decorated the cuffs and legs could only be fairy.

A few minutes later, Jacqui was ready to go, but she didn't say anything until they were outside.

"Twins." She slapped him on the arm, but she was grinning.

"It was the cup."

"I know. We should get a scan at twenty weeks; then they will look like babies."

"Really?" He wanted to look at the picture again.

"I'll get you a book. We should get a book." She stopped walking. "Are there midwives in Annwyn? I know they have to be born there to be fairies, but what if I need a doctor?"

"I'll bring one across. I'll bring you a whole staff if you want, but there has never been a problem with a baby born in Annwyn. Where there is death, there is life too."

"And love." She smiled at him and he placed a soft kiss on her lips.

"That would be the most important part." He hoped more fairies would discover their heart. "Shall we find a place to make this picture huge?"

She rolled her eyes. "I can't believe you are going to do that."

"Trust me, the Court will love it. They love anything new and intriguing."

———

He'd been right, of course. Felan had put the picture of the babies in a large frame and placed it on a wall for all to see. He was explaining his idea for new magic to anyone who'd listen, and there were a few who were more than curious.

Jacqui hoped that they'd be able to make the magic work—not that she was going to volunteer as a guinea pig. While she still didn't look pregnant, it was beginning to feel real with every passing day. And as the babies grew, Annwyn came to life a little more.

Soon Verden was going to come and get them for Christmas dinner across the veil, so they could celebrate with Felan's son. Verden had survived his injuries and as promised Felan's first act as King had been to lift the banishment. Verden and Taryn were living in Charleston with Caspian and Lydia, and were officially Caspian's Brownies. She was looking forward to crossing the veil to see Felan's family and hers.

Until then, she and Felan presided over the Yule festival, decked out like angels in gauzy silver. If she'd been anywhere else, she would have felt silly, but not here. Not when everyone else had also dressed up in silver and white with pretend wings attached to their costumes. Some showed more skin than others, and there was enough silver dust to make everyone sparkle in the firelight.

In previous years, snow had apparently been brought across, and Annwyn had been turned into mock winter, but this year it was too close to reality, so the much more subtle theme of winter angels had been chosen.

Felan broke away from the group, who was examining the ultrasound picture—Jacqui suspected there would be a rush on babies as they wanted to see this for themselves—and walked over to her, his sheer silver wings sweeping the floor and his crown of holly making him look the way she'd imagined fairies should look—beautiful, regal, dangerous all in one heartbeat. She caught her breath and he took her hand and lifted it his lips.

"The first dance, my love?"

"Every dance."

Acknowledgments

As always, this story wouldn't have been possible without the support of my hubby and kids. The wonderful WINK girls, who read all my early drafts and brainstormed any glitches with me. My editor, Mary Altman, and agent, Eric Ruben, for believing in my alternate worlds. While there are many people who touched the story on its way to becoming a book, I don't know them all by name, but I am grateful to all of them. And finally, my readers, as without them I wouldn't get to share my stories. :)

About the Author

Three-time ARRA finalist Shona Husk lives in Western Australia at the edge of the Indian Ocean. Blessed with a lively imagination, she spent most of her childhood making up stories. As an adult, she discovered romance novels and hasn't looked back. Drawing on history and myth, she weaves new worlds and writes heroes who aren't afraid to get hurt while falling in love.

With stories ranging from sensual to scorching, she writes paranormal, fantasy, and sci-fi romance. You can find out more at www.shonahusk.com. Also: www.twitter.com/ShonaHusk, www.facebook.com/shonahusk, and Newsletter: http://eepurl.com/lySiD.

The Outcast Prince

by Shona Husk

—⁓—

Just one taste is all it takes...

This was no ordinary mirror. Caspian caught a hint of color, a whirl of a waltz just past his reflection—a glimpse into the decadent Fairy Court of Annwyn. The home he could never have. It called to him, whispering temptation after temptation...if he would only reclaim his rightful heritage.

To be forever lost

Caspian has an even stronger reason to stay in the world of humans. He's just met a woman who captivates him like no other. But loving him has proven to be dangerous. And he will do whatever it takes to protect Lydia from the vicious, seductive world of Court—even if doing so requires the ultimate sacrifice: his soul.

—⁓—

"Brilliantly unique, beautifully sensual, *The Outcast Prince* had me spellbound from the first page! Shona Husk's engaging voice and vivid, creative world-building make every one of her books a must-read!"
—*Larissa Ione*, New York Times *bestselling author*

For more Shona Husk, visit:

www.sourcebooks.com

Lord of the Hunt

by Shona Husk

—◦◦◦—

Raised in the mortal world, the fairy Taryn never planned on going back to Annwyn, much less to Court. But with the power shift imminent, she is her parents' only hope of securing a pardon from exile and avoiding certain death.

Verden, Lord of the Hunt, swore to serve the King. But as the magic of Annwyn fails and the Prince makes ready to take the throne, Verden knows his days as Hunter are numbered.

When Taryn and Verden meet, their attraction is instant and devastating. Their love could bring down a queen and change the mortal world forever.

—◦◦◦—

Praise for *For the Love of a Goblin Warrior*:

"Ms. Husk outdid herself in this book…
Once I got into the story, I couldn't put it down."
—*Night Owl Romance* Reviewer Top Pick

"Husk has an amazing ability to weave a
mesmerizing story with a magical dark
fairy-tale feel." —*Love Romance Passion*

"An entertaining and unique read. Shona Husk
creates a dark yet delightful world where romance
and fantasy combine." —*Romance Reviews*

For more Shona Husk visit:

www.sourcebooks.com

Forged by Desire

by Bec McMaster

**Look for the fourth book in Bec McMaster's highly
acclaimed London Steampunk series.**

The captain of the Nighthawk guard has a deadly mission:
capture a steel-jawed monster who's been preying on women.
Capt. Garrett Reed hates to put his partner Perry in jeopardy,
but she's the best bait he has. Little does he realize, he's the one
about to be caught in his own trap…

Perry has been half in love with Garrett for years, but this
is not exactly the best time to fall in love—especially when
their investigation leads them directly into the clutches of the
madman she thought she'd escaped…

Praise for Bec McMaster:

"Bec McMaster brilliantly weaves a world
that engulfs your senses and takes you on a
fantastical journey."—Tome Tender

"[McMaster's] descriptive powers are flawless and her ability
to draw the reader in is unparalleled."—Debbie's Book Bag

For more Bec McMaster, visit:

www.sourcebooks.com

The Highland Dragon's Lady

by Isabel Cooper

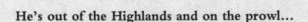

He's out of the Highlands and on the prowl...

Regina Talbot-Jones has always known her rambling family home was haunted. She also knows her brother has invited one of his friends to attend an ill-conceived séance. She didn't count on that friend being so handsome...and she certainly didn't expect him to be a dragon.

Scottish Highlander Colin MacAlasdair has hidden his true nature for his entire life, but the moment he sets eyes on Regina, he knows he has to have her. In his hundreds of years, he's never met a woman who could understand him so thoroughly...or touch him so deeply. Bound by their mutual loneliness, drawn by the fire awakening inside of them, Colin and Regina must work together to defeat a vengeful spirit—and discover whether their growing love is powerful enough to defy convention.

Praise for Isabel Cooper:

"Cooper's world-building is solid and believable." —*RT Book Reviews*

"Isabel Cooper is an author to watch!" —*All About Romance*

For more Isabel Cooper, visit:

www.sourcebooks.com